# BIKER DUDE

★ A NOVEL ★

RESTRICTED

R

BEN POVLOW

# BIKER DUDE

A Novel

**Ben Povlow**

Bucket List Book Publishing

This is a work of fiction. Names, characters, places, and incidents either are the product of the author's imagination or are used fictitiously. Any resemblance to actual persons, living or dead, events, or locales is entirely coincidental. No motorcycles were damaged in process of creating this story.



Published by: Bucket List Book Publishing. 1457 Kelly Road #255. Apex, NC. 27502

ISBN 978-1-7354223-8-1

For all the motorcycle enthusiasts around the world. Ride safe and party hard.

# Chapter 1

MOTORCYCLE RALLY SEASON IS in full swing, and the one they call Dude is loading camping gear onto his black 2017 Harley-Davidson Road Glide. He is getting ready to hit the road for another long weekend adventure. It's springtime on the East Coast and the weather is perfect for taking a long ride on a hot hog. The weekend forecast is looking great on the other side of North Carolina, but getting out of town is shaping up to be a wet one.

Dude will trade painting houses for riding in the rain any day. He's just happy to be out of his paint splattered work clothes. The work keeps him physically fit, but it's not something he would do for free. Going to motorcycle rallies is his way of forgetting about the daily grind of climbing ladders and dealing with whiney customers. Having his own business is stressful and painting is the last thing he wants to talk about when he is on a road trip. There is something magical about hitting the open road on a motorcycle that makes stress melt away, not to mention all the drugs and alcohol that will help to cause work amnesia. The past week will be a blur in no time.

Dude wipes his jeans and brushes dirt off the shoulder of his black Laconia shirt from 2010. Then he straps his blue camping chair, a tent, and a sleeping bag to his tour pack and, just as he finishes, he hears a voice from across the road. "Hi Dude, where are you going now?"

"Hey Vince, I'm heading out to Mud Hole for a four-day rally and I'm running late. What do you need?"

"Don't need anything. Just wanted to say hi and, uh, see what you're up to. Since you're going away, do you want me to keep an eye on your RV?"

"Yeah, that'd be cool. I'm not expecting any company, so if you see anyone creeping around, you know the deal. Shoot first and ask questions later. Just joking, I'm sure it will be as boring as always while I'm gone."

Dude's black 2012 Chevy Silverado is a 2500HD with ladder racks. The truck has no problem pulling his mobile home down the road. His RV can be easily hooked to the truck and moved on a moment's notice.

The twenty-eight-foot Jayco toy hauler can hold all his worldly possessions, including both of his motorcycles, his outdoor furniture, and his tools. Dude has made year-round campgrounds his home for the past twelve years. Private sleeping quarters, stove, sink, shower, toilet and plenty of seating and foldout bunks make the perfect setup for a single guy who likes to keep life moving.

Vince asks, "how long will you be gone for?"

"Well, the rally is four days, but I am on a mission to catch a thief while I'm there, so who knows. But listen man, I can't get into too many details because I'm really running late, I should have been on the road hours ago. I had a couple last-minute things to straighten out with this bike first. I need to be in Mud Hole, just above Boone, by five o'clock at the latest, or I'm going to miss a huge opportunity."

"What kind of opportunity are you talking about, Dude?"

"Well, I can't get into all the details because, like I said, I'm running late, but do you remember what happened to me in Daytona a couple of months ago?"

"No, I didn't hear that story."

"Well, it is a story I don't have time to tell right now. I will fill you in on the details when I get back. But the short version is, I made a fool of myself, and a video of it went viral."

"Oh boy, I can't imagine what that's about." Vince is now shaking his head from side to side with a vision of Daytona engulfed in flames flashing through his mind.

"Well, anyway, some DJ out in Mud Hole got wind of the story and a buddy of mine, who's friends with him, said I'd be at the rally this weekend and he wants to bring me on the radio to interview me. I asked him if he'd be okay with me getting the word out about George Walker's stolen motorcycle and the poker run I'm organizing, and he said, 'yeah, no problem.' So, If I can get the word out about the stolen bike ahead of the rally, I will have a better chance of catching the thief and hopefully recovering the classic Panhead. Plus, I need to raise enough money to give George a proper burial and, with this exposure, I can get locals to sign up for the poker run too. It will be open to anyone whether or not they are attending the rally."

"I remember George, he was a great guy. Sorry again for your loss."

"Thanks Vince."

"I hope you catch the bastard and raise enough money. Um, well, I won't hold you up any longer. The sky's looking awfully dark, you better get going."

"Thanks, Vince. Call me if you need anything."

"Will do, have a safe trip."

With his motorcycle fully loaded, Dude looks west towards a stormy sky and decides it would be a good idea to put on his rain gear and prepare to get wet.

***

All geared up now, he locks up his camper door, puts on his helmet, tightens the chin strap under his mostly brown beard, then hops onto the bike from the left side. With the bike he refers to as Angel now warming up, he gets his GPS set up with the address for the radio station in Mud Hole.

Dude takes such great care of Angel that he has had girlfriends get jealous of the shiny steel horse. Her chrome wheels and gleaming accent pieces get a lot of attention. Angel's snakeskin seat is used to being molested by the ladies.

His goggles are fogging up over his blue eyes; it's time to get moving. Dude squeezes the clutch, then pops the bike into gear. He raises the kickstand and pulls off his little patch of grass and onto the dirt road, then makes his way around the campground. He rolls along under the tall pine trees and past old man Archie's trailer, with its obnoxious bright blue paint job and an old wooden deck slapped up against the front of it. Every time Dude rides by, the old man gives him the middle finger. As usual, Dude squeezes the clutch and cracks the throttle a couple times just to piss off the old man as he rides away.

The two have had issues with each other ever since the time Dude was drunk and puked on the hood of the old man's car. He threatened to sue Dude for ruining the paint on his shiny red Cadillac.

After exiting the Happy Pines RV Park, Dude stops at a local gas station to top off his tank about a mile down the road before hitting the highway. None of that cheap shit, only 93 octane for his baby.

With a full tank of gas and almost two hundred miles ahead of him, Dude takes the on-ramp for route 64 west towards Greensboro. Within five miles down the road, the sky opens up and it is like having buckets of water dumped on his head. But with no time to spare, all he can think about is his friend George and all the good times they shared over the years.

George loved going to motorcycle rallies and partying his ass off. Dude can clearly picture George smiling and laughing at last year's Mud Hole rally with a fat doobie in his mouth. Dude is planning to party for two this weekend in memory of his good buddy. The only thing George loved more than partying was his red and white H-D Panhead. It was a 1963 Philadelphia Police Special. There are only a few left in circulation; it's no wonder someone wanted to steal it.

Last year, Dude and George rode to the Mud Hole Motorcycle Rally together. The rally has been going on for years, but they had never been to this event before. George had his classic Panhead in the bike show and it got a lot of attention. Obviously too much attention, because when they returned to camp after the last band finished on Saturday night, the antique motorcycle was gone. The police took a report, but the motorcycle was never found.

The following morning, everyone was packing up to leave before the pair had a chance to figure out who could've stolen the bike. Of course, Dude and George immediately asked everyone within an earshot the night it disappeared, but most people were up by the stage watching the band when it happened. Several people mentioned seeing a white van driving around the camping area, but it was nowhere to be found. The pair poked their heads into every trailer still on the farm, but there was no sign of the Panhead.

Internet research and local businesses provided some leads but nothing solid. Because most of the attendees were from the surrounding towns, the pair decided to go back to the scene of the crime this year to search for the thief and, more importantly, bring home the beautiful red, white, and chrome antique machine.

Two months ago, George passed away unexpectedly from a heart attack. His family had him cremated, but they don't have the money to give him a proper burial. George had planned to leave the antique motorcycle to his eleven-year-old son, George Junior. Dude is now on a mission to follow through with the plan he and George had to return to Mud Hole and get answers. They'd spent the past year having visions of hurting the thief or having them arrested. Dude is still not sure how he will react, if and when he comes face to face with the asshole who took George's baby.

Dude is planning to raise money for George's funeral on Saturday morning with the poker run he has organized. The money raised will go towards laying George to rest with the goal of raising enough money to cover all the burial costs.

With heavy rain pounding against his windshield, a bandana around his face and goggles snug tightly over his eyes, Dude is hauling down the highway like a raped date. He can feel his phone vibrating on his chest through the inside pocket of his black riding jacket. He thinks about who could be calling, but he has no time to stop and find out. He figures the call is most likely coming from his buddy Santa, who is already at the farm where the rally is taking place. He is pretty sure Santa is calling to tell him that there are titties everywhere, and he needs to hurry.

With his mind fixed on his first stop at the radio station, he can't help but to think, *damn, I shouldn't have drunk that last coffee, I really need to use the bathroom*. Then he forces himself to think of something else to keep his mind off the possibility of him shitting his pants. He turns his thoughts to the sights and smells of what is shaping up to be a beautiful weather weekend and one hell of a party.

With Dude getting in on Thursday night, a day ahead of anyone who didn't pay for camping, he will wake up to the sweet sound of thunder coming out of exhaust pipes on the first official day of the rally.

Friday's schedule for Dude is to touch base with the event staff about the poker run and meet Santa's nephew, who will work the registration table for him. Then the plan is to check out the vendors, rub elbows with the locals, and people watch as the motorcycles storm into the farm. You never know what kind of badass motorcycles you will see rolling through the gates. The bands take the stage in the afternoon and play all night.

Saturday, after the morning poker run, the agenda is jam packed with all the usual (and unusual) biker games, the wet t-shirt contest, a burnout pit, the bike show, and of course another full day of live music. There will be vendors selling everything from carnival food to motorcycle parts and anything in between.

***

After exiting off 64 west and on to 421 north, the sky clears up and Dude's staring at nothing but open road. While daydreaming about the days ahead, he cracks open the throttle to kick this trip up a notch. He's hauling ass as he leans into the sweeping curve of the inclined road. Just as he zooms under an overpass, he sees out of the corner of his eye those dreaded blue lights on the top of a car sitting about twenty yards behind the concrete barrier. Immediately, his eyes dart down to his speedometer, and he knows he's in trouble.

Sure enough, as his eyes cut over to the mirror again, the car was pulling out of its hiding spot. Dude's thoughts shift to, *should I just pull over now and wait for him to catch up to me or crack the throttle and ditch 'em?*

He decides to pull on to the shoulder, cut the engine and get off the bike.

Just as the police cruiser pulls up behind him, the door comes swinging open immediately and the highway patrolman, in a firm military voice, says, "excuse me Sir, what are you doing? Get back on the bike!"

With Dude standing there on the side of the highway as trucks scream by, causing him and his bike to sway with every gust of wind, the officer moves closer. Dude says, "I know what I did. Just give me my ticket so I can get going. I have an important meeting that I can't be late for."

"That's not how it works, we're going to do this my way. I'm the one asking the questions here, you're not in charge. First things first, let me see your license, registration, and insurance."

Dude pulls the paperwork out of his wallet. "I understand. Here you go Officer."

The officer grabs the documentation and then takes a hard look at Dude's driver's license. He looks up at Dude and then back down at the license.

"You don't look like you're two hundred and twenty pounds. And you look taller than five-foot, ten inches, and with the mix of gray, there's not much brown hair in your beard. Please take off your helmet."

"You got it, sir. I lost forty pounds in the last year, but that is me."

With the cop back in his cruiser, Dude is just standing there, hands on the bike, minding his own business and praying this whole ordeal ends fast.

After a few minutes, the officer gets out of his car, walks up, and says, "you don't have any warrants and all your paperwork checks out. But before I let you go; I need to ask; 'do you have any drugs on you or have you been drinking?' "

"No sir."

"I am going to give you a quick pat down anyway."

"Not a problem."

The officer starts at the top of Dude's shoulders and works his way to the wrists where he sees inked skin sticking out of his sleeve. "Are you part of a club?"

"No sir. I'm a lone wolf."

He moves his hands down around Dude's rib cage and across his waistband. Nothing yet. Then sure enough, the officer gets to Dude's pants pocket, and, like every other biker, he's got a small pocketknife.

"What are you planning to do with this blade?

"Nothing sir. Just in case I need it for something on the bike or, ah, you know, I will be using it to cut up my food when I'm camping."

"Open up your hand."

The cop pulls out the blade and lays it across Dude's leather-like palm. From the blue paint he used yesterday, his hands look like a dye pack exploded on him during a bank robbery.

"Seems to be under four inches. I guess I will let you keep it."

The officer puts the knife back in Dude's pocket and continues the pat down. He runs his hands down Dude's legs and into his dirty old black riding boot. With the officer bent down digging into his sweaty sock, Dude can't help but to think to himself, *please don't fart now, please don't fart now, oh god, please don't let me fart right now!*

A sigh of relief washes over Dude's face as the officer stands up straight and says, "do I need to start digging into your saddlebags too?"

"No sir. I have nothing to hide. I'm heading to a motorcycle rally. But I got an important appointment at a radio station along the way, and I'm not looking for any trouble. I've got nothing illegal on me. All the beer I need is waiting for me when I get there."

"Well, Mr. Sparks, you know you were speeding, don't you?"

"Yes sir. I'm sorry about that. I got a little carried away because I really need to use the bathroom and I'm running late, but I'm sorry and I won't let it happen again."

"You were doing seventy-seven in a seventy. Since you've been cooperative, I'm going to give you a ticket, but it won't carry any points. Make the payment and we can forget this ever happened.

"Sounds good to me, Officer. I appreciate the courtesy."

The cop goes back to his cruiser to write up the ticket. After a few minutes, which felt like an hour for Dude who was standing there with his legs crossed, with what felt like a prairie dog sticking its head out of his ass, the officer steps out of his car and on to the asphalt of the highway. Then he strolls up to Dude and says, "here's your ticket. Slow down and be careful."

"Will do. Thank you, sir."

Dude hops onto Angel, fires her up and, with a quick glance in the mirror, he sees a break in traffic. After gaining some speed on the shoulder, he merges his way back onto 421 north with only one thing on his mind; *how far is the next exit?*

***

Somewhere in western North Carolina, a fast-food restaurant was cleared out after Dude left the restroom. Walking out feeling about ten pounds lighter, Dude moves quickly back to his bike, strips off his rain gear, and then races his way back onto the highway.

Trying not to stress himself, he does his best not to think about how much time he lost between getting pulled over and the mandatory restroom break. Now Dude is thinking about ways he can make up some time without another incident.

With about fifty miles until he gets to the radio station, Dude focuses on how he's going to maximize this opportunity to promote the poker run and get the word out about the Panhead. He is also focused on how he can avoid embarrassing himself any more with these ridiculous questions he is sure DJ Bear is going to have for him. Bear is known for breaking balls and doing crazy shit on the radio, and Dude is pretty sure that today will be no exception.

***

After exiting the highway, Dude cruises the winding back roads of this sleepy little town nestled between ranges of mountains. With the smell of cow shit in the air, he rolls by a small pasture and then past a huge confederate flag, an entrance to the Blue Ridge Parkway, and then a sign pointing towards the town of Blowing Rock. The sun is now shining brightly, and the first leg of the trip is almost complete.

A few miles later, he rolls into the parking lot of the radio station. Dude is looking for the call letters BMRP 97.7 amongst the radio stations listed on a sign. He sees what he's looking for. Now knowing he's in the right place; he finds an open parking spot and backs into it.

Dude walks into the building, and then towards the elevator to his right. Once the elevator arrives, he gets in and pushes the button for the third floor. Just as the tiny metal box was about to close its doors, an older woman steps in with a bag of food. The aroma is so powerful; it tempted Dude to grab it from her and take off running. Instead, he thinks about all the delicious grilled food waiting for him at the farm, where he knows Santa will be cooking up a storm. Imagining the smell and taste of hot dogs, hamburgers, chicken, and steak cooked on an open fire drowned out the smell of whatever this woman has in her bag.

Dude steps out of the elevator and walks up to the reception desk. "I'm here to see DJ Bear."

The pretty young lady behind the desk wearing a Bad Company t-shirt and sporting a purple Mohawk says, "okay, do you have an appointment?"

"I do. The name is Dude."

She blushes and says, "You mean the biker dude who, um, you know, went viral at Bike Week in Daytona?"

With no shame in his game, Dude smiles and says, “yeah, that dude!”

She could barely look him in the eyes as she picks up the phone and says, “the guest has arrived.”

# Chapter 2

WALKING INTO THE STUDIO feels surreal as Dude steps through the doorway. He hears a bunch of laughing and then a raspy voice says, “holy shit, I almost didn’t recognize you with your clothes on. I’m Bear, it’s a pleasure to meet you, Dude.”

This tall, hairy beast squeezes Dude’s hand and shakes it for a few seconds before saying, “I can’t believe you showed up. Thanks for being here.”

It’s obvious where Bear got his nickname. He looks like he was plucked straight out of Yosemite National Park with his three hundred pound, six-foot five-inch monster frame. His black hair is pushing out of the top of his white short-sleeved shirt, and it looks like his arms were dipped in honey and then rolled across the back of a shedding dog.

“The pleasure’s all mine. Thanks for having me.” Dude is excited, but a little nervous at the same time. Not sure what to expect, he braces for the worst.

“Take a seat over here, grab the headphones, and get close to the microphone. We’re going to jump right into the interview as soon as we come out of this commercial break. We have about sixty seconds, any questions?” Bear is now chomping at the bit to get the details of what would cause someone to act like such a crazy person in front of thousands of strangers.

"Are you going to give me an opportunity to mention my poker run and the missing bike I was telling you about?"

"Relax man. I told you on the phone, I'll give you an opportunity to mention your stuff, but first I have a list of questions my listeners have been sending me they need answered. I can't stop playing the audio clip of you screaming 'where's my clothes' as the police were dragging you off that stage. That stunt you pulled in Daytona was crazy!"

"Yeah, yeah, I know, my phone's been ringing off the hook ever since the video went viral."

"I know you're heading over to the farm for the motorcycle rally this weekend, so, I guess my first unofficial question is, will you be drinking alcohol?"

Radio station employees are now gathering around the windows of the studio to get an in-person view of this long-awaited interview.

"Well, you know, it is a party, but I sure as hell don't plan on letting myself get as shitfaced as I was at Bike Week."

Everyone in the room laughs. Then the producer says, "all right guys, we're about to go live on the air. I'm going to count it down from ten. You ready?"

"As ready as I'll ever be," says Dude. "Let's do it."

***

10, 9, 8, 7, 6, 5, 4, 3, 2, 1…

"Welcome back to the Bear show. We are live in the studio with the one, the only, the infamous Daytona Bike Week Streaker; Naked Biker Dude."

"Don't worry listeners, I have all the questions you've been sending in, and we're going to get to as many of them as possible, so, let's jump right in. Dude, thanks for being here in studio. We really appreciate you going out of your way. How has your life been different since what happened three months ago?" Asks Bear as he stands up from his chair trying to get a good look at Dude's face in anticipation of what's coming.

"Thankfully, most of the people in my RV park don't really talk to me anyway, so, as long as I stay within the confines of my local area, not much is different, but if I get on social media, man, it's a shit storm."

"So, my listeners want to know, what were you on that night? Were you just drinking or were you on some serious drugs? Bear asks with an excited look on his face.

"Do I really have to give you all the details? I don't want to incriminate myself."

"That's what the listeners want to know. You don't want to disappoint the listeners, do you?" Causing everyone in the room and those pressed up against the glass to perk up.

Dude mumbles and then he blurts out, "well, it was a long day. I started early so I don't know what was still working inside my system by the time ten o'clock at night rolled around. But if I had to list the things I consumed throughout the day, I'd have to start with the couple cans of beer I had for breakfast. Then the whiskey I washed them down with. And you know how it is at the campgrounds during Bike Week. You can't walk five feet without someone passing you a joint. So, I had a few puffs with a guy named Spider, who was from Georgia."

"Hold on a minute. All this happened by what time?" Bear asks, with a glazed-over look on his face.

Bear has rock stars come into the studio all the time and they do some serious partying, but he doesn't spend much time with the average party animal when he is off air. Until this point, while watching the video of Dude, he just imagined a guy who was a lightweight and had gone out drinking on an empty stomach. Bear is quickly figuring out that what happened in Daytona was not a fluke.

"I don't know, I guess it had to be around noon by then."

"Wow! Were you planning to take a nap in the afternoon? How could you possibly think you could make it until midnight at that pace?" A puzzled Bear leans back in his chair.

"Who needs a nap when you can get energy drinks or speed?"

With the jaws of the spectators down on the floor and their eyes wide open, Bear jumps up and shouts, "that was your plan?"

"It's always part of the plan. How else do you think a middle-aged maniac like me keeps the party going all night? So, anyway, after the lunchtime smoke session with Spider, I rode out to the Cheyenne to meet up with friends and check out a local band while drinking a few more cold beers. I got a couple of burgers from the food truck that was in the bar's parking lot, and as I was sitting at the picnic table eating, Jackie boy offered me a line. And since I needed a pick-me-up, as soon as I finished eating, we headed to the restroom, and I did it without question. And sure enough, the second it hit the inside of my nostril, I knew it wasn't coke.

"Why, what was it?" A curious Bear couldn't wait to hear what this mysterious powder could have been. Being sober for years, Bear is out of the loop when it comes to street drugs.

"Rocket fuel like that could have only been one thing; Meth. I wasn't disappointed. My only complaint was that I didn't mentally prepare myself for that burning sensation in my sinuses. It knocked me out of my haze, that's for sure. Then it was time to head back to the campground to relax and get ready for a jam-packed night of partying on Main Street."

With many years of experience attending motorcycle rallies, Dude usually has a pretty good idea of what to expect. But no rally is ever the same, and every year the bikes and the personalities get bigger and bigger. Old bars close, and new bars open, so Main Street is always changing and the only way to know what's going on is to cruise up and down until your bike gets too hot. Then you park it and walk the street to get a closer look at the vendors, the bars, and always a showstopper; the half-naked girls selling cold beer out of horse troths.

"Back at my campground, after that kick in the pants from Jackie Boy, I was feeling pretty good. Then the young bucks that were camping a few tents down from me busted out a bottle of cinnamon whiskey and then twisted my arm to do a couple shots with them. And I'm sure that was what caused me to lose my shit; and my clothes!"

With silence in the studio, Bear wants to make sure he is hearing this right and asks, "so what you're saying is that you were drunk and high before you went out for the night?"

Obviously, Bear isn't aware of how much a beer can cost when you're buying it from a single mother wearing daisy dukes and a bikini top three sizes too small for her newly purchased breasts.

"You have to get primed up before you go out or it will cost a fortune to get a buzz on down there." Dude says like its common knowledge.

At this point, the whole studio is laughing their asses off and Bear is signaling to his producer to skip the commercial break and keep the tape rolling. He doesn't want to lose the momentum Dude has going and risk killing the flow. With a look of disapproval, the producer reluctantly gives Bear a thumbs up and motions for him to wrap it up soon.

"Ok Dude, now that you have made it down to Main Street, what happened next?"

"I parked my bike in front of the cemetery across from Boot Hill, then went into Main Street Station. There was a Lynyrd Skynyrd cover band rocking the stage out back, so I grabbed an overpriced beer from a short blond-haired girl who was young enough to be my daughter. Then I weaved my way through the sea of leather and found a stool with a view of the stage. When I heard the band start playing Free Bird, I knew they were about to wrap it up, so, I decided to keep it moving. It was getting dark as I made my way toward the front gate. I walked down to Froggy's where there were thongs and bras hanging from the ceiling and dollar bills stapled to the walls. The place smelled like stale beer and puke, so I only had one beer and split."

"It has to be getting late now. Tell us about what led up to the incident." Bear is now chomping at the bit to get the juicy details.

With the phone lines ringing off the hook and Bear ignoring all calls, the anticipation in the room is reaching capacity as people press their faces against the glass to witness Dude, now standing in front of his chair, headphones all disheveled, practically screaming into the microphone with his hands flying everywhere. It looks like they will have to drag Dude out of the studio at the rate he's going.

Then Dude slips. "I'm fuckin..."

"YO, YO, YO, you can't curse on the radio!" The producer screams across the speakers. "Please don't let it happen again or we will have to end the interview."

"Ok, my bad. Sorry about that. So, ah, anyway, where was I? Oh yeah, I remember. After I left Froggy's, I ran into a friend named Jessie I used to party with all the time back when I lived in New Jersey. I hadn't seen him in years, so we popped into this big tent to grab a beer and catch up. A few beers later, he asks if I want to take a couple puffs of a Moon Rock, which is one of the strongest forms of marijuana you can get. We hit the back alley and Jessie pulls out this fancy glass pipe and loads it up with a piece of this Moon Rock and then puts a lighter to it. With a delicious aroma in the air and smoke now coming out of Jessie's nose, he passes this smoking pipe to me. Wow! The taste was amazing and within a matter of minutes I was flying."

You would think someone who gets this high would need to wear a tracking device in case they get lost. With everyone in the studio staring in silence, Bear jumps out of his chair and with excitement in his voice he announces, "Dude, I bet that's what caused you to jump on stage naked!"

"Bingo! That and a little incentive from Jessie. He bet me five-hundred-bucks that I wouldn't do it and then he said he would make it one thousand if I stood there and played air guitar for sixty seconds. How could I pass on a deal like that? The band was rocking, and the lead singer was a hot chick, so I didn't think anyone would even notice me. I just went for it. I didn't notice the police at the back of the bar until I was standing up there on stage swinging my junk like a tripping Jim Morrison."

Laughing along with everyone else in the studio, Bear catches his breath and between laughs says, "man, you are nuts. And according to the video, you stayed up there for over sixty seconds, so I am assuming you collected the thousand bucks?"

"Yeah, it was reimbursement for the fine I had to pay. At least the Daytona Beach Police were nice enough to keep the price of my freedom fairly low. They let me use my credit card and I was out in a couple hours."

"How much longer did you stay in Daytona after you got out of jail?"

"Oh, not long. Angel was waiting for me in front of the cemetery when I got out, so we boogied straight back to the campground to catch some Z's before hitting the highway the next morning all sobered up."

"I received a ton of emails from people wanting to know, what the hell happened to your clothes?" Asking with a curious look on his face, Bear doesn't want the story to end.

"Great question. By the time they drug me to the police car, Jessie rushed over to throw me my jeans before the cops hauled my ass away. The two police officers were happy to let me put them on. One cop was all weirded out because my junk almost touched his arm."

"So, all you had on in the jail cell was a pair of jeans?"

"And my boots. Plus, eventually I had an orange Daytona Beach Police shirt the cops gave me to wear."

"That's too funny. So how come you haven't explained your side of the story to anyone since the incident? Bear asks with curiosity.

"There really isn't much to tell. I got wasted and made a fool of myself. No excuses. I mean, it's not like TV stations are lining up to interview a drunken biker who does dumb stuff for money. Plus, it's just another day on the roller coaster that is my life. It's not the first time I made a fool of myself in public and I'm sure it won't be the last."

"You mentioned your poker run, and I promised you an opportunity to let the listeners know about it. And you mentioned something about a missing motorcycle?"

The only reason Dude agreed to do this interview was for the opportunity to promote the poker run and get the word out about the missing antique bike. Thinking he should have made some notes for himself, he mumbles and then snaps himself out of the fog and, after wiping the sweat from his brow, his animated hands start flying again.

"The bottom line is, there is a poker run on Saturday morning. Five participating bars will open up at 9am sharp just for our people. Anyone can register at the rally's registration table. The cost is twenty bucks for a single rider and an extra ten for passengers. The winning hand gets five-hundred-dollars. The other half is going towards my good friend George's funeral. The other thing I want to mention is that last year at the Mud Hole Rally, George's motorcycle was stolen, and I have a one-thousand-dollar reward for anyone who has useful information about who took the red and white 1963 H-D Panhead."

Dude catches his breath; he is trying to think if there is anything else he forgot to mention. With every eye in the room fixated on him, the pressure to end on a high note is weighing on his every thought. Then he jumps to his feet, and with the look of a deer in the headlights he blurts out, "oh and uh, ladies, I'm single, come find me. Bear, thanks for the opportunity to let me share this info with your listeners. If anyone is going to be over at the rally this weekend, please stop by and say hi. I look forward to meeting you."

As Bear wraps up the interview, he says jokingly, "hey Dude, stay away from the whiskey and those Moon Rocks. These Watauga County Sheriffs are just waiting for someone like you to get out of control." Then he tells his listeners, "If you want to meet The Naked Biker Dude, he'll be at the Mud Hole Motorcycle Rally till Sunday. You can also find me there, too. I will be judging the bike show and broadcasting live Saturday afternoon. Look for the radio station tent and stop by for some free swag. We're giving out koozies, key chains, beer mugs, and a whole host of other prizes, including concert tickets to the biggest rock shows of the summer. Thanks again for coming in Dude, that's a wrap."

Bear pushes play on AC/DC's Highway to Hell, then he takes off his headphones and walks over to Dude and gives him a big bear hug and says, "I can't wait to hear about what kind of shit you pull this weekend."

# Chapter 3

THE SUN IS WORKING its way down as Dude cruises along the back roads of this mountainside town of Mud Hole. It's only a hop, skip, and a jump from the radio station to the farm. His last stop before he hits the rally's main gate, Dude pulls into a gas station to grab a case of beer and top off his tank. As he walks out of the gas station store, he sees a couple of young guys checking out his motorcycle.

Giving the guys a nod as he walks up, Dude sits the case of beer on the ground. Then he's taking off the gas cap when the shorter of the two young guys says to him, "hey, nice bike."

"Thanks."

The two guys step closer and within a matter of seconds, one of them asks, "are you The Biker Dude?"

Quickly shooting his eyes away from the pump handle and over towards the back of the bike, he asks, "What tipped you off, kid?"

The young buck with the black Harley t-shirt says, "your custom license plate gave it away." Then he tells Dude, "We just heard you on the radio with Bear. Great interview. You're a sick motherfucker."

Laughing under his breath, Dude smiles and responds, "stay away from that whiskey, it's a bitch."

Just the thought of drinking that liquid poison gives Dude a headache, but it doesn't stop him from drinking it. The young guys were interested in the rally and asking a ton of questions about the cost and what all would be going on. They say they're locals but didn't know the rally was happening until they heard him talk about it on the radio. Complaining about having to work on Friday, they want to know if it's worth going for only one day.

"Anyone is welcome." Dude tells them, "I think a one-day ticket costs around twenty bucks. Not exactly sure, I bought a weekend pass. Swing by, it's well worth the money. Saturday is the best day if you have to choose only one. There will be all kinds of crazy biker games, a bike show, a burnout pit, and some killer bands. And of course, the wet t-shirt contest. There will be topless chicks everywhere. If you make it over, stop by and say hi; you'll see my bike. And if you see my baby, you can be sure I'm not too far away. Tell your friends about the poker run."

He puts the gas cap back on, then goes into the saddlebag and pulls out a flyer for the missing motorcycle and hands it to the guy doing all the talking. "Please ask around about this old bike. Call me if you get any info." Dude warns the two guys to step back. "I don't want to blow your hat off when I fire up this hog."

They part ways with the two young guys being excited about the possibility of going to a real old school biker party. They tell Dude, Saturday sounds awesome, and they will try to stop by.

***

Ten minutes later, Dude rolls up to the main gate of the farm. A handful of workers are checking tickets and putting red wristbands on everyone's arm before letting them through the gate. There is a trailer set up on the left side of the dirt road with a registration table covered by a tent.

There are five bikes ahead of Dude as he rolls in. After he waits his turn in line, he pulls up to the short guy with the bright orange vest and arms covered in ink. Putting the bike in neutral, Dude reaches into his jacket and pulls his ticket from an inside pocket. Just as the guy is wrapping the red paper wristband around Dude's left arm, a voice from the distance echoes across the field, "yee fuckin haw! Dude, so glad you finally made it. Follow me."

The voice belongs to his buddy, Santa, who he met last year at the Mud Hole Rally; a local hillbilly who loves to party. The only presents he gives out, is in the form of beads when he throws them at girls who are willing to lift their shirts. With his long white scruffy beard, a beat-up straw hat, a pair of blue jean overalls, no shirt, and a neck full of beads; Santa is a chick magnet.

After getting the go-ahead from the short guy with the sleeves, Dude follows Santa off the dirt road and onto the grass to the right, through an open field littered with mostly tents and motorcycles lined up along the fence. The middle of the field is where the RVs and campers of all kinds are set up. Everything from Drivable Coachmen to tow behind Fleetwood's to old campervans form a semi-straight line up the center of the enormous field of freshly cut grass. Motorcycles are scattered everywhere.

The two ride in on the left side of the field between the tents along the fence and the row of campers up the middle. Continuing straight to the other end of the field where it loops around to the right, they make their way back down the other side of the campers until they see a black flag with a skull on it. Slowing down, Santa pulls towards the left and comes to a stop in front of two tents with a newly built firepit in the middle.

They haven't even been off their bikes for thirty seconds when Santa slurs, "I got a special treat for ya Dude."

"Ah, na, na, I'm still hungover from that shit you made last year."

"Don't you worry, my moonshine is as clean as it gets. Not like that store-bought bullshit."

The arm-twisting continued for a few minutes before Dude gave in and took a swig of this clear liquid out of a mason jar that smelled like lighter fluid. With fire in his eyes and his tongue hanging out of his mouth, Dude looks toward the sun setting over the mountains in the distance and lets out a thunderous battle cry, "THE GREAT OUTDOORS!"

Hooting, hollering and cheering erupt from campsites all around them. Dude feels right at home as people continued stopping by to introduce themselves to their new favorite loudmouth. Taking a break to *cheers* everyone who passes by is slowing down the process of getting his tent set up. He's hoping to finish before it becomes a pain in the ass trying to see in the dark.

With his mind shifting from alcohol to food, Dude lets Santa know he hasn't eaten all day. Without hesitation, Santa calls his old lady, "hey Sweet Tits, grab me a few burgers and dogs while I get this fire started." Kat gets the food out of the cooler and hands it to Santa. Then she turns to Dude and says, "oh, and by the way, you're famous around these parts. We heard you on the radio!"

Kat Miller stands at five-foot even with long straight brown hair, and tan skin with tattoos scattered all over her body. She looks like a spring chicken compared to most other women in their early fifties because of her tight skin, those plump breasts and that cute little ass on her skinny frame. Her feisty attitude tends to attract assholes who are only looking for a cheap thrill. She is currently off the market, so anyone who hits on her is risking a kick in the nuts.

She goes on for the next ten minutes, asking a ton of questions about what it was like to be in the studio and get interviewed by Bear. He told her it was a lot of fun and then he asked how it sounded over the airwaves. Kat let him know it was great and how much fun it was laughing and having a good time listening to the interview.

Finally unhooking the bungee cords off his luggage rack, Dude grabs his tent and starts rolling it out across the grass as he hears Santa trying to get his attention. "Here's a good spot for ya." Dude drags the tent over about ten feet and then starts assembling the poles. A few minutes later, a green and gray dome rises from the ground. And with the addition of a small pillow and a sleeping bag, Dude's weekend home is complete.

The sun is now buried behind the Blue Ridge Mountains, and the music from the stage radiates back to the camping area; a clear sign this rally is officially underway.

***

"Grab me a beer, it's been a long day. I could really use another cold one." Dude yells over to Santa as he gets the camping chair off the side of his saddlebag, then sets it up next to the firepit. "What time is your nephew going to be here in the morning? I want to get him set up at the registration table as early as possible so he can start signing people up for the poker run as they come in."

A grumbling Santa tells Dude, "Don't worry, Tommy is a reliable kid. He said he will be here by 7am, so that's when you can expect to meet him. You can give him all the details in the morning."

Two bikes pull up in front of their campsite and cut off the engines. Getting off the silver and black anniversary edition Harley Road King is a huge lumberjack who looks like he could be Paul Bunyan's long-lost son. Clocking in at six-two, two-hundred and eighty pounds, he towers over the blond-haired woman who is dressed like she is straight out of a comic book with the amount of padded riding gear she is wearing. Her three wheeled motorcycle has all the bells and whistles. The only thing missing is a rocket launcher to complete her apocalypse preparedness kit. The big man with the red beard leans down and gives her a kiss and a pat on the ass and says, "nice ridin' baby."

Santa climbs out of his chair to greet the couple. "I hope you two had a nice ride around Mud Hole. I'm looking forward to cruising some back roads tomorrow. Come over here, I got a friend that I want y'all to meet. He's your new tent neighbor. Chuck and Birdie, this is Dude, the guy we were telling you about."

There are handshakes and hugs between the new friends. Everyone is making quick work of getting acquainted. "We rode over from Tennessee. We got here early to set up our tent and then went out for a cruise and decided to hop on the Blue Ridge Parkway. What an amazing road! And the view from the lookout points is pretty damn cool too." Chuck tells Dude and then asks him where he rode in from.

Saying he rode over from Raleigh; Dude moves on to telling everyone about his ride across beautiful North Carolina. Acknowledging that it could have been worse, he talks about how it all started with the sky opening up and dumping buckets of rain on him for the first half of the trip. With his hands moving like a conductor of an orchestra, his voice gets louder as he lets the group know about him getting pulled over for speeding.

"I got felt up by a man on the side of 421 north."

With everyone laughing at the expense of Dude's misfortune, he gives the officer some credit and mentions catching a break and only getting one ticket with a small fine and no points.

"I guess it's a whole hell of a lot better than him putting me in handcuffs. Thankfully the cop didn't go in that right side saddle bag, or I would have been in trouble."

Santa perks up with curiosity. A quiet chatter breaks out among the group and then Chuck shows interest in what Dude is being so secretive about. "What do ya got? Let's see it." The natives are getting restless. Dude gets up and walks over to his bike and pops open the lid of the saddlebag and pulls out his rain gear, a sweatshirt, a pair of gloves, some extra glasses, a flashlight, and a bunch of other gear.

"Where's the good shit?" A buzzed Santa is now out of his chair and doing his best to see what Dude is up to.

After a small tool kit, Dude finally pulls out a can of brake cleaner and starts walking back towards the firepit. With flashlights in one hand and cans of beer in the other, their heads are tilted sideways as the group all shared the same puzzled look on their faces. Most likely wondering why someone would get in trouble for carrying a can of brake cleaner.

Flipping the can upside down with both hands, Dude starts twisting one hand clockwise and the other counterclockwise. Through the smoke coming off the fire, there is just enough light to see everyone's eyes widening as he unscrews the false bottom of the can and pulls out a plastic bag full of pre-rolled joints.

Dude proclaims, "Let's get this party started! This weekend is dedicated to George Walker. Cheers!" He pulls out two joints.

The entire group is smiling and laughing, while fumbling around in their pockets, seeing who can be the first one to pull out a lighter. Handing one joint to Santa and putting a second one in between his lips, Dude lets the group know to pass them to the right. "And please don't slobber all over them."

The crew eases back in their chairs as the music from the stage gets louder. With the sweet smell of cheeba spreading across the farm, Birdie asks if anyone is ready to walk over and check out the bands. With everyone in agreement, Kat puts cans of beer in a cooler bag while the rest of them fold up their camping chairs and get ready to head toward the stage.

Walking along the line of campers, the group stops to check out this wild custom trike parked in between two RVs. After a brief conversation with the owner of the trike, he tags along for the walk to the stage. With everyone walking, talking, and getting to know each other, Dude asks if anyone had been over to see the vendors yet.

Chuck mentions he took a spin around the main grounds earlier in the day when the vendors were just getting set up. He wasn't sure if any new vendors had popped up since around noon, but goes on about the ones he saw earlier.

"They got someone sewing on patches, a whole tent full of leather products, new and used motorcycle parts and I saw another guy selling beef jerky, turkey jerky, and he even got deer jerky. They've got a little bit of everything. We will get a better look at the vendors during the daylight tomorrow."

Needing to know if he saw the vendor selling rally t-shirts, patches, and pins, Dude looks over at Chuck who is banging his head to the music and with a raised voice lets him know, "I need a patch for my vest and a t-shirt for my collection. I have one from every rally I've ever been to."

Dude gets a Harley shirt from every dealership he comes across on his travels. He also collects the poker chips with each of the dealers' names and location on each side. They range from two-tone bright colors to traditional black and orange. Dude always gets an extra chip to mail to his niece in Florida. He started by getting the colors a female teenager would like, but with her collection growing so big, now he just looks for ones that are unique in an attempt to avoid giving her a color combination she already has.

Asking Chuck to remind him not to forget the shirt and patch, Dude talks about not wanting to wait till the last day because they always sell out of his size fast and by the time Sunday rolls around, there won't be any extra larges left and they will only have small sizes.

The closer they get to the stage, the louder the music becomes.

Entering the main grounds, with the stage at the close end and vendors on both sides and across the back, they head straight towards the stage. Being led by Santa, they make their way through the maze of leather and tattoos. Skirting around a blanket covered with people who are mesmerized from staring up at the stars, the group stumbles upon an open patch of grass in the middle of the crowd. With a good view of the stage, and easy access to the porta potties, the group stakes their claim with camping chairs and a cooler bag which was unzipped immediately after hitting the grass.

Approximately fifty feet from the stage and off to the right is where the crew plants their flag for the next couple hours. The band kicks it up a notch with a cover of Black Sabbath's song, *Paranoid*. As the imitation Ozzy begins singing, a short red-haired girl stands up on the seat of a motorcycle and flashes her titties to the crowd, causing cheers from near and far. Birdie shakes her head and lets everyone know that there is zero chance of her flashing anybody. And with a towering Chuck nodding his head in agreement, the message was crystal clear; don't bother asking!

As for Kat, taking off her shirt in front of people is no big deal. She was a stripper when Santa first met her. It only takes a little bit of liquor to get Kat going and you won't hear any objections from her old man. He is usually the one encouraging her to take it off.

Motorcycles and golf carts continue to pour into the main grounds to get ready for tonight's headliner. A cloud of smoke from the food vendors comes blowing by, bringing with it the smell of freshly cooked barbeque. Dude reaches his hand into the ice-filled cooler and pulls out a frosty can of PBR and then asks if anyone else needs one.

Now kicked back in his chair, Dude's eyes start scanning the crowd. With half-naked hotties in every direction, he's not sure whether to start taking pictures or go prospecting for phone numbers. One girl is getting everyone's attention. She has a fine ass and a cute face, but it's the 9mm pistol on her hip that is attracting all the eyes.

With the temperature hovering around seventy degrees at night, the daytime sun should be hot enough to get everyone out of their clothes. Speaking of heating things up, the night's final act is about to go on.

The Emcee of the rally takes the stage to introduce the band. "GOOD EVENING EVERYBODY! I'm Uncle Tucker and I am so excited to be your master of ceremonies for the weekend. We have an amazing line up for y'all and right now it is my pleasure to bring to the stage, America's number one AC/DC tribute band. Put your hands together for THUNDER BALLS!"

The first guitar cord comes screaming through the speakers and the crowd roars. As the drums kick in, the cheers get even louder and then the stage lights shoot out over the crowd. With a clear sky and the lights shining brightly, you can see a silhouette of the Blue Ridge Mountains behind the stage. Thunder Balls finds their groove and so does the crowd.

Thursday night's party is just what the doctor ordered for these hard-working blue-collar bikers looking for a good time. Seemingly without a care in the world, everyone is smiling and singing along to the good old-fashioned rock-n-roll.

A cloud of smoke hovers over the crowd, who is dancing the night away.

With a long travel day catching up to the group and the anticipation of an early morning looming, the five of them begin the trek back to their tents to rest up for the madness that tomorrow will bring.

The group walks through the barely lit camping area, discussing their agenda for tomorrow.

Santa speaks up. "Get some sleep. I'm going to take y'all on some beautiful back roads tomorrow."

# Chapter 4

THE SUN IS COMING up over the mountains and the bright light is shooting through the canvas of the tent, causing Dude to wake up sweating his ass off. He wakes to the sound of roaring engines and screaming pipes. The new arrivals are giving out wake-up calls to everyone in the camping area. Shortly after the rolling alarm clocks pass by, Dude dozes off for a couple more precious minutes of sleep. His dream is cut short when someone in a truck cranks up the local country station on their radio and gives a second wake up call to everybody within an earshot.

Dude's first thoughts are about getting Tommy set up for registering people for the poker run and then finding a cup of hot coffee. He unzips his tent and pops his head out. He sees smoke coming off the smoldering ashes of the fire pit and Kat sitting there by herself. She was up half the night because of the pain in her back. The random stragglers stumbling by making noise had her paranoid about someone messing with the bikes. Figuring since she couldn't sleep anyway, she got out of the tent to sit guard.

"Good morning, Dude. How'd you sleep?"

Standing up through the opening of his tent in his boxer shorts, Dude stretches his arms toward the sky. He lets Kat know he slept good until the mountain side wake-up calls.

"Shook me out of this dream I was having where I was banging some hot, young blonde. She was bent over the side of my motorcycle and a chicken was watching us go at it. Weird, huh?"

"Sounds like a fun dream to me. I'm pretty sure that big guy with the blue bike woke everyone up when he pulled in."

"It's no big deal. I have to piss anyway. Is Tommy here yet?"

Kat lets him know. "He is on his way now. Should be here real soon."

Dude puts on a pair of jeans and a black t-shirt from Six-Bends H-D in Ft. Myers, Florida. He steps out of the tent and kneels down to put on his boots. He grabs a bottle of water, his toothbrush and toothpaste from the tent, and walks to an open patch of grass, then brushes his teeth.

He lets Kat know he is walking to the port-a-potties and then he wants to find coffee. Kat tells him that there is a vendor selling coffee, donuts, and other breakfast food. She already had her coffee, but she tells him that Santa will need one when he wakes up.

Santa sleeps like a bear but it's almost impossible for anyone to stay zipped up in a hot tent past 9am. You have to be really drunk to sleep during the day with the endless amount of thunder that fills the air at a rally like this.

As Dude walks to the portable toilet, he can see bunches of motorcycles rolling through the main gate across the field. Tents are popping out of the ground everywhere like weeds. A bunch of people must have come in overnight because Dude didn't remember seeing this many people when he went to sleep.

Stepping out of the porta-potty, he pulls his shirt down from over his face and exhales. Desperate for fresh air, he takes a few deep breaths. Trying not to imagine what the plastic boxes will smell like later in the night, Dude walks away hoping his coffee doesn't run right through him.

As he's walking back to his campsite through a maze of tents, his nose perks up and then he sees a cute red-haired girl sitting in the driver's seat of a white Jeep Gladiator truck smoking weed from a pipe. Locking eyes, she motions to Dude, lifting the pipe and stretching her arm out towards him, "you want a hit?"

"Sure, if you don't mind sharing."

"Not at all. Come have a seat."

The door opens and a pair of cowgirl boots hit the ground. Dude's eyes follow her long legs up from the grass to her super short daisy dukes, followed by a flat, smooth stomach with the cutest little belly button. Turning her back to Dude for a moment, he sees a peek of a thong sticking up from her shorts. Trying not to get caught, he glances up at her boobs, which are peeking out of a small red and black plaid shirt with a knot tied in the bottom. Every part of her sixty-seven-inch body is packing a punch.

"Will do. My name's Dude. What's yours?" Following her to the back of the jeep, she drops the tailgate, hops up, and takes a seat. Dude follows suit and plants his ass right next to this cutie holding the pipe. Cozying up next to her, knees bumping into each other, she turns to him, "I'm Trixie. Thanks for the company. My girlfriends don't smoke."

He hadn't noticed her friends sitting in chairs on the other side of the vehicle. When Trixie calls her two friends over to introduce them, Dude is pleasantly surprised. "This is Dude." A short brown-haired girl stands up and with an exhausted look on her face says, "I'm married."

"Did your mom name you that?" Dude asks with a non-interested look on his face.

"Ha ha, very funny. You can call me Emma. Did your mom name you Dude? How'd you pick the name?"

With no husband in sight and a hot body like hers, that wedding ring won't have much power in stopping people from trying to pick her up this weekend. Her defense strategy must be to scare guys away with her miserable attitude.

"Growing up at the Jersey Shore, I spent a lot of time hanging around surfers. I went through a phase when I was calling everyone dude. Eventually

I had a couple friends who would mock me for it, and they gave me the nickname Dude as a joke, but it stuck."

Trixie lets him know as she looks him up and down, "I think it's cute. Since you are a tall handsome dude, I think the name is spot on."

Dude is only three inches taller than her, but he'll take the compliment.

Having just arrived this morning, they haven't made too much progress getting their camp set up. Only putting out their chairs so far, they need to unwind from their two-hour drive before taking on the task of unloading the jeep and setting up their tents.

From the passenger side of the jeep, a tall blonde appears wearing a bikini top and a tight pair of booty shorts. The huge rose tattoo on her upper right arm catches Dude's eye immediately. While rubbing sunscreen on her chest and belly, she peers over at Dude and says, "I'm Peggy. Nice to meet you. Perfect timing, uh, can you help us set up our tents?"

"I'd be happy to help. Seems like a fair trade. Smells good, what kind of bud are you smoking?

The cute redhead holding the smoking pipe lets Dude know, "this is OG Kush. I scored it from my cousin in Tennessee. He never disappoints. Here, taste it." She hands him the fancy handmade glass piece of art and a lighter. Dude takes a big hit and after holding in the smoke for a minute, he exhales and lets her know it tastes great. Then he calls it the real breakfast of champions.

"I'm glad you like it. Where are you set up at?"

Pointing towards where his tent is, Dude tells Trixie, "I'm just over there, not far at all."

Smoking and getting to know each other, it's clear Dude is interested in much more than just smoking her weed. Focusing solely on Trixie like her friends weren't even there, he asks common questions like, "where are you from, and how do you girls know each other?"

"We live in Asheville and all work together at a stupid call center selling magazine subscriptions to suckers. Coming here is our way of trying to forget about that place, so we have agreed not to talk about work while we're here." Followed by a big hit. Trixie is hoping that was the last time she would have to say the word *work* for the rest of the weekend.

The conversation was going great and then Trixie, with flirtation in her voice, asks Dude, "what are you riding? Maybe I can stop by later to check out your bike."

"Sounds great. I'd love to see you later. I'm on a black 2017 Harley Road Glide. You can't miss me."

"There are a lot of black motorcycles here. What makes yours stand out?"

"Besides the snakeskin seat and some shiny chrome details, my name is on the license plate. It has a nice comfy spot for a passenger if you're up for a ride later."

“I’ll consider your offer.”

The potential of getting Trixie on the back of his bike has motivated Dude to pop up off his ass and ask the girls to get the tents out of the jeep. Unpacking the tents, Dude asks the girls to stand in the spot where each one wants theirs to go. Squeezed between a trailer hooked to a blue Chevy and the camp of an older couple who were sitting there minding their own business, each girl picks her spot. One by one, Dude assembles each tent and places it in the spot of choice. The appreciation of the threesome is overwhelming. “You are so helpful. Stop by anytime.” Peggy extends an invitation Dude will surely take her up on.

As much as Dude would like to drag his tent along the grass and put it smack dab next to Trixie’s, he resists the temptation. After thanking them for the wake and bake, he lets the girls know he’s heading over to get a coffee and asks if any of them want one.

Trixie responds for the group with a smile on her face and a devilish look in her eye, “no, thanks, were good for now. We have energy drinks in the cooler. We are just going to relax and check out the bikes, and the guys as they roll in.”

“Don’t be cheating on me.”

Trixie smiles and says, “we’ll see about that.” With Dude now walking away, she yells, “nice ass!”

He looks back with a smile and throws up a peace sign with his hand.

***

Back at his bike, shuffling through his tour pack, Dude is a happy camper. He can't wait to tell Santa and the crew all about Trixie and her girlfriends. But he's trying to play it cool, so he doesn't mention them yet.

Everyone is now awake and sitting around a pile of ashes, talking about their plans for the day. Then Dude notices a fifth person sitting next to Santa.

"Is this Tommy?" Dude's eyes widen as he realizes that it's time to get to work on raising money for George's burial.

"This is my brother Billy's kid. Tommy meet Dude. He is the one you will be working for this weekend."

Tommy pushes up the sleeves of his dirty green shirt and reaches for Dude's hand. "It's a pleasure to meet you." In his mid-twenties, Tommy is built like a brick shithouse with a short blonde crew cut. He remains standing up with an anxious look in his eyes. "I'm ready to get started."

"Sounds great. Follow me down to the registration table." Dude gets on his motorcycle and Tommy gets into his red Chevy pickup, then they make their way through the camping area.

The registration table for the rally is covered with people coming and going, but there is only one person Dude is looking for: Tex Anderson. He is the man in charge of the whole rally and Dude's contact person for getting Tommy a seat at the registration table.

After a quick chat with Tex, Dude unloads the supplies from his saddlebag. With his hands full, he moves under the white tent and drops everything on the table. Tommy will spend the day next to a large woman named Hammer, who looks like she just broke out of prison yesterday. Her dark curly hair is wildly puffed out in every direction and her leather skinned face looks like it could be a mask. Her abundance of silver metal bracelets is drawing attention to her left hand, which is covered by a pentagram tattoo.

"Tommy, sit here on the end. This flyer has all the info about the motorcycle that was stolen from my friend last year. Ask everyone if they know anything about it and if they do, have them call me. The sign-up sheet sits here next to the flyer, explaining the details and rules of the poker run. When someone signs up, make sure they put their name and phone number, and be sure to ask them if they will have a passenger who wants to play also. Once they sign the sheet, take their money, and put it in this pouch, then zip it. Then you put one of these yellow wristbands on their arm. This lets us and the participating bars know who is with the poker run group. If you have any questions, call me, here's my number."

Dude gives Tommy twenty dollars up-front and lets him know he will get the other eighty at the end of the night. Dude is paying him another hundred bucks tomorrow to man the finish line and document each riders' cards as they check in. Dude will announce the winner from the registration table at high noon, just before the bike show gets started.

With the business end of the day delegated to Tommy, Dude makes his way back to camp to see what time they will be heading out for a ride.

He has George on his mind as he plows across the grass. Reflecting on the good times they spent together over the many years. Thinking to himself, *what would George do?* He knows if George were here, he would be on the hunt for the missing Panhead, but Dude also knows that nothing would stop George Walker from having a good time. He loved to smoke weed and cigars. George only drank two things: beer and coffee. His favorite food was anything deep fried. When it came to motorcycle rallies, George loved the bikes, but he went for the party. Dude knows George wouldn't want him moping around all weekend. George would want his life celebrated; not mourned over.

Dude thinks to himself. *If it's a party George would want; it's a party George will get! I dedicate this weekend to the life and memory of George Walker.*

***

Still craving coffee, Dude announces to the group that he is walking over to get a hot cup. Santa offers to take the walk with him. After a deep breath, the old man tugs up on his pant legs and pushes himself up and out of his chair.

The two make their way through the camping area on foot. Trying not to seem too interested, Dude purposely takes a different route to avoid passing by Trixie and her friends.

Walking the long way around the camping area, Dude is taking in the sights of this enormous property. Surrounded by mountains, the farm spreads well beyond the areas being used for the rally. Cows appear tiny on the hills in the distance. Roads appear to be carved into the side of the massive tree-covered mountain across the road from the farm. Looking like the size of ants, cars move through the trees. The rolling hills of the property allow Dude to see the tops of the vendor tents as he and Santa make their way past the registration table.

The main rally area of the farm has a grand entrance featuring a set of tall hand carved wooden logs standing in an upright position, and a steel sign connected on each side to the post. Inside of an arched metal frame, reads the name of the farm in rusted metal lettering.

Passing under the Lone Ranger's Farm sign, the boys are greeted with a wide-open field with motorcycles parked in the middle, the stage to their right, and vendor tents set up along the outside edge of the other three sides of the main rally area. People are scattered everywhere. Trash from last night's affairs remain littered in front of the stage. The smoke coming off the food vendors' trucks at the far end of the field is the next thing Dude notices.

Along the line of vendors, people are coming and going and checking out what's for sale. Starting with the first tent, where a woman who is surrounded by patches with a spider tattoo on her neck, is sewing the letters USA onto the chest of a black leather vest. Beside her tent is a man selling handmade jewelry.

A dark-skinned woman smelling like coconut oil walks up to Santa and starts stroking his long white beard. "Hey sugar! Can I take a ride on your sled?"

Loving the attention and more than happy to flirt, Santa would never cheat on his old lady. He glances down this woman's shirt as she cops her feel and then he keeps it moving. They are on a mission to get coffee. Just before they arrive at the food vendors in the back, they pass the last tent on the left where the radio station is set up. The street team is giving away radio station swag and they have a prize wheel set up. Dude asks the young girl when Bear would be around.

"Tomorrow around noon."

He thanks her and spins the wheel. He wins a black 97.7 BMRP t-shirt with a picture of a guitar on the front and the radio station logo on the back. Dude swings the shirt up over his shoulder as he walks away with a big smile on his face. The sun is reflecting off his sunglasses as he walks up to the kitchen on wheels to order his coffee.

Speaking through a small open window, a little old lady with a Trump 2020 hat on asks, "what'll it be?"

"Large coffee with cream and sugar and an order of biscuits and gravy, please. Hey Santa, what do you want? It's on me."

"Black coffee and a plain donut would be great. Thanks Dude."

They take a seat at a nearby picnic table with their food and drinks. Reminiscing about last year's rally and how miserable it was because of the rain, the two of them are thanking the biker gods for providing such nice weather this year.

"Me and Kat are looking forward to getting out and riding some back roads today. I'm not sure about Chuck and Birdie, but what's your plan, are you coming with us?"

"Yeah, I told you I'm up for a ride. And guess what, I may even be bringing a passenger if I play my cards right."

Dude tells Santa all about what happened this morning on his way back from taking a piss. Getting excited just talking about Trixie, he stands up then moves his hands in the shape of an hourglass to describe her body. He offers a fifty-dollar bet to Santa to show how confident he is that she will be on the back of his bike when they roll out. Reaching out his hand, "you're on." Santa makes the wager official.

There is nothing like a southern breakfast to get the day started off right. Rubbing his belly and unbuttoning his pants, Dude is ready to walk back, but his body needs a few more minutes. Taking in the sights, sounds, and smells of everything the main grounds has to offer, the two plan their next move.

They decide to check out the vendors along the back and then clockwise around the field to see what's on the other side. A female mannequin wearing a bulletproof vest catches their attention. It was standing in front of a twenty-foot-long trailer with two openings exposed by the hatches that were lifted up. Inside is a large man sitting behind a small table, taking apart a gun. Next to him is a heavyset woman standing in front of a wall of bullets, trying to get the attention of people walking by. It looks like she is wearing a Dog the Bounty Hunter Halloween costume. She has handcuffs hooked to her belt loop, and a taser holstered on her right hip.

Noticing a glass case full of knives, Dude walks over to get a closer look.

Pulling out his money to pay for a traditional green camo pocketknife with a matte black blade that flips out, the lady behind the counter says, "I will give you two for thirty dollars." The moment he looks back down into the case, a pink camouflage knife catches his eye. "Sounds good. I will take the pink one for my new redheaded friend."

Thinking the gift will increase the chance of winning the bet, Dude gloats to Santa as they continue their stroll down vendor row. Stopping them dead in their tracks is a box truck with a law firm logo on the side and two smokin' hot blondes handing out free can koozies.

"Yes, please. Whatever you're selling, sign me up." Santa says to the girls as he pushes his way in front of Dude. Dressed like gothic Hooters girls, if these two were standing on the side of a highway, they would definitely cause an accident. They may even cause a few guys to break their neck or drop their motorcycle trying to get a look. Hoping to see one of these girls again in tomorrow's wet t-shirt contest, the guys walk away before one of them says something obnoxious and gets themselves slapped.

They step up to the guy with blankets full of used motorcycle parts. Dude scans the lot of parts for anything related to a Panhead. Nothing catches his eye. Stepping out from the rear of a blue pickup truck is a fragile old man with a flannel shirt and denim blue jeans that are being held up by a pair of black and gold suspenders. He identifies himself as Willie, then tips his sunglasses down onto his nose. He peers over at Dude and asks if he is looking for anything in particular.

"Yes sir, I am. Anything from a 60s Panhead."

"I have nothing for a Panhead, but I have a set of rocker covers for a Shovelhead if that helps you any."

Dude asks the guy questions about whether he has heard anything about an old police bike being sold in this area in the past twelve months. Dude hands Willie a flyer with the details of the missing motorcycle. The old man's eyes light up when he sees the one-thousand-dollar reward. "I haven't seen or heard anything about it, but I will be sure to ask around. I will call your number if I get any info."

With the prospect of having Willie putting his feelers out, Dude's level of optimism just clicked up a notch. He is relying on the locals for info and who better than the man who is wheeling and dealing motorcycle parts.

Dude and Santa head straight back to the camping area to relax before they head out for a ride. Santa is still worked up from the sexy lawyer girls. Immediately upon getting back to camp, he takes Kat in the tent to have her finish what the two blondes started.

# Chapter 5

THE GROUP DISCUSSES THEIR plans for the day while sitting around the fire pit. Chuck and Birdie want to relax and take in the sights at the farm since they were out cruising around yesterday. Santa and Kat are planning a scenic ride to downtown Blowing Rock for lunch. They invite Dude to join them. He is excited to take the ride, but with some hesitation, he tells the couple he will be right back.

Dude walks like a man on a mission while rehearsing his pitch to get Trixie on board for the ride. Approaching the white Jeep, at first, he doesn't see anyone. Getting closer, he sees Trixie's tent door wide open with her sitting up on an air mattress with her legs crossed. She looks up at Dude as he walks toward her alongside the jeep. He hears *American Kids* by Kenny Chesney streaming from her tent as he gets closer. Knocking on her tent as if it were a door, Dude jokingly asks if he is interrupting anything.

"I'm just sitting here, bored out of my mind. We were supposed to walk over to the main grounds to check out what's going on, but I'm still waiting for these two to get their crap together. Emma has been on the phone with her husband for over an hour and Peggy said she was only taking a quick nap, but it's been a while."

"Sounds frustrating. I have an offer that will cure your boredom but before I forget, I bought you a gift."

Dude pulls a black rectangular shaped box out of his pants pocket and extends his arm through the unzipped door of the tent. Somewhat reluctant to grab the box, Trixie looks at it like a snake will pop out when she opens it. He assures her it's not alive.

She blushes as she takes it from his hand. "Thank you. This is very flattering. Whatever it is, you really didn't have to."

"I thought of you as soon as I saw it. Open the box."

A surprised look comes over her face as he mentions thinking about her.

"My ex never bought me gifts. You're so sweet."

"Does that mean you are single?" Dude asks and then holds his breath, anxiously waiting for her answer.

"It does. We broke up six months ago."

A huge sense of relief comes over Dude. He has a smile from ear to ear as he leans in toward Trixie, who is now on her knees preparing to open the mysterious box. With Dude down on one knee and Trixie opening a small suspicious box, this has all the makings of a redneck proposal.

"I do, love it! Thank you so much." Trixie shows her appreciation by leaning forward and giving Dude a long hug and a kiss on the cheek. She grabs the pink camouflage handle with her right hand and unfolds the shiny metal blade with her thumb. Wielding the knife like a pro, Trixie makes stabbing motions like she's taking out her cellmate with a shiv. Dude slowly backs away from the tent and asks her to step outside.

"The weather is too nice for you to be cooped up in that hot tent. How would you like to cool off by getting some wind in your face?"

She takes a few seconds to process what he means, then asks, "are you asking me to go for a ride on your motorcycle?"

"Absolutely! It will be great. I'm about to go for a scenic ride with my friend Santa and his wife, Kat. They're great people, you will love them. We're leaving soon. Are you in?"

With excitement written all over her face, she glances toward the tents of her friends as if she was looking for their approval. Emma, who can be heard from fifty feet away, continues to chirp into her phone and Peggy sounds like she is sawing wood. Trixie asks a few questions about where they're going and how long they will be gone for.

Dude tells her about how beautiful Blowing Rock is and lets her know they would be back in a few hours.

Determined to have fun and forget about reality for the weekend, Trixie gives Dude a resounding yes. He moves in for a celebratory hug, which she embraces.

"Just put on a pair of long pants and bring a jacket. I will swing by to pick you up in half an hour."

Dude is practically skipping through other people's campsites he is so excited. At every rally, there is one girl that captures his attention above all others. He is getting good vibes from Trixie, and a ride on the back of Angel is sure to seal the deal.

Storming into the camp like a bat out of hell, Dude announces he and Trixie are going for the ride. Then he turns to Santa and tells him to pay up.

"I don't see a girl on the back of your bike."

"You'll see her when we stop by her camp on our way out."

"Who is this chick?" Kat wants to know what's going on.

Dude cracks open a cold beer to celebrate his minor victory. Passing one to Santa, they bang their cans together and say *cheers*. He tells Kat about how he met Trixie and her girlfriends. He says she is a fellow stoner, and everyone is going to love her.

"If she has nice tits, I like her already." Kat slaps Santa across the mouth and tells him, "Watch it old man."

Impatiently waiting next to Santa's bike, Kat is ready to go.

Santa bungees a small cooler bag of beer to the tour pack of his red '96 HD Ultra Classic. He mounts his sled and Kat climbs on behind him.

Dude fires up his bike and lets it idle as he scans through the radio stations looking for anything but a commercial. A brief clip of *Stairway to Heaven* was all it took, and he was good to go. He popped Angel in to first gear and yells over to Santa.

"Hey, I will lead us to her campsite and then we need to stop by the vendors before we can roll out. We'll check on Tommy and then you can be our road captain once we hit the asphalt."

As they approach Trixie's campsite, Dude sees her standing in front of her jeep with her ginger hair in a ponytail, wearing cowboy boots, skin-tight jeans, and a low-cut top with her cleavage fully exposed. With a white jacket in one hand and her thumb sticking out like a hitchhiker with the other, Trixie is ready and waiting. "I thought you guys left without me."

Dude squeezes the clutch and over the rumbling of the engines, he attempts to introduce Trixie to Santa and Kat.

Waving and screaming "girl power" to Kat, Trixie makes her way over to the left side of Dude's bike. He instructs her to put her left foot on the passenger peg and swing her right leg over the seat to climb on. She slides her chest down his back as she lands on the seat and presses her back against the snakeskin covered backrest. Picking the wedgie out of her ass and making herself comfortable, she leans forward and gets close to Dude's ear with her lips and tells him she is ready.

Before they can exit the farm's property, they have a couple of stops to make. Riding into the main grounds, they weave in and out of the people wandering around. They park their bikes in the center of the field surrounded by motorcycles of all makes and models.

"What's wrong? I thought we were going for a ride." Trixie is confused by the two-minute ride.

"We need to get you a lid."

"A what?"

"A helmet. And Glasses. It's the law."

The two get off Dude's bike and he tells Santa to hang tight. He remembers seeing a table of helmets for sale. So they head straight for the guy selling what they need. Standing in front of the table, Dude tells Trixie to try one on. Limited to only a few choices, she immediately reaches for the white one. The first helmet she puts on is too big. She gets the smallest size available and then Dude takes her hand and guides her to the rack of sunglasses.

"You look good in those. How do they feel?"

"Comfortable enough. Let's get 'em."

Unzipping her purse, Dude reaches out and puts his hand on Trixie's arm. He looks into her beautiful green eyes. "Your money is no good here. I'm paying."

Cocking her head slightly to the right with a surprised smile on her face, she squeezes his hand and pulls him tight up against her body. Their eyes are locked together, with their noses only inches apart. She bats her eyelashes and with a soft voice, "thank you. I am so excited. I haven't been on the back of a motorcycle for more than a year."

"It's my pleasure. Thanks for trusting me."

They approach the bike holding hands. Santa takes one look at their childlike faces and spits out, “Yo, Dude and Dudette, get a fuckin’ room!”

“Your just jealous old man. Doesn’t she look good in her new safety gear?”

“Yeah, yeah. Let’s go playboy. Kat is starving.”

Trixie’s small purse and jacket get tucked away in the saddlebag and across the field they go. They pass behind the empty stage, then down the rocky dirt road to the registration table. They stop to check on Tommy. He tells Dude he’s already signed up a bunch of people and things are going great. Hammer puts her hand on Tommy’s shoulder and with a devious smile on her face, she tells Dude, “I will take good care of him. Don’t worry, I won’t let anyone give him a hard time.”

Trixie sits on the back of the bike trying to make sense of the conversation Dude is having with the workers.

The two bikes slowly follow the road around a curve and out the front gate. On the asphalt road running across the front of the property, Santa and Kat pull ahead with Dude and Trixie falling in behind them. A right turn at the first stop sign leads them onto a road with a steep incline. Both girls have their backs pinned to the tour packs.

Dude can feel his breakfast being squeezed out of his stomach by the arms of his passenger. They hit a stretch of flat road just before the biscuits and gravy make their exit. She loosens her death grip and leans forward to apologize. “I’m sorry, that hill caught me off guard. I will be ready next time. I hope you don't mind me holding you tight."

"You can hold me however you want. Just remember to lean with me on the curves."

He feels her relax, then put her hands on his hips. She looks at his face in the mirror and smiles.

Traffic slows down in front of them. The flashing lights ahead are attached to a slow-moving tractor. Now moving at a snail's pace, Dude turns his head and asks Trixie if she is okay. He checks to make sure she is comfortable. A kiss on his neck followed by, "this feels amazing," is her response.

Winding through the back roads comes to an end as the motorcycles reach a red stoplight. A sign with two arrows hangs from a pole. Straight ahead for Blowing Rock and Downtown Boone to the right. A large red and yellow sign saying General Store catches Santa's eye. He puts his right turn signal on. In front of the General Store is a bench with a bronze statue of a man playing a guitar. A sign saying welcome to Main Street gives off a great American small-town vibe. Kat sees a diner, then taps on Santa's shoulder and points to a sign for food.

Small mom and pop shops line both sides of the street. One lane of traffic goes in each direction. They come to a stoplight and Dude points ahead and to the right. "That's the Squirrel's Nest. It's one of the bars participating in the poker run tomorrow."

Trixie's ears perk up. "What is a poker run?"

The light turns green, and the rumble of the two bikes gets louder as they start rolling. "I will tell you about it later"

The girls have their heads on a swivel as the guys focus on the road. With the colorful marquee of the local theater in their rearview mirrors, they come to a fork in the road. Santa leans left and Dude follows suit. Kat is signaling to Trixie by making hand motions as if she is eating a bowl of soup with a spoon. Trixie mouths the words, *I'm getting hungry too*, back at her.

Dude gets a glimpse of the hand signals going back and forth between the girls. He cocks his head to the right and asks Trixie if everything is okay back there. She lets him know both girls are hungry. Pulling up beside Santa, Dude lets him know, "we need to find somewhere to get lunch."

"I know a great spot. We're heading to Blowing Rock." Santa screams over the rumbling of the engines. Now it's three against one. Santa must give in and lead the group to food.

Putting his hand on Trixie's knee, Dude turns his head and declares, "if he doesn't pull over soon, we will just do our own thing."

Around tight turns, the bikes ride alongside a rock wall; the guys are laser focused. Meanwhile, the girls' heads are spinning, trying to capture a glimpse of the many unique businesses on each side of the road. In rapid fire succession they pass a zip lining adventure company, a wild west theme park with a train riding along the side of a mountain, a suspicious-looking place called Mystery Hill, followed by a kayak rental store.

All the twists and turns in the road bring them to the top of a mountain looking over the entire town they just rode through. Everything looks so small.

They continue down the other side of the mountain, passing houses that look like paintings. The smell of fresh flowers fills the air for a moment. An old wooden barn marks the bottom of the hill.

A right turn puts them on the cutest little Main Street Trixie has ever seen. She thinks the only thing that could make it better was if it were decorated for Christmas and there was snow on the ground. Small shops fill the old stone buildings lining the right side of the street. A historical sign sits in front of the Methodist Church on the left side as they approach the heart of Blowing Rock.

Cars are parked along the right side and then Santa sees a few parked motorcycles in the mix. With room for two more, Santa puts on his turn signal and motions for Dude to slow down. He backs into the curb next to a maroon Gold Wing, then Dude backs in on the other side of him.

Everyone is off the bikes and the girls waste no time getting acquainted. They embrace each other with a big hug and then some secretive giggling breaks out. Dude opens the saddlebag and grabs Trixie's purse. He puts their helmets on the mirrors and turns to walk away. Neat little storefronts line the sidewalk. The group begins their stroll, looking for a place to eat.

Santa sees the sign he was looking for and points it out to the others. “There it is.”

***

A round sign for the Tree Top Brew Pub becomes clear as they get closer. The group is greeted by an outdoor beer garden sitting in front of a building from the mid-1900s. A North Carolina state flag hanging from the building blows in the wind. Large wagon wheels line the path to the entrance of the old building.

The group is seated in the dining room at a table in front of a large window overlooking a beautiful mountain landscape. The breathtaking view has Trixie in a trance as the server approaches their table.

Santa orders a burger and a beer. Kat gets a grilled chicken sandwich and a sweet tea. Dude requests an order of soft pretzels for the table to share and then gets himself an order of fish tacos. With their large house beer selection, Dude is having a hard time choosing only one. He goes with an IPA Flight containing four different beers. After staring at the menu while everyone else ordered, Trixie has made a decision. “I will have an order of barbeque chicken wings and a White Claw.”

The young waitress says, “The wings I have, but I’m sorry, we don’t sell any hard seltzers. I can get you a cider if you’d like.”

“Sounds good. Thank you.”

“I will be right back with y’all’s drinks.”

While waiting on their food, all eyes point to the new girl. Santa rifles off a few questions at her before Kat jumps in and tells him to back off. "I like her. Don't scare her away. Plus, I think these two make a cute couple."

Dude looks down the table at Kat to let her know. "Now *you* are going to scare her away. We just met. I wouldn't call us a couple just yet."

"Whatever. I can see the potential."

Trixie is acting like a fly on the wall taking in the conversation. Dude quickly changes the subject. "Hey Santa, what band are you looking forward to seeing most this weekend?"

The server returns with the drinks. "Our classic lager for you, sir." She sits a frosty pint glass full of golden liquid in front of Santa. Placing the wooden flight board in front of Dude, she identifies each of the four beers in the little glasses. She sits the tea and cider in front of the girls and lets them know she is coming right back with the appetizer. The group raises their glasses and clinks them all together.

Dude says, "Cheers to a great weekend and new friends! And to George, may he rest in peace."

Trixie Stone shoots a curious look towards Dude. "Who is George?"

He has been so enamored with Trixie's good looks and southern charm that he never got around to telling her about George and his mission for the weekend. Her presence has been a useful distraction to this point, but now he has to catch her up to speed.

"George is… was, a really good friend of mine. He recently passed away. The poker run I mentioned earlier is something I organized to raise money for George's funeral."

Still confused about what a poker run is, she leans over and gives Dude a hug. "So sorry for your loss. It sounds like he meant a lot to you. If there is anything I can do to help, just let me know."

He thanks Trixie and lets her know how much he appreciates her support.

He doesn't want the conversation to be dominated by dwelling on the memory of George, so he changes the subject. Dude asks Santa again about what band he wants to see most.

"I hear the Confederate Outlaws kick ass. They cover all the good southern rock I grew up with."

Trixie blurts out, "tomorrow night's band, Carolina Country, is the reason I'm here. They're from Asheville and I love them. They put on a great show. I've seen them a few times back home. I just love their music. It got me through some rough times over the past couple of years."

Kat reaches over and grabs her hand. "Awe, that's really cool. I can't wait to see them."

The server walks up to the table and puts down a basket of freshly baked soft pretzels that smell amazing. "Your lunch will be out shortly."

The guys get into a debate over which is better; the batwing fairing or the shark nose. The girls start their own conversation.

The smell of the food arrives moments ahead of the four delicious looking plates. The handmade burger topped with cheddar cheese and bacon on a round roll with all the fixins' comes off the tray first. It all looks amazing. Asking each other what they think of the food, no complaints, everyone is happy with their choice. The table gets quiet as the hungry guests chow down.

Aside from a small amount of chit chat, once the plates hit the table, it was all about the food. Stuffed like turkeys, they sit back in their chairs and contemplate their next move.

The girls vote for checking out some shops. Santa talks about the route he has planned for the ride back to the farm. His detailed directions along a river sound amazing.

Trixie leans in close to Dude and puts her hand on his thigh.

"I'm not ready to go back yet. Can we ride more first? Please."

With no reason to deny this beautiful woman's request, Dude turns to Santa and lets him know that he and Trixie are going on a different scenic ride. "We will catch up with you back at Lone Ranger's Farm."

With a childlike look on her face, Trixie adds, "But I still want to stop in a couple of these cute little shops before we leave."

***

Out the front door, passing the row of wagon wheels, the group turns right and heads away from the bikes. Trixie gets her way and Kat isn't ready to leave yet either. Checking out all the charm Blowing Rock has to offer; the group moseys down the sidewalk. They are only window shopping until a hand carved sea turtle catches Trixie's eye. She becomes enamored by the handcrafted wood sculptures of sea creatures in the window of a gallery. "Let's go in here."

They all walk inside, and an employee welcomes them into the store. He is telling the group that everything in this shop was handmade by one person. A unique young artist who is unfortunately not in the building at the moment. The group of four peruses the aisles admiring the one-of-a-kind art. Trixie gets her sea turtle, but no one else buys anything.

In and out of a few more stores they go before Santa calls it quits and announces to the group that he is ready to go. The couples agreed to part ways. The girls hug each other, and the guys shake hands. Dude says he's going to take Trixie up onto the Blue Ridge Parkway.

With excitement in her voice, Trixie speaks up to tell them, "I have been on that road before but never on a motorcycle."

Dude tells her, "It's a totally different experience. You're going to love it." Then he turns to Santa and Kat. "We'll see you guys back at camp. Please check on Tommy for me. Ride safe."

# Chapter 6

DUDE AND TRIXIE HANG around eating ice cream cones and getting to know each other before leaving downtown Blowing Rock for their scenic ride. What started out as just sharing their common interests is now getting into personal details. Dude slowly slices up Trixie's questions with his imaginary sword, then turns the questioning onto her. "Tell me about yourself."

She tilts her head forward and looks over the top of her sunglasses at Dude. "I rarely open up to people I barely know, but there is something about you that makes me feel at ease." Trixie goes on to tell him that although she dabbled with weed in high school, she didn't become a regular smoker until after she lost her mother to breast cancer two years ago. "It really helps me cope. She passed away one month before my fortieth birthday."

Placing his hand on her shoulder, he lets her know, "I am really sorry for your loss. I have some of that funny smelling medicine with me, but we're going to hold off on firing it up until we get somewhere a little more private."

"Thank you. Sounds good."

He also doesn't usually open up to just anybody. Talking about his past has a tendency to scare people away. But somehow, Trixie is softening him up.

"I also lost my mother, when I was thirteen. Then my dad passed away when I was twenty-two, which would have been, uh, um, twenty-three years ago. We had a rocky relationship when I was a kid, but we got along great as I got older. He took me to motorcycle rallies and showed me the ropes when it came to riding. He loved to ride, and he left me his old Harley Sportster when he died. I had my fair share of issues after he passed, but I don't want to scare you away with the details."

She puts her shoulder against his as they sit on a bench. "Awe, baby, that is so sad. You must have been devastated."

"Losing loved ones caused issues with depression and led me to using drugs and, uh, you know, that led to trouble."

"Speaking of lost loved ones, tell me more about your friend George and this poker run." She seems to be genuinely interested, so Dude breaks it down for her.

"George was the first person I met when I moved to North Carolina seven years ago. I needed some work done on my other motorcycle and he worked at the repair shop I took it too. He became my mechanic. We started hanging out and became fast friends. He had always been going to motorcycle rallies by himself and I was doing the same, so we started hitting the road together."

"Awe, that is such a sweet story."

"Last year, we came to this Mud Hole rally for the first time, and his antique motorcycle was stolen from the farm. We had plans to come here together this year to find the bike and who stole it. He passed away two months ago from a heart attack. His wife, Julie, and his son, George Jr. could only afford to have him cremated. I organized this poker run to raise enough money to give him a proper burial and hopefully raise a little extra to help them as well. The way it works is, registered bikes go to five different bars and collect one playing card from each bar. The staff member writes the person's name on the card and when they have all five, they return to the registration table. The person who has the best five card hand at twelve noon wins five-hundred-dollars. Make sense?"

Trixie eyes puddle up as her bottom lip quivers. "You are such a good friend. And such an amazing man. George is surely smiling down on you from heaven. I want to play this game of motorcycle poker. You can sign me up if I can ride on the back with you."

"That would be awesome. Your seat has officially been reserved."

"This sounds like so much fun. Thank you."

She looks into his blue eyes. "Can I please just ask you one more question? What is the name your mama gave you when you were born?"

Squirming in his seat, Dude thinks for a minute before answering. He usually makes up an alias when random people ask him that same question. If he thought she was just going to be a one-night stand, he would give her a bullshit answer. But he sees potential here. She could be a keeper and he doesn't want to start things off with lying.

Her truth serum seems to be working on him.

He turns to her, "I will tell you my real name now, but the rest is going to have to wait until later. Let's move towards the bike."

He takes her hand and helps her up from the bench; they start walking. He's pointing at trinkets in storefront windows in an attempt to change the subject. She picks up on what he's doing and makes a fake coughing sound. "Ahem, you were saying?"

Knowing the future of this budding relationship is hinging on truth, he goes for it.

"According to my birth certificate, I was born with the name, Russell Robert Sparks."

"Awe, that is cute. I like it. Does anyone call you Russell?"

"Very few people. Kids in school called me by my middle name, Bobby."

"Bobby is a great name. Can I call you Bobby?"

"It's such a common name. I like to be unique." Trying not to get defensive, he walks up to his motorcycle and turns on the ignition, then hits the start button.

"Um, ah, let me think about that one." He hands her the white helmet, and he puts on the black one covered with stickers. He climbs on first and then she grabs his shoulder and pulls herself up and throws her leg over the seat. He looks down at a map on his phone to get the quickest route to an entrance for the Blue Ridge Parkway.

***

The smell of fresh cut grass fills the air as they cruise along a golf course on a winding road. The sun is glaring, and the breeze feels great. With Trixie's seat sitting four inches above Dude's, her chin sits perfectly on his shoulder. She has a front-row seat to the magic picture show unfolding before her eyes with every turn.

They made their last turn, giving them a straight shot to the Blue Ridge Parkway. They are riding uphill on a four-lane road that runs between two very tall solid rock walls. With a similar style and shape on each side, you can tell that a huge section of rock was cut out to make room for this road to pass through. A large American flag blows in the wind.

They pass under the parkway overpass, then take the exit on the right, looping them up and around onto it. Thick pine trees line the sides of the on-ramp. Keeping his eyes on the road, Dude slightly turns his head to the side and asks Trixie, "Which way; right or left?"

She says left, and at the stop sign, he turns left.

They feel the temperature drop as they make their way down the tree covered road. Trixie leans forward to ask if they could pull over to get her jacket out of the saddlebag.

"I will stop at the next overlook spot."

She wraps her arms around his waist and lays her head against his back to hide from the wind. He turns up the volume on the radio and then leans into the curve of the road with Trixie in sync. She goes where he goes. She is stuck to him like chewed gum to an old payphone.

A small concrete post with the numbers *254* carved in it vertically passes them on the right side of the road. They exit the tree tunnel and are greeted with bright sunshine and fluffy white clouds. Trixie pokes her head up to take in the view. She secretly admires Dude's face through his mirror, finding him sexier by the minute. Moving both of her hands down onto his thighs, she puts her chin on his shoulder and raises her voice to tell him, "This is freaking amazing!"

He brings his left hand down on to hers and locks their fingers together. They are cruising fifty miles per hour on an open stretch of road when they see a sign reading *lookout ahead*.

An exit on the right side of the road leads them to a long narrow parking lot overlooking mountains for as far as the eye can see. There are a handful of cars, one RV, and three other motorcycles parked at the far end. Most people are standing outside their vehicles, taking pictures. One young couple has a blanket laid out and they are sitting on it having a picnic. They ride to the far end and pull headfirst into an open spot next to the three Harleys. Dude gives the bikers a nod as he waits for Trixie to climb off. He sees them checking out her ass and just smiles.

A walkway and a two-foot-high stone wall are the only things separating the parking lot from the valley below. Just beyond the wall sits a wooden sign with the words *Grandview Overlook, Elevation 3,240.* Looking straight down, all they see are trees. The valley of rolling hills extends for miles. White puffy clouds cast shadows over the many shades of green. Tiny looking buildings are scattered throughout the landscape. Mountain ranges in the distance frame this beautiful picture. The smell of flowers fills the air.

Trixie steps up onto the wall with her camera phone in hand. Snapping pictures in every direction, she looks down at Dude and asks him to hold the back of her shirt. The view is amazing, but she doesn't want to risk rolling down the hill for a few snapshots. He wraps his hands around her hips and slides his index fingers through her belt loops. A pair of hawks crisscrosses above their heads. Looking up, they both stare silently, taking in the view together.

One Harley engine roars, then another and another. The guys parked beside them break the silence. Dude takes Trixie's hand and helps her down off the wall. He walks toward his bike, and she follows. He pops open his saddlebag and digs for his can of brake cleaner. He turns and sees the puzzled look on her face.

"Is something broken?"

"No, we're all good. This is where I keep my stash."

Silent and staring at the can, she looks confused. He unscrews the bottom of the hollow can and pulls out a zip-lock bag. Holding it down low so no one else could see it, he unrolls the bag to show her what's inside.

"Isn't this the coolest place to smoke a joint?"

"Yes, but there are people around." Trixie looks nervous as she scans the parking lot to see who's watching them.

"Relax, we're going to take a walk downwind, over there in the trees." Dude points to the wall of trees at the end of the parking lot.

"You're a risk taker, that's sexy." She reaches over and squeezes his bicep. "And you work out?"

"Planet Fitness." He flexes.

She purrs.

"Stop teasing me."

"I'm not a tease. I just know when I see something I like."

With a smirk on his face, he jokingly says, "you're going to get me into trouble. I can't risk another public indecency charge. If we go into the woods to smoke, are you going to get high and try to molest me?"

She laughs out loud. "You wish."

"Just checking. Then let's fire up."

The pair walk just inside the tree line and Dude pulls out his lighter. He offers her the opportunity to do the honors. She passes, so he lights it ablaze.

Trixie jokes, "I hope Smokey the Bear is not around."

Dude takes a couple of puffs and passes it to her. She hits it, holds in the smoke for thirty seconds and exhales, followed by a light cough. As she hands it back to him, their eyes lock together, and they both start laughing.

She says, "I can't believe we are here."

Caught up in the moment, he blurts out, "I can't believe how much I like you."

Blushing, she leans in for a kiss. "I like you too."

"Listen to us like a bunch of grade schoolers." Dude makes light of the reality that these two stoners have a great connection.

She laughs. "Do you want me to write my phone number on a piece of paper and slip it to you under the desk, or do you want me to just put it straight into your phone?"

"My phone please." He pulls the phone from his pocket and hands it to her.

She stores her number in his phone with a heart next to her name. "There you go, I hope you call." Handing the phone back to him.

He quickly puts it away before she has a chance to change her mind. After a few puffs each, he puts out the joint by rubbing it on the bottom of his boot.

They get bottles of water out of Dude's tour pack, and they find a spot on the wall to plant their asses. Sitting close together on the rocks with their feet in the grass, they gaze out into the distance.

"I'm intrigued by you." Trixie breaks the silence. "Are you sure there is no wife at home?"

"I'm sure. I have no strings attached. No kids and never been married. I'm free as a bird."

"And you wouldn't lie to me, would you?"

Dude hesitates to make the verbal commitment. He thinks long and hard before answering, "I was engaged once before, but it never happened. And as far as kids go; I guess I never found the right woman."

Trixie smiles and reassures him she is honest, trustworthy, and loyal. Then she reluctantly tells him, "I don't have any kids either, unless you consider my tabby cat, Boots. But I was married once. It was a long time ago; I was young and naïve. My high School sweetheart, I'm sure you've heard this story before."

"It's all good. Is your cat home alone?"

"Slow down Peta, I put out extra food, water, and litter."

"Jeez, you don't need to get defensive. What I'm really asking is, do you live alone? By the way, I do like cats. I had one for years, rest in peace, Pancake. He loved riding on the motorcycle." Dude sips his water.

"Awe, I'm so sorry about your cat. Cute name. I feel guilty leaving her home alone, but really, Boots is fine. And yes, I do live alone."

Dude thinks *good to know*. Then he looks for an answer to something else he's been wondering about. “From where I’m sitting, I don’t see any tattoos on you. Where are you hiding them?”

“Wouldn’t you like to know? Just joking, I don’t have any. By the way, I like how you only have a bunch of smaller ones, not like these guys with sleeves or whatever they call it.”

Amazement washes over his face. He can’t think of a single girl he’s ever met at a motorcycle rally that didn’t have at least one tattoo. He lets her know she is a unicorn.

“You may be the only girl at the rally without one.”

Trixie takes it as a compliment. She tells him this is her first official motorcycle rally.

“I have been to a couple bike nights, but nothing where I had to camp out.”

He looks at her like she is the Virgin Mary. He fights the urge to think about how bad of an influence he’s going to be on her. He asks if she knows what she got herself into.

“I wanted to see Carolina Country, and I needed to get away. I looked at the rally’s website and saw pictures from last year and it looked like a good time. I convinced my two co-workers to go with me because I didn’t want to come here by myself.”

“How well do you know those girls?” Now Dude is intrigued.

“We are really friendly at work, but we’ve only hung out a handful of times. They both really like Carolina Country too. We all went to another one of their shows together a couple months ago.”

The pair continues getting to know each other when Trixie checks her phone and says, "Speaking of the devil." She has a text message from Emma asking if she will be back soon.

Sitting on top of the world around them, they take in the view for a few more minutes before returning to the bike. He tells her they will continue down the Parkway until the next overlook, then they will turn around to work their way towards the rally.

With the wind in their faces, Trixie's head pivots back and forth, trying to take in the view on both sides of the ridge. She feels like she's riding on a chariot with her wavy ponytail blowing in the wind. A sign reading *America's Scenic Byway* passes in a flash. She relaxes into her seat.

Twenty miles down the road, Dude pulls into another overlook. This time on the opposite side of the road with a different but equally amazing view. They take a few pictures but keep the stop short. With her girlfriends getting antsy and the night's festivities looming, although he doesn't want this ride to end, he's ready to return to the party.

He loops out of the parking area and back in the direction from which they came. Something small comes running out of the grass on the left side of the road and runs across the lane. With not much room to swerve on this two-lane parkway, he accidentally runs over a mouse. He looked at Trixie in the mirror and thankfully; she didn't see what happened.

In his mind, this ride has been a huge success. He hasn't put his foot in his mouth, and he senses only good things to come. He wants to end this ride on a high note and get her back safely.

Back on the local roads, they twist and turn their way towards the farm. They cross over a fast-moving river of rapids and past an old lumber mill. Small signs with the words *bike rally* and an arrow begin to appear repeatedly, directing them to their destination.

A left turn onto a dirt road reveals what appears to be the parking lot outside of a NASCAR race. Flags of all kinds are flying from the tops of RVs. The camping area has really filled in since they left five hours ago.

The black Road Glide comes to a stop in front of the registration table. Tommy has three guys and a girl pressed up against his table signing up for the poker run. A heavyset guy with a denim vest is dripping sweat from his mangy beard as he leans down to write his name and phone number on the sign-up sheet.

The group walks away with their bright yellow bracelets and Tommy looks up to see Dude and Trixie sitting there on the bike.

He adjusts his hat and with excitement in his voice, he waves his hand and yells, "Dude, it's going great. We have almost fifty people signed up so far."

"You're the man Tommy. Great job. After I park the bike and get settled, I will be by to give you a break, so you can get something to eat and wander around."

Trixie rubs Dude's back as they make their way through the pedestrians and turn onto the grass of the camping area. Slowly riding along, Trixie leans forward to tell Dude how much fun she had and how appreciative she is for him taking her for the ride.

Playing it cool, he reaches back and puts his left hand on her leg. "Anytime. I will text you later. Maybe we can hang out."

She lets him know she would love to catch up later in the night. He brings the bike to a stop in front of her white Jeep. She reminds him that her purse is in his saddlebag. He gets off and pops the lid. She takes the purse and gives him a big squeeze and a peck on the lips.

As he mounts the bike, she turns to see her friends anxiously waiting for details. She's not usually one to kiss and tell, but the excitement on her face is hard to hide.

When Dude pulls up to his camp, his friends are nowhere to be found, but people have filled in around them. He dismounts the bike and says hi to his new neighbor with an old rusty blue Panhead. He eyes the bike up and down and then makes a beeline for the cooler next to Santa's tent and grabs a beer. He pulls out the other half of the joint they smoked earlier and plops down into a chair facing the new neighbor. With visions of George's red and white '63 racing through his mind, he can't help but to think this Panhead parking next to him has to be a sign from above.

Since the guy popped a tent, Dude thinks he will be around for a while. He doesn't want to walk over and immediately start interrogating the guy, so he plays it cool and just says, "hey bro, nice bike."

Dude tries not to stare at the blue Panhead as he thinks about the amount of sign-ups Tommy said he had. He daydreams for a minute, wishing he could rub the rusty antiques' gas tank and answers would fly out.

He changes into a gray 2002 Biketoberfest t-shirt and puts on deodorant. He puts on a black Harley baseball hat with an orange bar and shield on the front. He turns the hat backwards, then rides up to the registration tent with an open beer in his cupholder.

# Chapter 7

TOMMY POPS OUT OF his chair when he sees Dude pull up next to the table. Motorcycles are coming and going in every direction with the rally in full swing. Dude asks Tommy to fill him in on how things have been going.

"One of the guys who signed up for the poker run has info about the missing bike." Tommy points to the name *Martin Woods* on the sign-up sheet.

"Excellent work Tommy! You are the man." Then Dude hands Tommy a twenty-dollar bill and tells him to take a break and go get something to eat.

Dude pulls out his phone and immediately dials the number for Martin. He gets no answer but leaves a voicemail.

Hesitant to sit next to Hammer, Dude opts for standing up in front of the table. He makes small talk with workers who are checking for the red bracelets as bikes enter the farm. When a new person stops to get their ticket checked for the rally, Dude approaches them with the poker run information.

A group of five motorcycles, two with passengers, stop to receive their red bracelets. As rally staff places the last bracelet on the arm of a passenger with a long blonde ponytail, Dude makes his move.

"Hey guys, welcome to the rally. I just want to let you all know that we are doing a poker run tomorrow morning to raise money for a good friend who recently passed away. It's twenty for each bike and ten for a passenger. Are any of you interested?"

Dude holds out the flyer to show them which bars are included and then he points at the five-hundred-dollar prize. He signs up three out of the five, including one with a passenger. He puts on their yellow bracelets and asks them to spread the word.

He is astonished by how many people Tommy registered since he cruised by with Trixie. After he added in these four sign-ups, the tally is up to seventy-nine.

Dude is striking up conversations with everyone walking by. He's got a flyer for the poker run in one hand and a flyer for the missing motorcycle in the other. He's asking everyone a list of questions: if they were at this rally last year, do they live locally, are they into antique motorcycles, and a bunch of random stuff mixed in. He has people telling him he's looking for a needle in a haystack.

An older couple comes shuffling by, kicking up dust and rocks as they approach Dude. The woman is short with curly white hair, wearing a pair of baggy jeans with a chain going from her belt loop to her wallet. The man who appears to be her husband is wearing denim overalls and a beat-up straw hat. Dude says hi and the man stops to introduce himself. He blows cigar smoke into the sky and then, in a raspy voice, he reaches out his hand and tells Dude, "I'm Buck, Buck Jones, and this is my wife, Gretchen. Nice to meet you. I can see that piece of paper in your hand, nice machine. How much are you selling it for?"

Dude passes the missing motorcycle flyer to Buck. "It's not for sale; it was stolen. Were you here last year?"

"As a matter of fact, I was. We have been coming for the past three years. We only live twenty miles away but we camp-out so we can drink and have a good time without having to ride home."

"Take a good look at this picture. Do you remember seeing this Panhead in the bike show last year? In the antique class. It took second place."

"It looks a little familiar. What happened to it?"

Dude tells him the story of how it disappeared at last year's rally. He tells Buck about all the online research they've done over the past twelve months. Dude shares the names of some people he and George contacted, and all about dead ends they followed. He lists all the motorcycle shops they checked in the weeks following the theft. Then Dude mentions the name Henry, and the old man's eyes widened, then a blank stare came over his face. It's like you can see him thinking.

He snaps out of his trance and starts shaking his index finger at Dude. "Henry Schultz? That's a name I recognize. I've lived in this area my whole life and that's the only Henry I know. Been a while since I've seen him around. We've never been good friends, but I know a couple guys who drink with him at the local watering hole. Have you been in touch with Henry?"

"No. But not for a lack of trying. He is a hard man to get ahold of. I was told he was here with a white utility van last year. Do you remember seeing him here? What is the name of the bar he drinks in?"

"Yes, he was here. But I don't remember seeing what he was driving. He was just walking the vendors when I saw him. I think the bar is called Jack's Pub. It's over on Mountain View Road in Boone."

"Have you seen him here this weekend yet?"

"No sir."

"If you do, please call me. I think he may be able to help me. If anything comes of it, I will give you a cash reward. Anything else you can find out for me would be great. Thank you very much."

"Sure, I will keep an eye out for Henry. I will also ask around about the bike. No problem."

Dude reaches for his cold beer as his hot lead walks away. He raises his can toward Hammer, and gives a hearty, "CHEERS! We got action!"

His celebratory moment is interrupted by the vibrating phone in his pants pocket. "Hello."

The man on the other end of the line identifies himself as Martin Woods. Dude's eyes widen to the size of the sun. "Thank you for calling me back."

Martin is in his fifties and has been toying around with motorcycles since he was a kid. His love for the two-wheeled machine is second only to his dog,

Spike. His deep voice echoes through the earpiece of Dude's phone.

"There is a guy here selling motorcycle parts. I saw him at a swap meet six months ago and I bought a few Panhead parts from him. Have you been by to question the guy yet?"

A stunned look comes over Dude's face. He can't believe he let Willie off the hook so easily. "Yeah, I talked to him, and he said he knew nothing about it."

Martin tells Dude. "Go back and remind him of the parts he sold me last year at the swap meet in Boone at the firehouse. He knows more than he is telling you."

"Thank you, Martin. I look forward to meeting you tomorrow morning. I owe you a cold beer. Have a great night."

Tommy strolls up, raving about two girls he just seen topless with their boobs airbrushed. "They had eyeballs painted on them. It was like their boobs were watching me."

As exciting as these bouncing eyeballs seem to be, Dude is all business. He jumps right into telling Tommy about Buck and the lead Martin just gave him on the suspected bike thief. "Make sure you're showing everybody this flyer and asking if they know anything about this missing motorcycle."

Dude tells Tommy to get out from behind the table and approach any new bikes rolling in for the first time. "Don't be shy. After the event staff gives people their red bracelets, walk over and talk to them before they pull away. Talk to everyone that walks by too. About both, the Panhead and the poker run." He shows Tommy how it's done with the next group of bikes that pull in.

Tommy looks at the sign-up sheet and smiles when he sees how many people Dude signed up while he was gone. "Wow, we're up to ninety-seven and there are still two hours of daylight left."

"Keep up the good work Tommy. I'm going to take a walk and grab a beer and something to eat. Be back in a little while." Dude leaves his motorcycle parked at the registration tent and makes his way into the main grounds.

Dude heads straight for the old man selling the parts. He imagines breaking the legs of this fragile old man would be much like splitting the wishbone of a Thanksgiving turkey. His mind is racing faster than his feet can move. *Did this old man lie to me, or did I not ask the right questions?*

Dude goes plowing across the blankets full of motorcycle parts. "Hey Willie, we need to talk!"

Slightly hunched over, the fragile senior citizen shuffles in Dude's direction. The tunnel vision caused Dude to kick a green gas tank and step on a chrome exhaust pipe. Willie's beady eyes are level with Dude's shoulder when the two men come toe to toe.

Looking down at Willie's leather skinned face, Dude wastes no time with small talk.

"Do you remember the swap meet at the firehouse in Boone last year?"

The old man's eyes get googly, and he is looking everywhere but at Dude. He nervously looks down at his greasy boots before he mutters, "uh, um, ah, ma-ma-maybe."

"You recognized that bike when I showed it to you this morning, didn't you?" Dude pulls out the flyer to refresh Willie's memory.

"Okay, okay. It looks familiar. But I'm no thief. I swear to God. Please believe me."

"Tell me what you know."

"Ok. Um. I may have had a few parts from a Panhead like that last year."

"Where did you get those parts?"

"I get all my stuff from swap meets, yard sales, flea markets and junk stores."

Dude's patience is running thin as he lowers himself to Willie's eye level.

"It's a rare '63 police bike. You don't just stumble across these every day. If you didn't steal the bike, tell me exactly where you bought the parts from. This is a small town, don't play stupid with me. I know you remember. Willie, I will give you one thousand dollars for the name of the person who sold you those Panhead parts."

"Okay. I may be able to help you, but you have to swear not to tell anyone you heard this from me."

"I swear. Keep talking."

"Every so often these two brothers show up at swap meets and flea markets with whole motorcycles' worth of parts. No frames, and no engines. They have other random parts mixed in, but you can tell most of what they have came off the same bike. There is no rhyme or reason to how they operate. Most people have the same spot at the flea market every week, but not these guys. They show up randomly."

"Thank you, Willie. I really appreciate you sharing this with me. Do you have their names?"

Willie shuffles in place as he dips into deep thought. You can almost see smoke come out of his ears. "I know they are related because they look like they could be twins. But I don't know their names. Here is what I will do; tonight, I will make a few phone calls. Stop by and see me tomorrow and I will let you know what I find out. Deal?"

"Let's shake on it." Dude extends his arm to make the agreement official.

***

Dude's mind is now racing even faster than it was before he had talked to Willie. *Who the fuck are these twins?*

He walks away just in time to see the 80s hair band tribute, Loud as Thunder, come on at seven p.m. He's been told they cover everything from Motley Crue to Jackyl.

The main grounds are packed with bustling people and motorcycles spread out everywhere. The rumbling in his stomach directs Dude to the food trucks. Not sure what he wants, he previews each of their menus and then settles on a pulled pork sandwich and two cups of beer.

Uncle Tucker introduces the band. They strike the first chord of Metallica's classic, *Ride the Lightning*, and the crowd goes wild. People rev their engines. The whole place is buzzing. A lady covered in tattoos rides by on a golf cart with no shirt or bra; only wearing a neck full of beads. People are coming and going in every direction as Dude stands alone in the shade, eating his sandwich and taking it all in.

He sees a tall green flag with *Delta 8* spelled out vertically in white. He walks over to the vendor tent the flag is attached to and looks into the glass case on the table. Behind the table sits a woman in a chair with white hair wearing a tie-dyed shirt. Standing off to the side is a tall guy with a long black beard and a weed leaf tattooed on his neck. He walks up to the table and introduces himself to Dude. "Can I help you?"

At first dude was just browsing but then something caught his eye; edibles. "Tell me more about these."

The man reaches into the case and pulls out a brownie, a cereal bar, and two jars full of chewy candy. He has all types of sweets. Everything looks good to Dude.

The guy says that all these products contain Delta 8 THC.

"Are they strong?"

"Compared to what," asks the guy.

"Compared to me smoking a joint."

The big, bearded man explains the milligrams and all the details of how much THC and CBD are in each product. "Delta 8 is the only legal THC in North Carolina."

The man is going on and on with all this scientific jargon when Dude says, "I'll take one brownie to try it. If I like it, I will be back for more."

Dude hands over the money and immediately takes the brownie out of the wrapper and starts eating it. The guy warns him not to eat the whole thing, so he only eats half and puts the rest in his pocket. "Pretty tasty. Thanks bro, this is the perfect dessert." He washes down the last bite with a sip of beer.

Dude pulls the vibrating phone out of his pocket just in time to answer a call from Santa, who is wondering if Dude made it back to the farm yet. Over the loud music, he only catches a few words; *near the Bounty Hunter*. With a pretty good idea of what Santa meant, Dude walks towards the trailer full of knives and bullets.

Still twenty feet away, he sees Chuck's orange beard towering over the crowd. Kat and Birdy are huddled together sitting on the grass, engaged in a focused conversation. Dude walks up behind Santa and pokes his finger into his back and says, "give me all your money." They both have a good laugh and then shake hands.

"I thought you rode off into the sunset with that redhead. When did you get back?"

“We’ve been back awhile. I sat in for Tommy so he could take a dinner break. He’s doing a great job. Thanks for hooking me up with him. We have a ton of people signed up for the poker run, and I connected with a local who knows that guy Henry I was telling you I haven’t been able to find. Plus, Tommy had a guy sign up for the poker run who gave us another hot tip. Guess what? That motherfucker selling the parts lied to us this morning!”

Santa says, “let’s talk. Take a walk to the beer tent with me. Hey Chuck, do you need one?” Then he leans down to ask the ladies if they want anything. They look up to see Dude standing there and Kat asks, “How was your ride? Where is Trixie?”

Dude lets her know the ride was great, and he dropped Trixie off at her camp a couple hours ago. Kat is asking for details when Santa pulls Dude away. “He is coming with me to get beers. You can interrogate him later.” Kat flips her hair back, rolls her eyes, and gives Santa the middle finger.

The pair makes their way through the maze of people, motorcycles, and golf carts in a way that could make someone dizzy. Which is exactly what is happening to Dude as they reach the beer tent. “Hey Santa, do you feel the ground moving?”

“What the fuck are you talking about? No, the ground is as solid as a piece of plywood. Are you already drunk?”

A little confused himself, Dude has to think about it for a minute. “I’ve only had a few beers. How can I be drunk? Oh shit, I know what's happening. No, I'm not drunk. I ate a THC brownie, but I didn't expect it to be this strong and kick in this fast."

"Dude, you're going to be a mess. It's not even dark yet."

Considering he may have eaten too much of the brownie, he offers Santa the other half.

"No thanks. I'd like to stay on planet earth tonight."

The music echoes inside Dude's ears. He quickly realizes that he better get his bike from the registration tent and move it back to his campsite before the brownie fucks with his motor skills.

"I'm going to skip this beer and go move my bike before it's too late."

He moves through the crowd like a moth to a flame.

He walks straight up to his motorcycle and climbs on. "Tommy, how are you making out?"

Tommy assures him it's going good and the number of poker run sign-ups continues to climb.

"Awesome. I will be back in a flash. I just need to get the bike back to camp."

He becomes one with Angel and uses all his focus to slowly make his way through the campground. He rolls past Trixie and her friends and without coming to a full stop, he yells over, "hey girls. Having fun yet?" He keeps going and doesn't hear their response. Then he sees Trixie step out into the open grass in his rearview mirror. He tells himself, *damn, she is cute, but keep your eyes forward.*

He successfully pulls up in front of his tent and slowly lowers the kickstand. *Holy shit, what a ride.* Feeling like he was floating on clouds, he plants his feet safely in the grass. He stares at the snakeskin seat as the scales appear to be moving. Now he's thinking, *I could charge people money for a ride like that.*

He bends down to grab a bottle of water from the ice filled cooler. He looks up at the darkening sky and pours the cold water over his face. Shaking his head from side-to-side, like a dog who just got a bath, he sprays drops of water in every direction.

Trixie comes walking up. "Are you okay?"

"Uh, I think so. Just need to chill for a minute."

He can only imagine what he looks like through Trixie's eyes. *Do I look wacked out?* He brushes his salt and pepper beard with the palms of his hands when Trixie's concerned stare burns a hole in his face. "You looked a little wobbly when you went by."

He thanks his lucky stars for not dropping the motorcycle on the short ride across the grass.

"My bad. I just needed to bring the bike back from the registration tent before I got too messed up to ride it."

"Jesus. How drunk are you?"

"It's not from alcohol. There is a vendor selling THC edibles. I ate half of a brownie about an hour ago."

Trixie is struck with relief as she relaxes into a chair. "I'm glad you're okay."

"Thanks for your concern. I guess I wasn't expecting it to be this strong. I still have the other half. Do you want a piece of it?"

She ponders his question as she sits in a chair and crosses her fair skinned legs. Trixie Stone is not usually spontaneous. Dude's go with the flow style is something she rarely experiences personally. She wishes she had the courage to just go whichever way the wind blows. This weekend rally took her months of planning. She stares at the cows in the distance and imagines letting herself be impulsive for a change.

Dude silently looks at the blank stare on Trixie's face and approaches her with the brownie in his hand. She looks up at his face and lowers her voice. "Maybe a small piece?"

"Help yourself." Dude hands her the brownie in its clear wrapper with the label on top. Trixie quickly glances at the small writing and sees 250mg written in bold black letters. "This is strong." She squeezes her index finger and thumb into the open end of the wrapper and pinches off a corner of the brownie. She holds it up by her lips, but before she puts it in her mouth, she looks into Dude's eyes. "Now you're stuck with me for the night."

"Fine with me. I just have to check on Tommy before we get lost in the sauce."

# Chapter 8

THE SUN IS FALLING fast, and the sky is turning purple with an orange glow outlining the mountain tops. Lights are coming on around the farm as Dude and Trixie approach the registration tent. Tommy is talking to a guy sitting on his idling European adventure bike.

Dude notices the man wearing a yellow bracelet as he rides away. “Great work Tommy. I want you to meet Trixie.”

“Thanks. Nice to meet you.” Tommy hands the clipboard to Dude and shakes Trixie’s hand.

“Holy shit. Damn, you’ve been a busy boy.” Dude shows Trixie the sign-up sheet.

Her eyes light up. “Wow. This is awesome. Can I please sign up now?”

“Absolutely. You can be number one twenty-two, and I will be one twenty-three.”

She takes the sign-up sheet and leans on the table to write her name and number. She turns to Tommy and hands him a ten-dollar bill. Dude follows suit and hands over a twenty.

Trixie takes a phone call from Peggy. “We need to wait here; the girls are walking over.”

Tommy tells Dude that a bunch of people said they will sign up in the morning if they can wake up early enough to participate. He shows his appreciation for Tommy's hard work by handing him five twenty-dollar bills. "I think we're done for the night. Let's wrap it up. It's time to have some fun, Tommy. Let's go find your uncle."

Emma and Peggy find their way to the registration tent and Tommy checks them out from head to toe. The pair get introduced to Tommy, and he gets caught staring directly down Peggy's shirt. She acts like she didn't notice. Her long legs, short shorts and cowboy boots have Tommy mesmerized. Emma is wearing black sneakers, skintight capri pants and a white V-neck t-shirt showing just enough cleavage to be a tease. She flashes her wedding ring as she reaches out to shake Tommy's hand. "Nice to meet you."

The group makes their way under the Lone Ranger's Farm sign and into the main grounds. A golf cart decorated with multicolored Christmas lights being driven by a topless woman catches Tommy's eye. Dude and Trixie play grab ass like school kids. Emma is secretly giving them the stink eye. Peggy thinks it's cute, but not cuter than Tommy. She is secretly eyeing him up every time he looks the other way. Trixie's constant giggling and playfulness are a sure sign that the brownie has kicked in.

Dude points to the far side of the crowd. "They were over there a little while ago." He takes Trixie's hand and guides her through the crowd with Tommy and the girlfriends in tow. They pass through a cloud of cigar smoke and around a row of camping chairs squeezed together. A guy sitting on a parked motorcycle passes a bottle of vodka to a woman wearing a shirt that says *No Beard, No Booty*. Trixie notices the shirt, then reaches over and strokes Dude's hairy chin. He shoots her a smile, then raises his voice. "There they are."

Kat pops up off the ground like someone lit a firecracker under her ass. She pulls Trixie in for a big hug, then introduces her to Birdie. Trixie excitedly pulls her friends forward. "Kat and Birdie, meet my friends, Peggy and Emma." The friends are introduced to Santa and Chuck, then the five girls quickly form a circle. They separate themselves from the guys before the gab session kicks into high gear. Kat breaks the ice by asking Trixie about her motorcycle ride on the Blue Ridge Parkway.

The four guys form a circle of their own as Trixie giggles and glances over at Dude to make sure he's not looking. "Oh my god, it was amazing, and so is he. I was vibrating in all the right places. I can't wait to get back on that bike tomorrow morning." Kat Miller cracks a smile from ear to ear. "He is a great guy. I'm happy you two found each other." Peggy nods her head in agreement while Emma's face is covered with skepticism.

The swooning and drooling over the thought of the vibrating seat made Trixie thirsty. "My mouth is really dry. Does anyone want to walk to the beer tent with me?" She may as well have said she was going to the bathroom when all the females' hands went up. Like a mother duck with her ducklings, Trixie begins walking and the line of girls follows.

"We'll be back." Kat lets the guys know where they're going.

The conversation in the guy's circle started similarly. Santa applauds Dude for the nice catch. "You found yourself a sweet little redhead. And her friends ain't bad either. How was the ride after you two ditched us following lunch?"

Dude tries to resist showing his excitement. He doesn't want to jinx anything he has going with Trixie. "She does make a great passenger. We had a nice ride."

Santa can see straight through his bullshit answer. "I get it. You don't want to kiss and tell. Whatever, Dude. Your face tells me everything I need to know anyway."

Tommy jumps into the conversation. "Wait, you just met her today? What's up with her friend? The tall blonde: not the chick with the wedding ring stuck up her ass."

All the guys laugh.

Dude gives Tommy the scoop. "Yeah, I met her first thing this morning. The blonde is Peggy. I'm pretty sure she is single, and I think I caught her checking you out. Go for it."

The stage lights flash across the crowd as the band wraps up their set. The intermission music is like an iPod on shuffle. One song is rock, and the next song is country. The stage crew is swapping out the drum kits when Uncle Tucker taps on the microphone. “Ahem. Ahem. How is everybody doing out there? Let’s give a big round of applause for Midnight Jacks.” Horns honk and headlights are flashing. “Grab yourselves a cold drink and get ready for our next band. Don’t go too far. I will be back in thirty minutes to bring you tonight’s headliner, the Confederate Outlaws.”

A lightbulb goes on in Dude’s head. He tells the guys he will be right back and then takes off toward the stage. He weaves his way through the crowd to arrive at the side of the stage just as Uncle Tucker hits the bottom step.

Breathing heavily and sweating, Dude introduces himself.

The man with the black bandana on his head and a long-braided goatee looks up at Dude with confusion. “Are you okay brother?”

“Yeah bro, I’m good. I have a huge favor to ask you. Tomorrow morning, we’re having a poker run to raise money for the family of a fellow biker who recently passed away. I will be at the registration table at seven a.m. and the bars open at nine. I will give away five-hundred-dollars to the best hand at noon. Can you please make a quick announcement about it for me when you go back up on stage?”

Uncle Tucker asks a few quick questions before saying, “I should be able to make it happen.” Then the two men shake on it.

Careful not to overplay his hand, Dude says thank you and zips his lips. He shoots himself back into the crowd with a tremendous sense of excitement.

He stumbles up to his friends and drops to the grass to catch his breath. He looks up to see Trixie's wide eyes looking down on him with concern. "Are you okay?

"I'm fine. You guys won't believe what I just pulled off. I want it to be a surprise, so I'm not going to tell you yet. Let's fire up an early celebration joint. Hey Trix, can I please have a sip of your beer?"

She passes him the beer, and he hands her the joint. "You do the honors."

*Chicken Fried* by the Zac Brown Band comes pumping out of the speakers. Trixie reaches down to pull Dude up from the grass. "Let's dance!"

The pair are smoking and dancing like they are in a world of their own. Peggy gets envious and grabs Tommy's hand. "I hope you can dance."

"I can sure try." Tommy moves like the whitest of whiteboys but follows Peggy's lead. She pulls him close and whispers something into his ear. He smiles and slides his hands down onto her ass cheeks. Tommy's uncle Santa is silently cheering him on in the background.

Trixie looks over at Peggy and gives her a thumbs up, then mouths the words, *he's cute.*

The song fades out, and the whirling couples come together. Dude winks at Tommy, and the girls scatter off holding hands.

Santa whips out a jar of moonshine and asks the group, "who's thirsty?" Chuck is first to take him up on his offer, then Birdie slides up next to him for a swig of her own. The mason jar gets passed around until it lands back in Santa's hands.

A tapping on the microphone gets the crowd's attention.

"Before we bring out tonight's headliner, I have an announcement to make. For those of you who would like to support a good cause, there is a poker run tomorrow morning. Look for a guy named Dude at the registration tent. He will be there at seven a.m. and the bars open at nine. The best hand wins five-hundred-bucks. The winner will be announced at noon just before we get started with the bike show. Get y'alls scooters shined up. We have a jam-packed schedule tomorrow. Ladies, don't forget to sign up for the wet t-shirt contest. We also added porta potty races to the agenda this year and you don't want to miss that shit show. No pun intended. Okay, enough about tomorrow, let's keep this night rolling. Everybody get on your feet and welcome to the stage, THE CONFEDERATE OUTLAWS!"

Motorcycle engines rev, people scream, then the stage lights flicker and flash. The crowd bounces off their feet with the first kick of the drums.

Trixie grabs Dude by his biceps and starts shaking him. "Holy shit. How the hell did you do that?" The entire group joins in on the questioning.

"I just felt compelled to ask. I'm almost in shock that he did it. Tommy, we need to be up bright and early tomorrow morning. Cheers everybody! The next round is on me." He raises his joint to their beers. It looks like he just won a dick measuring contest the way the high-fives and pats on the back are flying in. Dude's spirits are almost as high as he is. Trixie wraps her arms around his waist and jams her tongue into his mouth. Dude's hands caress the bare skin of her lower back as they make out like a pair of teenagers at a high school dance. Two minutes pass before they come up for air.

The music is cranked up to ten, and this night just went into overdrive. Everyone in the group is shaking their asses; even Emma is getting in on the action.

A nearby onlooker who has been discreetly watching the group celebration approaches Dude. He emerges from behind the group wearing a white Indian Motorcycles t-shirt under a black leather vest covered in patches. "Are you the guy in charge of the poker run? The same dude that was on the radio with Bear yesterday?"

The whirlwind of today's events made yesterday feel like it was a week ago. High as a kite, Dude stutters, ah, yea, yeah, that's me. He reaches out to shake the man's hand. "Nice to meet you."

"I thought you sounded great on the radio. Funny stuff. Can I buy you a beer?"

"Sure bro. Thanks."

The stranger rambles for a minute. Then he tells Dude he is already signed up for the poker run and he might have some helpful info about the missing Panhead. Dude straightened up in an instant. "About that beer, let's take a walk." Dude tells Trixie he will be right back. She had been listening to their conversation and as Dude turns to walk away, she pulls him in for a quick peck on the cheek. "What the heck were you doing on the radio?"

"I will fill you in when I get back. This guy might have info about George's missing motorcycle."

The two men weave their way through the crowd in search of the beer tent. Dude is still in a bit of a daze, so he just listens to the guy before he dives in with questions. The younger man identifies himself as Anchor. He's a local who rides with a club. He tells Dude that his club has their ear to the street when it comes to stolen bikes. He is sure to make it clear from the start. "We didn't take the bike. But I may have an idea of who could've done it."

"Thanks for being willing to step forward. You know I'm giving a thousand-dollar reward to the person who leads me to the thief?"

"Honestly, that's the main reason I'm willing to help you."

The two men are standing around talking and drinking beer when Santa comes walking up. "Everything okay, Dude?"

"All good. Santa, meet Anchor. He's a local who is going to help us catch the thief."

Santa slurs. "Thas great fucckinn' news."

The group of stumbling individuals agree to revisit this conversation in the morning when they're all sober. Dude ushers Santa back to the group and lowers him into a chair.

The Confederate Outlaws are blowing the crowd away. Everyone in the crowd, except drunken Santa, is on their feet dancing and having a good time. He's having his fun by sitting eye level with three sets of shaking ass cheeks. Santa smiles in his stupor.

Kat declares Santa better get back to camp before he passes out in the chair, and they have to carry him. Chuck and Birdie second the motion. Chuck has had to carry Santa before; he'd rather not have to do it again.

Since most of them have an early morning anyway, the decision is simple. Dude invites Trixie and her friends back to his camp for a nightcap. "We can get a fire going and have a few more drinks." Everyone agrees, so they make their move. The group of people to the right are chomping at the bit to spread out their stuff as soon as Dude and the crew roll out.

The music from the stage radiates back to the camping area as the group of nine make their way through the dark maze of tents and campers. The group makes a quick stop at the girl's camp so they can grab their cooler and chairs. A beam of light from a nearby RV shines through their campsite.

***

Santa drops into his chair. Kat helps the three visiting females get comfortable. Chuck and Birdie go straight for their toothbrushes. Tommy digs a tent out of the back of his truck and looks for a place to set it up. Dude grabs a cold beer and heads for his tent.

Trixie offers Kat a hard seltzer. "Mmm, I've never had one before."

"They are delicious. You will love it. Here, take a sip of mine." Trixie puts the can up near Kat's lips. "It smells good, like watermelon." Kat takes a small taste, followed by a big gulp. "Ahhh, that is good. Like liquid candy. Yes, please." She reaches her hand out for a can of her own.

Santa pops out of his chair and lunges at the firepit. "Let me get this started." He has a thing for being in charge of the fire; he doesn't let anyone else touch it. He could have pyro in his blood; nobody knows.

Dude is kneeling into his tent with a flashlight when Trixie walks up and slaps him on the ass.

"Is there room for two in there?"

He looks back. "Let's climb in and see."

Trixie sucks on her bottom lip. "Maybe later." She gets a chill and wraps her arms across her chest. If there were more light, Dude could see her nipples poking holes in her shirt.

The two love birds pump the brakes and make their way to the circle of chairs around the fire pit. Emma is staring at her phone while Peggy and Kat have a chat about Tommy, who is on his knees wrestling with his tent.

Santa successfully gets the fire going, then reaches for his mason jar of celebration juice. Chuck and Birdie wipe the toothpaste residue from the corners of their mouths. Chuck ducks through the tent door. "See y'all bright and early." Birdie waves and blows kisses to the girls.

Peggy walks over to lend a hand to the effort of getting Tommy's tent popped up. She wraps both hands around his bicep and asks how she can help. He asks her to *hold this*. He puts his pole in her hand. "Stick it through that hole." Tommy points with his right index finger while pulling the canvas with his left hand. He is trying not to step on the tent with his boots. He guides the pole out the other end of the tent as Peggy pushes. They repeat the process for pole number two and pop goes the weasel; the dome shaped shelter rises out of the moist grass.

Santa gets up to take a piss and almost stumbles straight into his precious firepit. A close call. Too close for Kat. "You need to go to bed. Nobody wants to drive your drunk ass to the hospital. I will be in soon. Say goodnight to your friends." Santa mumbles under his breath, then gives in. "I hear ya." He pisses behind Tommy's truck and then gives his nephew a hug on his way to the tent. "Goodnight fuckers."

Tommy and Peggy move two chairs close together and sit down laughing. Emma rolls her eyes while she fiddles with her phone out of boredom.

Trixie signals to Dude and pats her hand on the empty red chair next to her. "Come sit with me."

Smoke from the fire is blowing toward Kat, so she moves her chair while coughing.

Trixie turns to Dude and asks for the details of what he was talking about with Anchor. “The part about you being on the radio. Are you a DJ?”

Dude goes into the story of why he was on the radio when Kat cuts him off and turns to Trixie. “You don’t know what happened?”

“What do you mean, *what happened?*”

“Tell her, Dude, the whole story, don’t leave out any of the juicy details.” Kat sits up on the edge of her chair to watch him squirm.

“It all started a few months ago in Daytona Beach, Florida. I embarrassed myself for money and the incident went viral on the internet. DJ Bear, from 97.7 wanted to interview me about how it all happened. I went there yesterday to let him pile on the humiliation in exchange for promoting the poker run and getting the word out about George’s missing motorcycle.”

Kat stands up and tells him to stop holding out. Dude hesitates, as he knows this story could be interpreted a few different ways.

“Uh, um, well, the thing is… fuck it! During bike week, I jumped on the stage of a packed bar and played air guitar naked. There, I said it. You happy now Kat?”

Trixie wears a blank stare as she tries to wrap her mind around what she just heard. Emma struggles to bite her tongue. “See, I told you he was some kind of player. I bet he does this stuff all the time. He probably hooks up with a different girl at every rally. Trixie, he is just being nice to get in your pants.”

"Stop Emma. Why are you always so negative? You're just jealous. Besides, we are just having fun, it's not like I'm planning to marry the guy." She turns to Dude. "No offense."

"None taken. Seriously Emma, what's your deal?"

Tension fills the air when Kat decides to tap out. "I am really sorry if this is my fault. I'm going to bed now. Really sorry." She gives Trixie a hug.

Emma snaps. "The both of you." She looks at Peggy, then Trixie. "You're hooking up with these random guys we just met. If I knew it was going to be like this, I would have brought my husband."

It feels like the fun has been sucked out of their bodies. If this was *Survivor*, Emma would be getting voted off the island right now. She caps off her spiel by saying she is ready to go back to their own camp and she didn't want to go alone. "I really just want to go home." Emma is officially throwing a tantrum as she folds up her chair. After some back and forth arguing, the three girls decide to call it a night.

Dude barely makes it to his feet when the threesome starts walking away. "I guess I will see you in the morning?"

Trixie looks back with a discouraged look on her face. "Maybe. She makes some valid points."

He waits until they are far enough away to express his frustration.

"What the fuck! Thanks Kat."

A whimpering voice emerges from Kat's tent. "I really am sorry Dude."

# Chapter 9

THE SUN IS STILL behind the mountains but providing just the slightest hint of daylight as Dude rolls out of his tent. He barely slept and his blood is still running hot from the way last night ended. He takes a piss behind Tommy's truck, then grabs a beer to cool himself down. Sprawled out in a chair, he stares up at the sky and watches the stars fade as the minutes pass by. Wearing only boxer shorts, his bare feet are wet from the morning dew covering the grass. He adjusts his nuts as he slides deeper into the damp chair.

With so much to do today, Dude starts planning how he will get it all done. He recounts all the people he talked to about George's missing motorcycle. The early sign-ups for the poker run won't raise enough to cover George's funeral costs. Dude is fighting to get out of his own head. Thoughts of running out of time creep into his mind. *Today is the last full day to make it all happen.*

He gives himself a pep talk to shake the doubts away.

Dude pours cold water over his head and then brushes his teeth with what's left in the bottle. He pulls a black 2018 Sturgis t-shirt over his head, then runs his fingers through his thick brown and gray hair. He sits in his tent and pulls on his blue denim jeans, followed by long white socks and his black Harley riding boots.

He scratches his fingertips on the canvas of Tommy's tent. "Cock-a-doodle-doo. Time to make the donuts." It sounds like a rat rummaging through garbage as Tommy rolls around in his sleeping bag but doesn't answer.

Dude decides to give Tommy a few more minutes, then walks over to his bike and unlocks the ignition and all the saddlebags. He pulls out the poker run papers and glances over the sign-up sheet. He does some quick math in his head, and the numbers just aren't there. *It looks like I may have to get naked again to foot this funeral bill.*

The tip of the sun peeks over the mountain top causing Dude to squint and reach for sunglasses. His eyes squeeze so tight that his beard lifts with his cheeks.

The sound of a tent unzipping gets Dude's attention. He swings his head around, hoping it's Tommy and not Kat. He is still pissed and hoping to break camp before she pops her head out of that nylon gofer's hole.

"You're the man Tommy. Good morning. I'm going to ride up to the registration tent and get us set up. Take your time."

He lets Angel warm up for a few minutes while he wipes the dew off the snakeskin seat. The rumble coming out of the exhaust pipes draws criticism from one of Dude's camping neighbors. "Shut that fucking thing off or ride away asshole."

Dude lets the comment roll off his back as he slowly rides away from his home base. He totally understands people being upset when they get woken up at six-thirty on a Saturday morning. Trying not to piss off anymore neighbors, he slowly makes his way through the camping area.

He slows down as he approaches Trixie's camp. He feels confused. *Am I going the right way?*

The white Jeep is gone.

Three tents occupy the space but no Jeep.

Dude's mind runs wild. *Would they just take off and leave their tents? What the fuck!* He tries to act like he doesn't care. *Whatever, I don't need this girl drama slowing me down today anyway.*

He weaves his way through the smoke of smoldering campfires and past a porta potty with its door stuck wide open. The smell gags him and causes a swerve in his front wheel.

He circles the registration tent then pulls up beside it with his shark nose faring pointed at the dirt road. The two long connected tables sit empty aside from a few rocks used to keep papers from blowing away. Dude opens the lid of his tour pack and pulls out all the paperwork. He puts the flyers down on the end of the table closest to his bike and sits the rocks on top of them. The poker run flyer and sign-up sheet are on the left and the missing bike flyer is to the right.

An older couple walks by with steaming hot cups of coffee and Dude's nose perks up. Two motorcycles come out of the camping area and head into the main grounds. The hum of running generators comes from the vendor tents as they take the tarps off their merchandise. The people heading towards the coffee truck look like zombies dragging themselves to the caffeine.

Dude is sitting in a chair with his head on the table when two guys startle him. They are standing over the table reading the flyers when Dude looks up.

"Good morning fellas."

The two men nod, then the taller of the two opens his mouth. "If I win but I'm not here at noon, what happens to my money?" His stare is burning a hole in Dude's forehead.

"Not a problem. If the winner is not present when the name is announced, I will call them and hold the prize money until they come get it. I'm not going anywhere. You put your phone number right here." Dude points to a blank space on the sign-up sheet.

The two men talk to each other for a minute before pulling on the chains attached to their wallets. "Okay, we're in."

Dude is wrapping the yellow bracelets around their wrists just as Tommy pulls up in his truck.

"Perfect timing. I'm going to grab us coffee and sandwiches. Be right back." He hands Tommy the money pouch and makes a beeline for the food vendors. He is stopped by the man who sold him the brownie. "So, what'd you think of it?"

He gives the guy a blank stare as it takes a minute to register in Dude's brain. "Oh, the brownie. Yeah, it was good." The tall man tells him to stop by later. "I can give you a good deal on stuff to take home with you."

"Okay, we'll see. Thanks." Dude brushes him off with the quickness and keeps moving in the coffee's direction. He kicks an empty beer can and steps over a half-eaten sandwich from last night. His saving grace is now straight ahead.

A large woman wearing a small apron pops her head out of the food truck window. "What can I do you for?"

Dude stands back a couple feet from the window and raises his voice to order. "Two large coffees and two of your ham, egg and cheese biscuits please." A small line is forming behind him, so he pays for his order and then steps to the side.

With the coffee and sandwiches in hand, he stops by Willie's parts tent on his way back to Tommy. The old man is spreading parts across a blanket when Dude walks up. "Good morning Willie."

The hunched over senior turns to see who is talking. "Oh, it's you. Good morning. I didn't expect to see you this early."

"I have a busy day. I just wanted to stop by really quick to see if you were able to make those phone calls."

Willie straightens himself up and waves Dude to come closer. “Everyone I talked to, mentioned the same two guys I was telling you about. They have been known to steal motorcycles, but apparently, I was oblivious. I didn’t realize I was buying stolen parts. I would really like to help you catch these guys, but don’t tell anyone you’ve been talking to me. I am waiting on a call back from a friend who is working on getting us an address to where you can find these guys.”

“This is great news, thank you. I’m heading out for the poker run soon, but I will check back with you later in the day.” Dude trusts Willie is telling the truth this time. He offers him one of the coffees, but Willie declines and Dude walks away with a pep in his step.

He gets back to the registration tent just in time to watch another group of people walking away with yellow wristbands.

“You’re the man Tommy.” He hands him the coffee and sandwich. Tommy digs in and just as Dude gets ready to take a bite of his sandwich, he remembers to tell Tommy about the girl’s mysterious disappearance.

“You won’t fuckin’ believe this. Trixie and her friends are gone. At six-thirty this morning, I rode by, and their jeep wasn’t there. Their tents are still set up but there was nothing else around. I think they abandoned their tents and went home.

Tommy is in disbelief. “That’s crazy. I didn’t even get Peggy’s phone number.”

Dude stands there with his phone in hand, debating if he should call Trixie or not. After a few minutes, he sends her a lighthearted text message saying that he hopes she didn't get abducted by aliens. He tucks the phone into his pants pocket and eats his sandwich in three bites. He washes it down with a few gulps of coffee and then grabs the flyers off the table and walks into the middle of the dirt road. He cranks up his sales pitch for one last big push before it's time to roll out.

A poker run is much different than a toy run because motorcycles don't need to line up and wait for the first bike to go. This is a self-guided situation. People can go to any of the five participating bars in any order they want. As long as they come back with five cards before noon, it's all good. Tommy will stay behind to write down which cards people have when they come back.

Motorcyclists with yellow wristbands are starting to leave the farm in spurts. Dude is hoping that Trixie's Jeep will come rolling down the road any minute, but it's not looking good. Dude needs to get going soon because he needs to meet with the bar manager at each place. He must cover the cost of the cards and pay the bartenders for their time.

He checks his phone one last time, hoping for a response from Trixie, but it's not there. He gives Tommy some instructions and then climbs onto Angel. He jumps in behind the next group of wristbands that ride by. Not knowing where he is going first, he keeps a safe distance behind the bike in front of him and goes with the flow.

The group twists and turns through the tree lined back roads. The smell of fresh cut grass fills the air. A train horn drowns out the sound of the motorcycles. The cool morning air tastes like freedom. The incline of the road requires some extra throttle. They are heading straight for cloud nine.

Dude is slightly jealous of the motorcycle in front of him as he watches the passenger's hair blow in the wind. *Damn it Kat!* Then he wonders if Santa is going to crawl out of his tent in time to get five cards.

The last turn brings the group to the first bar, Rocco's Place, in the town of Seven Devils. The building looks like it was made from recycled trees. It has big plate-glass windows with neon beer lights bright enough to see in the daytime. There are already twelve motorcycles in the parking lot when the group pulls in. A few guys linger by their bikes smoking cigarettes before they walk inside. Dude introduces himself to the guys who parked next to him, then heads in through the side door of the building.

The smell of sawdust overpowers the smell of stale beer upon opening the door. Mirrors cover the wall behind the bar lined with shelves full of liquor bottles. The bar top is made of sticky wood as if nobody ever bothered to remove the sap before laying it down.

The bartender is a tall female with brown hair and brown eyes and a black tank top with the words *Rocco's Place* plastered across her swollen chest. She drops a coaster on the bar top in front of Dude and asks what he wants.

"A bottle of Bud and a shot of Jack." She asks for his ID so she can write his real name on a ten of hearts. He asks her to rub it for good luck, then sticks it in his back pocket.

Dude knocks back his first round and then asks for the manager. An overweight man with a cane comes limping out of the back office. His hair is disheveled, and his suspenders are holding onto his pants for dear life. "Can I help you?"

"Yes sir. I'm Dude, I owe you some money."

The man seems pleasantly surprised that he didn't have to chase Dude down for his cash. "Awfully honorable of you, Dude. Hey Sandra, this is the man paying you to be here this early. Give him a cold beer on me."

A short biker with a large piston patch on the back of his leather vest puts money in the jukebox. The first song to play is *That Smell* by Lynyrd Skynyrd. The guys at the pool table raise their sticks when the song kicks in.

The rumble of motorcycles backing into the parking spots against the building shakes the bottles behind the bar. Sandra grabs the vodka before it vibrates off the shelf.

The group of guys who just shook the bar walk through the door. They're all wearing the same club patches on their backs. There's a round patch with a pair of brass knuckles in the middle, the words Strange Riders above it, and North Carolina underneath. The last patch member to walk through the door is Anchor. Dude tells Sandra to give them all their first beer on him.

Sandra hands the men their bottles of beer and points to Dude. "The first round is on him." The guys raise their beers in his direction, and Anchor recognizes his face. "Thanks Dude!" And then he walks over to shake Dude's hand. "I got another handful of my brothers to sign up this morning."

The bar is filling in, and it's starting to feel more like Saturday night than Saturday morning. The cracking sound of pool balls breaking radiates through the box shaped bar.

Dude breaks the ice with small talk. "How about this weather?"

Anchor orders a shot of whiskey and taps his bottle against Dude's. "Cheers. It's shaping up to be a great day."

Anchor glances around to make sure nobody can hear him, then he leans in closer to Dude and drops his voice. "I'm going to be straight up with you. Sniffing around to find stolen bikes could cause you more problems than it's worth. I can point you in the right direction, but watch your ass if you go digging. There's another club in the area known for stealing motorcycles, the Tortured Men. Stealing is not our thing; ours is drugs."

"I appreciate you being straight up with me. I'm not looking for any trouble, but I do plan on following any leads I can get. What can you tell me?"

The minute of silence feels like an hour.

"Their clubhouse is in Banner Elk. They send their prospects to rallies to lift bikes while everyone is busy partying. If you took the cops over there, I am sure they would find what you're looking for. Just saying. And you didn't hear this from me." Anchor looks paranoid with his head on a swivel.

"For sure. No worries, my lips are sealed." Dude responds with suspicion running through his mind. *I think I know what's going on. Play it cool and then get the fuck out of here.*

Anchor rummages around in the inside pocket of his vest, then taps on Dude's leg. He flashes a small bag filled with an off-white powder. "You want to meet me in the shitter?"

Dude shoots his eyes down under the bar. His mind races in circles. *If I say no, he will think I'm a cop. If I say yes, I may not sleep for two days. Decisions, decisions.*

The last thing Dude would ever want to be called is a cop, and since he didn't get much sleep last night, the decision wasn't too hard to make.

Dude finishes his beer and slides a ten-dollar bill under his empty bottle. "Sure, I have to piss before I leave anyway." He stands up and makes his way through the smoke-filled room, around the pool table and through the flimsy wooden door labeled *Dudes*. It is next to another door labeled *Chicks*. He can't help but to think he's meant to be here. *I mean come on; I basically have my own personal toilet.*

Thirty seconds after the door shuts behind him, it swings back open. Through the door comes Anchor, grinding his teeth. His eyes are bulging, and they look black because his pupils are dilated to the max. Crumbs from his breakfast decorate his mangy yellowish beard. It looks like he has a homeless Christmas tree hanging from his chin.

The two men come belly to belly in the tiny shoebox. Anchor uses his sleeve to wipe off the front edge of the sink. He dumps out a pile of powder, then uses the blade of a knife to turn it into two jagged lines. Dude clears his sinuses as he watches over Anchor's shoulder.

Anchor glances back. "Roll up a bill."

Dude looks at himself in the murky mirror. *You're in for a long night.*

Anchor reaches back for the bill, then does his line. He comes up holding his nose with his head tilted back. Dude waits to see if there's any blood before he reaches out to grab the rolled up twenty. Anchor lets out a sound that only a wounded calf could make. His eyes are closed when he extends his arm toward Dude. With no blood in sight, Dude reluctantly takes the bill. He wipes it on his pant leg, then stuffs it in his back pocket. He pulls out a new bill and quickly uses it to make his line disappear.

The infamous burning sensation causes Dude to have a flashback from Daytona. That was the last time he touched the hard stuff. Feeling like a dragon breathing fire, Dude thanks Anchor for the blast and turns toward the urinal. "I'll be out in a minute."

Dude washes his hands and splashes cold water on his face before making his way back to the bar. Anchor is hovering around the pool table when Dude squeezes past behind him.

Sandra refreshes Dude's beer just in time for him to use it as a mouthwash. He snorts, then gurgles the beer until he feels his sinuses drip down the back of his throat. The numbing sensation should dissipate by the time he gets back to the farm.

Dude polishes off the last of his beer and pushes the empty bottle and cash forward. "Thanks for everything Sandra. I hope you have a great day."

He pushes open the side door as he nods at Anchor. The sunlight is blinding. It seems way brighter than it did forty minutes ago. Dude stands next to Angel, trying to figure out which bar is next. Just a hop, skip, and a jump down the road is a hole in the wall called Topless Larry's. It's not technically a strip club, but it *is* Dude's next stop.

***

Red pasties with dangling tassels cover the nipples of a gothic blonde with purple stripes in her hair. She stands behind the bar wearing black leather booty shorts and tall matching boots. "Hey cutie, what can I get you?"

Dude's eyes are still adjusting to the darkness of the rectangle shaped room. There is only space for the bar and it's fifteen stools. No room for amenities like the pool table at Rocco's Place.

Dude orders a beer and scans the room looking for any familiar faces. A shot girl wearing a nurse's hat, pink pasties covering her nipples and a white mini skirt is selling syringes filled with a red liquid. The bloodlike concoction is *Sex on the Beach.* Not really a biker's preferred cocktail, but from her; they will suck it down.

Dude pulls out his phone to find out where Santa is at. In this dark bar, a ray of sunshine shoots out of his phone in the form of a waiting text message from Trixie. All it says is, *I just woke up. We are at a hotel. Please call me.*

Dude is confused and concerned at the same time. He just met Trixie, but for some reason; maybe her cute ass, maybe her soft lips, he's relieved that she's okay and still wants to see him. He wastes no time getting his questions answered. He dials her number; she says hello in a timid voice, then he jumps in. "How the hell did you end up at a hotel?"

# Chapter 10

DUDE STEPS OUT THE backdoor of the bar so he can hear what Trixie is saying through the phone.

"First, I want to apologize for Emma being a psychotic bitch. I'm sorry for leaving your camp like that last night. We all had trouble sleeping in the tents, so we went down the road to a hotel. It was the only thing I could do to avoid going home early. Of course, Emma was the one who kept saying she wanted to leave. Now she just wants to stay at the hotel until the band comes on and then go home after they're done. Peggy could go either way. I don't want to go home tonight. I told them I would pay for another night at the hotel to keep them from begging me to drive home after the show. I want to drink and have fun and be with you. I don't care what you've done in the past. As long as you treat me right, I want to hang out with you. I can't wait to get back on that machine with you. Can you come pick me up? I will let them take the jeep. Please?"

"I'm already at the second bar. I don't have time to take you back to get your other cards."

"I don't really care about the motorcycle poker. I just want to be on the bike with you."

"I have to square up with the manager and finish my beer. Text me the address to the hotel and get yourself ready. I will be on my way soon."

"You're the best. I am stripping my clothes off and jumping into the shower right now."

Dude looks at the shot girl but pictures Trixie topless instead. The shower scene playing out in his head causes his jeans to rise. A hand slaps down on his shoulder and snaps him out of his daydream.

"Ain't you the guy who put this whole thing together?" A big burly man smoking a cigar spins Dude's stool in a half circle.

Hesitant to answer, Dude looks up to see who's asking. It's an unfamiliar face; familiar to people who watch horror movies but not to Dude. He answers with reluctance. "Yup, that's me." Then he leans back in his seat to get a better angle in which to see the ugly mug of this oversized man. The next words that spill out of the man's mouth surprise Dude.

"I think you're doing a good thing. You know, helping to raise money for your friend's family and all. I read your flyers. How are you making out with finding that missing Panhead?"

"Thank you. I've gotten a few decent leads so far, but nothing concrete. Do you happen to know anything that can help me?"

The big man unfolds his arms. He tugs on the collar of his worn-out t-shirt and starts shaking his hand from side to side. "No, I'm sorry, I'm not from around here and it's my first time at this rally. If I did, I would tell you. I had a motorcycle stolen from me before, so I know how it feels. I just wanted to come over and commend you on your efforts. Good luck."

Dude breathes a sigh of relief once the big man walks away. He asks the bartender to find him the manager so he can put this bar in his rearview mirror.

***

He puts the address to Trixie's hotel in the GPS. She is in Boone, close to the bar Henry Schultz supposedly drinks in. He plans to pick up Trixie and then ride by the sixth bar on the way back to his original third stop.

He pulls into the hotel parking lot to find Trixie standing in front of the lobby with her helmet on and purse hanging from her shoulder. Dude has never dated a girl who could get ready as fast as Trixie. She's wearing those sexy cowgirl boots, light blue jeans and a tight red shirt with a glittery horseshoe bedazzled across her always amazing chest. In one hand she holds a white wicker cowgirl hat, and the other hand holds a jean jacket. She has two braided ponytails shooting out from the bottom of the helmet, one draped over each shoulder.

Dude barely comes to a full stop when she runs up and wraps her arms around his neck and gives him a wet kiss on the mouth. Her lip-gloss tastes like strawberries. Dude slides his right arm around her waist while holding the front brake with his left fingers.

"Let me put the kickstand down and get off." By the time he swung his leg over the seat, she was already on the left side of the bike waiting to grab him again.

"Seriously. I'm really sorry about last night."

He tries to ease her conscience. "Don't worry about last night. We all have crazy friends. You standing here in front of me right now just made my day. We have a bunch of stops to make. Are you ready?" He puts her hat, jacket, and purse in the tour pack. Then he puts the address to Jack's Pub in the GPS.

Trixie bites her bottom lip as she wiggles her ass on the back seat to get comfortable. She intentionally brushes her hand against his crotch as she wraps her arms around his waist. He pops a tent in his pants and then pops the bike into gear.

They twist and turn through the tree covered back roads until they reach Mountain View Road. A left turn puts them along the edge of a cliff, looking down over the town below. The narrow two-lane road takes every bit of focus Dude can muster. Between the beautiful distraction rubbing her hands on his back and his mind racing from the chemicals, the sign for Jack's Pub couldn't have popped up at a better time.

They pull into the parking lot of the cozy log cabin bar with its breathtaking views. There is only one car in the parking lot. It's immediately obvious that the bar is closed. But since there is nobody around,

Dude decides that it's a good place for a smoke break.

He parks in the back of the lot, and they climb off the bike. They find a large fallen tree trunk to sit on with a magnificent view of the surrounding mountains. Pine needles cover the ground under their feet. They both sit quiet until Dude lights up a joint.

More stress leaves Trixie's body with every puff. She goes on to tell Dude that she almost had an anxiety attack in the middle of the night while arguing with Emma.

He waits for her to relax and then asks the question that's been boggling his mind since six-thirty this morning. "I'm so sorry. I hope you're okay now. One question. Why did you girls abandon your tents?"

With a look of embarrassment on her face. She turns to look at Dude and asks him if he promises not to laugh. He puts on his best poker face and lies through his teeth. "I won't laugh."

"So, what happened is, um, we wanted to take the tents, but we didn't know how to fold them up." Dude tries to keep a straight face, but it just wasn't possible. He tries to pass it off as if he is laughing with her, and not at her. She punches him in the shoulder and tells him it's not funny.

"Don't worry, they were still there when I rode by this morning. I will help you take them down later."

The back door of the log cabin bar swings open and startles the smoking couple. A man emerges with a mop and a bucket of dirty water. His nose perks up and his eyes shoot to the motorcycle, then to the characters sitting behind it. “Don’t mind me. I’m just cleaning up the mess from last night.”

Dude pops off the log and walks toward the man. “Hey, I’m looking for a friend who hangs out here. Do you know Henry Schultz?”

The man puts down the mop and turns off the hose. “You mean Hank?”

Dude takes a second to think. “Yeah, if that’s what they are calling him nowadays. We are just passing through town, and I haven’t seen him in years. Do you know where I can find Hank? I’d like to surprise him.”

The man is seemingly unsuspicious, as Dude’s calm approach seems to be working.

“I don’t have his address, but I’m pretty sure I know where he lives unless he moved without telling me. He is over in Mud Hole. He has a corner property where 321 north and Mason Road come together. He has a rusty Ford pickup truck rotting away on his front lawn. You can’t miss it.”

Dude thanks the janitor and asks Trixie if she minds adding one more stop to their morning adventure. Her response catches him off guard. “I will go wherever you take me. But first, while I have you alone, can we talk for a couple minutes before we leave?”

He braces himself for the heart-to-heart conversation he senses is coming next. “Sure. What’s on your mind.”

"I don't know how to say this any other way, so I'm just going to spit it out. I'm not a prude, but I am far from a slut. My friends know that about me and they're just concerned. It has taken every bit of willpower I can muster not to rip off your clothes. Girls have needs too ya know. My friends know I don't have one-night stands; I'm not that type of girl. I really like you, but I need to know that you will still want to talk to me when the rally is over before I can go any further."

He knows that the next words out of his mouth can either seal the deal or send her packing. Dude thinks long and hard before answering. He takes Trixie by the hand and looks into her sexy green eyes.

"I can appreciate your friends watching your back, you're lucky to have them. Since you're being so forward with me, I will shoot straight with you too. I'm not the man whore Emma thinks I am. Have I hooked up with girls at rallies in the past? Let's see, I have been going to motorcycle rallies for over twenty-five years, so, yes, there has been a few. But I have also been in long term committed relationships as well, and when I'm in a relationship, I am faithful. If I had a girlfriend, we wouldn't be sitting here together right now. I'm looking for someone who is ready for an adventure; someone who wants to have fun and travel the world. I can sense that adventurous spirit in you and I would move these mountains to keep you from running away from me again. Trixie, I think you're special. I will move my RV across the state if it means I will get to see more of you."

Trixie crosses her legs to keep Dude from seeing the wet spot emerging from her crotch. She chews on her strawberry flavored bottom lip for a minute before she blurts out, "I know this sounds crazy, but I have never felt such an attraction to any other man in my life. Please don't break my heart."

With her feet still planted on the ground, she lifts her butt from the tree trunk and swings it onto his lap. She wraps her arms around his neck and moves in for a tongue tangled kiss. Dude's hands slide up under her shirt with no objection from Trixie. She grinds her ass on his lap as the passionate make-out session rages on. They come just short of dropping into the pine needles together when she breaks the lip lock. "I want to, but not here."

The disheveled couple slowly rises to their feet in sync. Their bodies are still pressed against each other, and Trixie can feel his erection poking her in the stomach. She puts her hand between his legs as her body quivers. "We can finish this tonight in your tent."

Dude nods in agreement with a smile from ear to ear. "Do we have to wait until tonight?"

She gives him a love tap on the shoulder. "You're naughty. Don't worry, it will be worth the wait."

***

Trixie's arms are wrapped around Dude's waist, locking her two hands together on his small beer gut. They are on their way to do a ride by on Henry Schultz's house.

After coming to grips with the fact that Trixie was gone, this turn of events is throwing Dude for a loop. His lifelong quest of trying to understand women continues to elude him. His focus had been set on taking care of the poker run, but now his mind keeps going to tent sex with Trixie. He wants to reach his hand behind his back so she can sit on it. He would rather it be his face, but he will settle for a hand in the meantime. He pushes past the urge and cracks down on the throttle.

They're on 321 north looking for the rusted Ford when the eyesore shows up at a red stoplight. The corner property could easily be mistaken for a junkyard. The Ford by the road was a drop in the bucket once Dude pulled into the empty driveway.

Cars, trucks, and junk are spread out across five acres of grass. None of the vehicles look like they run. It's all shit. The long gravel driveway causes a wobble in Dude's tires, so he rides onto the grass toward the house. Flaking paint is falling from the wooden siding. Five steps lead to a shaky porch where there is a window on each side and a brown door in the middle.

Dude parks the motorcycle and tells Trixie to "wait here" as he makes his way toward the steps. He grabs for the railing that isn't there and almost trips on a broken plank. He peeks in a window but doesn't see anyone. He knocks on the door. With no answer after a few minutes, Dude walks to the back of the house.

He approaches the garage behind the house with caution. He looks around and then presses his face against the garage window. A project car sits in the middle, surrounded by more piles of junk. Then a handlebar catches Dude's eye. After a closer look, the handlebar is attached to an old Honda Scrambler. There is a toolbox in the corner covered with cobwebs, and a rusty motor oil sign hanging above it.

There is no sign of anything red, white, or chrome anywhere on this property. Dude kicks empty beer cans as he zips through the piles of junk covering the path back to Trixie.

Shaking his head with disappointment, he signals to Trixie. "Let's get the fuck out of here before I need to get a tetanus shot."

Trixie pants like a puppy as she waits for him to climb onto the bike first. She swings her ginger braids to the back and uses Dude's shoulder to pull herself up. Her ass drops onto the seat and Dude lets out the clutch. He notices his tire tracks across the grass as he watches the house get smaller in his mirror. They pull out of the driveway and down a steep hill.

Trixie can see the discouragement in his face through the mirror. She massages his shoulders to help him relax and then he sinks down into the seat. Dude thinks about getting a hot shower, then he daydreams about Trixie taking the shower with him, then the curve of the road snaps him into reality. She leans when he leans. Trixie is the perfect passenger. Motorcycle companies could make a fortune if they included a Trixie with every bike purchase. It would be the single man's dream come true.

Now Dude needs to take a piss and he's kicking himself for not just pissing on Henry's junk piles. The beer is running through him. The debate in his mind of whether to stop now or wait ends quickly. He pulls behind an abandoned restaurant to drain the main vein before he soils the snakeskin. If Dude only knew Trixie is secretly trying to sneak a peek, this stop would last much longer, but he keeps it brief.

A few remaining turns are all that separates them from bar number three. Trixie is excited to see what this motorcycle poker fuss is all about. Her mouth is getting dry, and a cold drink can't come soon enough.

# Chapter 11

TRIXIE HOLDS ONTO HER braids as she turns her head to look down at a dead deer on the side of the road. Her face turns sour as she lifts her head. Dude looks at her in the mirror and chuckles under his breath.

Coming down from the top of a hill, they can see the cozy little Main Street of downtown Boone straight ahead. The down slope allows Trixie to see clean over the top of Dude's head. She looks like a puppy with its head hanging out of a car window. Not even a forty mile per hour breeze can wipe the smile off her face. The sunshine makes her white teeth sparkle. The happy couple comes to a stoplight at the bottom of the hill. Dude can see a group of motorcycles parking along the curb in the distance.

In front of poker run bar number three, the Squirrels Nest, Dude backs into the curb, squeezing himself between a pair of crotch rockets; a black and red Yamaha GSXR 1000 and a chromed-out Suzuki Hayabusa.

Trixie's boot almost clips the Busa as she swings her leg over the seat. Dude is pleasantly surprised with the number of motorcycles lining the sides of this quiet street.

From the outside, the Squirrels Nest looks like it was plucked straight out of an old western film. On the inside, not so much. Gaudy decorations are covering the long wall running down the right side of the room opposite the bar. A long row of stools leads to a back room with dart boards and a pool table. The big window next to the front door allows in just enough light to see the bartender. Behind the bar is a short guy in his mid-twenties. He has spiky blond hair and the type of blue eyes that make girls weak in the knees.

The amount of people drinking in a bar this early in the morning has Trixie in disbelief. She tugs on Dude's shirt as they make their way into the bar. "I didn't even know bars were open this early in the morning."

They plop down on a pair of stools and Dude waves his hand to get the bartender's attention. He spins himself on the stool to face Trixie. "No, not usually. I am paying them to open early."

The bartender asks what they're drinking. Dude orders a beer, and Trixie gets a Bloody Mary.

Dude scans the smoke-filled bar and notices a few of the people he personally signed up in the back room. He feels good about the turnout. He takes a minute to think about George and how much he loved poker runs. Dude knows George is with him in spirit.

The bartender brings their drinks and offers them a playing card. Trixie Stone is all smiles as the cute blonde-haired guy lays a Jack of Clubs next to her pint glass with celery sticking out of the top. He asks for her ID, and she bats her eyes with confusion. "Do I look that young?"

He says, "I'm supposed to write your name on the card."

"Oh, okay. Sorry, I thought you were just trying to flatter me."

She takes a sip of her drink. "Yum. This is really good. Do you want to try it?"

She puts the straw up to Dude's mouth, so he gives it a taste. Trixie picks the green olives off the tiny plastic sword and lays them on her tongue in slow motion. Dude drools as he watches her roll them around in her mouth. He puts his hand on her knee and asks her to stop teasing him. She looks Dude in the eyes and then chomps down on the little green balls. Dude thinks *ouch* and then reaches for his nuts as if he could feel the pain.

*Single Saturday Night* by Cole Swindell comes blaring out of the jukebox, then Trixie pops off her stool and starts dancing. She grabs Dude by the hand and pulls him away from the bar. She turns her back to him and starts grinding her ass against his junk. Dude has his hands on her hips as they move with the music. Trixie spins around and throws her hands in the air. "This is so much fun."

She's rubbing Dude's bicep when she remembers to ask about his shirt. "I was sitting behind you on the bike, admiring the picture of Mount Rushmore on the back of this Sturgis shirt. Have you been there?"

"Three times. Sturgis is the mother of all rallies; Mount Rushmore is cool too. The rally is insane, and the riding out there is spectacular. It happens every year in August. If you're not busy in two months, maybe we could go together." Dude winks with his left eye.

Trixie cracks a half smile. "If I'm not on the side of the road with a broken heart by then, I will consider it."

Dude says, "Unless you secretly have a penis in your pants, you don't have anything to worry about."

The lovebirds are lost in time when Dude sees a Miller Lite clock on the wall showing eleven a.m.

"We need to keep it moving. Let me find the manager and then we have to get out of here. If you need to use the bathroom, do it now."

Dude feels the pressure of the twelve o'clock deadline looming. He is both nervous and excited for the poker run to be over. Dude puts a pep in his step as he and Trixie head out the front door of the bar. Two stops remain before they can return to the farm and give away the prize money.

Trixie waves her Jack of Clubs at Dude and tells him, "I'm saving this souvenir."

The next stop, the Boone Roadhouse, will put them five miles closer to the farm. Trixie is oblivious as to where they are going now. She continues to climb on the back of the bike without asking any questions. He could be going to Tennessee, and it wouldn't matter to her. She is floating on clouds back there. It's like an endless rollercoaster ride that will only cost her one golden ticket at the end of the night.

Trixie begins standing up while they are still moving when she sees the front of the roadhouse. It has country written all over it. There is a steer's skull above the handcrafted wood door with a lasso hanging from one of the horns. Light colored wood shiplap wraps the exterior of the building. There is a huge outdoor bar on the side, and it's packed with bikers. The parking lot is covered with motorcycles. The party is in full swing. The bar normally opens at eleven, so their regulars are now mixing in with the poker run crew.

Dude and Trixie go straight to the outdoor patio bar. To their surprise, Santa and Kat are sitting around a picnic table with Chuck and Birdie. Dude gets the attention of a waitress who is buzzing between tables with a tray of beers in her hand. He asks her to come back when she gets a minute. He points to where he will be sitting. Trixie notices the group at the table and when Dude turns around, she is squeezing her way through the crowd. She scares the shit out of Kat Miller from behind. Santa slides himself off the bench and gives Trixie a big hug.

"You guys just getting here?" Santa reaches out for Dude's hand.

"Yeah, I tried calling you an hour ago. How long have you been here?"

Santa pulls out his pocket watch. “About forty-five minutes, I guess. Great place, I don’t think we will make it back to the farm by noon.”

The girls are embracing each other with hugs and kisses. Kat immediately starts apologizing for last night. Trixie responds by apologizing for Emma. Dude decides to get in on the action and he apologizes to Kat. “I’m sorry for being a dick.”

Trixie looks at him, wondering why he would say such a thing. “What did you do?”

“I may have been a little frustrated after you girls left. I’m pretty sure I gave her an attitude.”

Kat accepts his apology and then tells Trixie, “A little frustrated would be an understatement. I heard him cursing to himself in the tent for an hour after you left. He was sad to see you go.”

Trixie smiles. “Awe, you really do care.”

Dude blushes and tells Kat, “Luckily they didn’t leave for good, and I was able to pick her up from the hotel.”

Kat is confused. “What do you mean, hotel?”

Dude just realized that nobody at the table knew about the girls leaving the farm. He asks Trixie to tell them what happened.

“Basically, we fought for hours and then we went into the tents and none of us could sleep. Emma was begging me to take her home and the only way I could get her to calm down was when I said the word hotel. Emma and Peggy are there now. They’re going to stay at the hotel until it’s time for Carolina Country and then they will drive over in my Jeep.”

The group looks shocked. To them, this sounded like something out of a book. Their collective thought is, *Who the hell would leave the great outdoors for a boring ass hotel room?*

Kat asks, "Where are you going to sleep tonight?"

Trixie looks at Dude, and then tells Kat, "Hopefully in *his* tent."

The waitress walks up to take their order. Dude pays for beers for anybody who wants one and orders himself a hamburger. The girls break off to the side of the guys and start a private conversation. Dude sits down next to Chuck and asks how the run has been going for him. Chuck pulls out two cards: a three of spades and a five of hearts. He turns to Dude. "I think I'm out."

The smell of pine blows through the patio. Chuck stands up and looks out into the forest behind the building. The waitress is back with the drinks. The group clinks their bottles together in comradery.

Dude tells the guys about him and Trixie riding by Henry's house. He catches them up on that lead from Anchor. "He is fuckin' trying to play me. The dumb fuck must be crazy if he thinks I bought that bullshit story he was selling. Like I'm stupid enough to have his rival's clubhouse raided by the police. They would kill me!"

Trixie comes out of the inside bar raving like a lunatic. "Oh my god. It's like a real honky-tonk in there!" She grabs Dude by the arm. "Come check it out with me."

"Okay. Real quick, we can't stay here long."

There's a poster on the glass door promoting line dancing every Sunday night. Trixie's eyes are as big as bottle caps as she scans every inch of the poster. Walking through the door, the couple are greeted by an empty stage on the left and a mostly empty, very large dance floor straight ahead. Mounted animal heads are spread out across the walls. A painted mural of a wagon train glows behind the bar. Pictures of teepees hang above the bathroom doors. The room has the smell of wood, beer, and dirty socks. All the female bartenders are wearing cowgirl hats and boots, daisy dukes, and plaid bras, no shirts.

Trixie is in heaven while Dude stands there speeding, looking for a clock. He tells her, "I'm really sorry that we can't stay longer. I still have to see one more manager and get back to the farm by noon. Those extra stops really set me back. You look around while I find the manager." Trixie's bright white smile fades fast.

The pair head back out onto the patio to find Dude's burger sitting on the picnic table. He is hungry, but his stomach is in knots from Anchor's speed, so he has it wrapped to go. They say bye to their group of friends. Dude explains the urgency, and the crew bids the couple farewell.

Trixie talks in Dude's ear all the way to the last bar. She can't stop raving about the Nashville style honky-tonk. "It reminds me of Rippy's on Broadway."

Dude is intrigued. In the parking lot of bar number five, he turns off the ignition and asks Trixie how many times she has been to Nashville.

"Um, ah, I don't know. A bunch. My ex was in a band, and they played there all the time. I would always tag along. It's been a while; I can't wait to go back again." To which Dude replies, "I like Tootsies the best."

With not enough time for a beer, Dude leaves Trixie by the bike and runs inside the Mud Hole Pub to see the manager. The parking lot is packed with motorcycles. The building looks like a square box of stucco with two tiny glass block windows glowing with neon beer signs. Three guys linger next to the front door, smoking cigarettes.

Dude asks the bartender, "can I please speak with the manager?"

The short woman with long brown hair covered with tattoos responds to Dude's question. "You found her. How can I help you?"

Dude towers over her from the opposite side of the bar. "I'm here to cover the expenses of you helping me with this poker run. Thank you for opening early for us."

The woman insists on giving Dude a beer as he pulls out his cash. He tries to refuse, but she looks insulted, so he pounds it down and sits the empty bottle on the bar. She hands him a seven of diamonds after writing the name *Dude* across the card with a black marker. The guy sitting on the stool next to him was eavesdropping on the conversation, then he puts his hand on Dude's shoulder. "Hey buddy, thanks for giving me something to do this morning. Here's my cards, I won't make it back by noon."

Dude looks down at the busted flush. "Keep them as souvenirs."

The small building is vibrating from all the commotion. It's definitely Dude's type of party, and he wishes he could stay longer, but duty calls. His commitment to seeing the run to the end is unwavering.

He walks out the door to blinding brightness. Trixie looks like a pin-up leaning against the motorcycle. Dude drools and stares a hole in her chest as he moves closer. He wraps his arms around her waist, then squeezes her ass cheeks. Trixie's heals come off the ground, and she gets a couple squeezes of his ass in return. They kiss for a minute before Dude pulls away. "You're going to give me blue balls."

Dude pulls out of the parking lot feeling relieved with the last stop behind him. The music is cranked up on Angel and she is running hotter than a bikini model laying on the beach in Miami. The next stop is Lone Ranger's Farm; or so he thought.

A mile from the Mud Hole Pub, there's a guy standing next to a maroon and white Indian Chief on the right side of the road. He looks like he's broken down, so Dude pulls over behind the Indian. The man walks up to Dude and tells him that the Indian is out of gas. Dude notices the man wearing a yellow wristband and offers to go get him some gas. The guy tells Dude not to worry, he already has somebody on their way with a can. The man only has three playing cards and will clearly not make it back to the farm in the next twenty minutes to qualify anyway.

Angel is back on the move, but the couple will be cutting it close. Dude has a pet peeve about being late; he tries to avoid it at all costs. He said he would give away the prize money at high-noon and his mission is to keep his word. Plus, the bike show, followed by the biker games, starts around noon, and he wants a front-row seat.

Dude turns onto the dirt road entering the farm. He comes around the curve and sees a cluster of people and motorcycles gathered around the registration tent. He only has five minutes to spare. He passes through the crowd and pulls into the center of the main grounds, which has a section wrapped with caution tape for where most of the day's events will take place. He pulls up to the yellow tape with black writing and drops his kickstand.

After a short walk, Dude and Trixie are welcomed to the registration tent with cheers. A few people make comments about him giving them the money. Everyone thinks they have the best hand. Tommy is the only person who knows who the winner is. Dude thanks Tommy for all his hard work and asks to see the paper with the winning name and which cards they have. Tommy points to the name circled on the paper and tells Dude it was really close between three people. There are two people who have four of a kind, but there is only one person with a straight flush.

Dude pulls out the five hundred in cash and holds it over his head. “First of all, I want to thank each and every one of you for supporting this poker run. I’m not sure yet if we have enough to cover the funeral costs, but I appreciate every dollar that was raised. Your money is going to a good cause. Everyone here is a winner, but only one person is going to get paid for it. That lucky person has a straight flush, all hearts, from seven to jack. And the prize money goes to, Michael Smithfield.”

There is a synced grunting sound from the two men who had four of a kind. Then, from the back of the crowd, a small celebration erupts. Michael climbs off his rusty 1977 Harley Shovelhead to approach Dude and collect his winnings. The two men shake hands and Dude gives Michael a big hug. “Congratulations Michael. You had this strongest hand, so you get the money.” Dude puts the pile of cash into Michael’s left hand and then raises his right arm like he just won a boxing match. The crowd goes wild.

Michael closes his hand on the money and proceeds to give an acceptance speech. “I had a lot of fun riding these beautiful back roads this morning. I would do it for free any day. This cash is just a bonus. Dude, when I signed up, you told me the story of your friend George. I think you’re doing something special, so I want to donate half the money back to George's family."

Cheers and whistling break out. High-fives start flying in and then Dude gives Michael a giant bear hug. Trixie's eyes puddle up. Tommy is standing on a chair, pumping his fist. Emotions are running high throughout the crowd. Comments of how generous Michael is being swirl. Dude releases Michael from his death grip and asks the people to give one more big round of applause for Michael and everyone who took part in today's run. The gathered crowd lets out a collective roar as people begin drifting toward the bike show.

Dude, Tommy, and Trixie come together for a group hug. Dude kisses Tommy on each cheek like a mob boss. The three are all smiles. Dude doesn't want to know the final numbers just yet. He considers the poker run a success, regardless of the amount of profit. He provided a good time for a great cause, and that's what the motorcycling community is all about.

He helps Tommy pack everything up and then the three of them climb into Tommy's truck and head back to their camp.

Before counting the money, Dude looks over the sign-up sheet. The total amount of people who participated in the poker run was two-hundred and forty-seven. There were Two-hundred and thirteen riders plus thirty-four passengers. Bringing the total incoming money to forty-six hundred and ten dollars. Minus the expenses of printing the flyers, buying the bracelets, covering the cost of the cards and the bartenders, plus paying Tommy. The total overhead was seven-hundred and seventy dollars. Adding in the two-hundred and fifty dollars that Michael donated back to the cause, the grand total going towards George's funeral is, four-thousand and ninety dollars.

A tremendous sense of relief comes over Dude's body as he sits on Tommy's tailgate. He's trying to process the fact that this should be enough money to provide George with an official final resting place. Before they walk to the main grounds for the bike show, Dude makes a phone call to George's wife, Julie, to tell her the good news.

# Chapter 12

BACK AT CAMP, TOMMY is taking a nap. Dude just got shot down by Trixie when he made a second suggestion about getting some daytime action. He pushes down on his stiffy and starts limping toward the bike show. Trixie trails slightly behind him while adjusting her bra from Dude's most recent time on second base.

The game of grab-ass continues as the horny couple makes their way through the camping area on foot. They stop to admire the three vacant tents that remain standing at Trixie's camp.

Dude asks her, "do you want me to break them down now?"

"No. Not yet. I told Emma to park the Jeep here. We can deal with this crap later." Trixie is ready to keep walking.

They pass the registration tent where Dude nods at Hammer through what looks like the smoke from a three-alarm fire. Every time a truck or bike rides on the dry dirt road, they leave a trail of dust. The main road coming into the farm has a huge cloud of dust hovering over it from all the traffic coming and going. Trixie puts her arm over her face like she is running into a burning house to save a cat.

The couple passes under the Lone Ranger's Farm sign and are greeted with vendor tents overflowing with people around the edges of the main event area. Moving people and motorcycles fill the space between the vendor tents and the caution taped area in the middle. Most motorcycles are parked facing the middle of the field. People are setting their chairs along the caution tape for a front-row seat of the day's festivities, which will continue for the next five hours.

A steady stream of custom paint and shiny chrome fill the large section in the center of the field for the bike show. This same area will be used for the biker games once the bike show is over and the nicest motorcycles on the farm clear the area.

Dude sees the entrance to the bike show on the other side of the field. He walks straight ahead to check on Angel before he and Trixie walk around the caution taped area. A row of people are admiring the show from the seat of their pants.

On their walk around the caution tape, Dude points at the Delta 8 tent. "Hey Trixie, how about a snack?"

She laughs. "Are you just trying to loosen me up so I will cave when you try to get laid again?"

Dude jokingly acts like he is offended.

Trixie says, "ask me again when the sun goes down."

They make their way to the table of trophies sitting at the bike show entrance. Gold plastic trophies topped with miniature motorcycles will be given to the top three bikes in each of the seven classes. Only one bike will be crowned the best of show and win a cash prize of three-hundred dollars and a lap dance from the wet t-shirt contest winner. Uncle Tucker, who is walking around with a microphone, tells the growing crowd that if the girl who wins doesn't want to do it, he will nominate his old lady to give the lap dance.

Uncle Tucker looks like he runs with an L.A. street gang. His pants are being pulled off his ass by the weight of the chain attached to his wallet, which is ripping through his back pocket. His red Chuck Taylor's and bandana make it clear which side he would be on if he were to start gang banging. His long-sleeved black and white flannel shirt is buttoned at the top and flapping in the breeze at the bottom. His braided beard hangs down to the top of his bubble of a belly. You can see the word *Sturgis* peeking between the open front of the flannel every time the wind kicks up.

Uncle Tucker weaves his way in and out of the parked motorcycles, shaking hands and kissing babies like he is the Pope.

Entering the judging area, past the trophies, there is a table where three cute blondes hand out clear sandwich bags containing eight tickets: one for each class and one for the best of show. The girls are representing the bike show sponsor, NC Biker Lawyers.

Every person attending the rally gets eight little paper tickets, each a different color. Each color ticket has the class written on it with black marker. Each class has its own section within the caution taped area. Small signs designate where each class starts. There is a bucket sitting in front of every bike for people to put their tickets in. Each person drops the related color ticket into the bucket of their favorite motorcycle in each class.

***

Entering the judging area, past the table of blondes, people walk up and down the wide strip of grass to examine the bikes lining each side. At the far end, there is a big section where the trikes and sidecars sit like tanks.

Lined up along the left side, the first section is for the sport bikes. There are six tricked-out crotch rockets fighting it out for the top spot. First up is a carbon fiber and silver 2004 Buell Blast. Its skinny front fairing cuts through the wind like a ninja. Custom airbrushed skulls cover the next bike in the line. It's a 2012 Suzuki Hayabusa with an extended chrome swing arm that separates this bike from the next four, which are all similar makes and models but with different paint jobs and chrome accent pieces.

Next in the line is the bagger class. A white Harley Street Glide is up first, then a silver Road Glide. Two Indian Chieftains, one is a Black Hills silver with marble accents, the second Indian is a two-tone black and tan with fringed black leather saddlebags, sit side by side. A fully dressed dark blue Yamaha V-

Star with white accents and all the bells and whistles, literally, is up next. A decked-out Victory Highball with matte black paint and red pinstripes rounds out the baggers.

People are filling into the bike show area in droves. A man and woman pass a joint back and forth while they slowly make their way to the front of the line to get tickets. Cans covered with foam koozies seem to be the popular choice for drinking beer with the temperature in the mid-eighties. The smell of BBQ blows across the crowd.

The last class on the left side is the rat bikes. One of the main rules of the bike show is that all bikes must be ridden in. It's a ride-in bike show; no trailering and no pushing bikes in. So, even though these rat bikes look like piles of shit, they all run.

First up is a Harley Sportster that has been chopped down to the bare minimum. It has drag bars and a solo seat. The paint job looks like it was done with a can of rust orange spray paint and the whole ass end is covered with what looks like mud. While everyone else in the bike show spent the morning washing and waxing their rides, this jackass must have been riding around in the cow pasture.

The second rat looks like it used to be a Honda Rebel before someone took a torch to it. What's left of the Rebel amounts to about twenty dollars' worth of scrap metal.

The third rat is a bare metal 80s Shovelhead. There are holes drilled into the tractor fenders and the seat is just a metal pan. It has no front fender, and the kick starter has a pedal from a children's bicycle. The guy who owns this rat is sitting on a cooler behind the bike drinking a PBR pounder and picking food out of his mangy beard. Because only three bikes entered the rat class, even the pile of scrap metal will leave with a trophy.

The big section at the end of the row starts with a stock Harley trike. Its female owner is leaning on the handlebar like a proud mother. Next to mama trike is something custom made with a Volkswagen engine and a triple seat. The wide ass-end has two sweeping exhaust pipes shooting out between the pair of car tires. The fiberglass one-piece fairing wraps around the machine like a dune buggy.

Rounding out the three wheeled machines is an Army green World War Two era military Harley-Davidson WLA and its sidecar. It is complete with ammo boxes and a fifty-caliber machine gun mounted to the front of the sidecar. This classic is getting all the attention. The fourth trike was disqualified because it was seen being pushed off a trailer. Since there are only three in the class, everyone is a winner.

The judges are making their rounds. The three judges each have a clipboard containing the criteria for how they will score each bike. Judge number one is Uncle Tucker. Judge number two is the man in charge of the entire event, Tex Anderson. Judge number three is the man, the myth, the legend, DJ

Bear, from 97.7. The three men examine each motorcycle from top to bottom, front to back.

Dude runs into the judges while they examine the crotch rockets. He thanks Uncle Tucker for last night's shout out, then lets him know about the success of the poker run. Bear hears Dude's voice and swings himself around from the Buell to congratulate Dude on the good news.

Bear extends his hand in Dude's direction. "Any word on the missing Panhead yet? Did you see the black and white Pan over there?" Bear points at the vintage class bikes.

He lets Bear know that they just walked up, and he is making his way around to the antiques. Then he introduces Trixie to the judges.

Uncle Tucker asks Trixie to sign up for the wet t-shirt contest. She doesn't have to think twice. "No thanks. If anyone is going to see these puppies, it's only going to be *him*." She squeezes Dude's ass.

"I can respect that. How about you two signs up for the weenie bite competition?" Uncle Tucker pushes Dude's chest. "Don't be scared. She looks like she'd be good at it."

Trixie looks to Dude for an explanation. "What is a weenie bite?"

"You would be on the back seat when I ride under a hanging hotdog, and you would lift yourself out of the seat and bite the raw hotdog without using your hands. The girl who bites off the biggest piece of the weenie wins."

Trixie's jaw drops and then she punches Uncle Tucker in the arm. "What makes you think I would be good at that?"

He hesitates to answer, then takes a step back and says, "that pretty little mouth of yours…"

"You pig! Bobby, are you going to let him talk to me like that?"

Dude doesn't know who to address first. "Oh no, you're not going to start with that Bobby shit, are you? Yo dude, can you please apologize to the lady?"

Uncle Tucker says sorry and then turns away as the two lovebirds hit another snag. Trixie likes Dude's nickname, but in her mind, calling him Bobby makes him feel more like a boyfriend and less like some dude who is going to get in her panties and then disappear. Dude knows this name thing is important to Trixie, so he lets her know she can call him whatever she wants.

"So, what do you think? Should we sign up?" Dude has always loved watching the weenie bite, but he's never had a chick willing to deep throat a hotdog from his back seat before.

The jury is still out in Trixie's mind. "I don't know yet. I think I need to see what it looks like first."

***

With the weenie bite idea on the back burner for now, the pair makes their way past the trikes and down the other side to the group of choppers.

Five front tires stick out farther than all the rest. The long front ends cause a tripping hazard for the drunks not paying attention to where they're walking. The chopper with the Sugar Bear forks immediately catches Dude's eye. It has psychedelic paint covering a coffin style gas tank and rear fender with twisted spoke rims and a yellow frame.

The second chopper looks like a Jessie James special. It has an iron cross headlight and a solid gloss black paint job with a joker's face airbrushed on the sides of the stretched gas tank. A sweeping set of exhaust pipes shoots out of the side of a chrome S&S motor.

Trixie asks Dude questions as she points at different parts of the bikes with curiosity. She pulls out her phone to take a picture of the row of choppers, and a lightbulb went off in her head. "Let's take a picture of us together." She pulls Dude close and takes a selfie. Then she says something that catches Dude by surprise. "I would like to learn how to ride a motorcycle someday."

"Really? Have you ever ridden anything with two wheels and a motor before?"

Trixie is full of surprises today. "When I was a kid, my dad showed me how to ride a homemade minibike with a lawn mower engine and I did okay on it. In recent years, I have ridden a couple of four wheelers, but that's about it."

Dude supports her idea of riding solo until he realizes it would cause a vacancy on his back seat.

"I'm sure you can do it. Maybe one day I will teach you."

They drift past the remaining three choppers when the custom paint class catches Trixie's eye.

"Dang, that must have been expensive." Her head tilts sideways, trying to follow the flowers weaving throughout the airbrushed paint of a '02 Harley V-Rod. There are even roses painted on the center of the solid mag wheels. Trixie bends down to get a closer look. The guy walking up behind her acts like he's also looking at the wheels until Dude catches him staring at Trixie's ass. Dude gives him the evil eye and motions for the perv to keep walking. Keeping guys from drooling on Trixie has now become a full-time job.

Realistic flames jump off the Harley Fat Boy that is next in line. Two bikes away, a much less impressive flame job gets no love. He may get an *E* for effort, but definitely not a trophy for that lackluster paint. The sun causes the last custom painted bike to sparkle. It's a Suzuki GSXR with flip-flop paint. From the front it looks purple, but as you walk towards the back of the bike, it turns blue, then it looks red when you're standing behind it. Dude tries to explain how it's possible to Trixie, but it's like talking to a deer staring into headlights; she is mesmerized.

Approaching the vintage class, the age of these classics can be seen from a mile away. A photographer has a long camera lens pointed at a knucklehead engine. The man's ass is dangerously close to the black and gold Norton parked next to the Knuckle. If he knocks over the Norton, it will fall into the ‘69 Triumph Bonneville on the other side of it. One stupid move could cause this photographer to be shitting film for the next week.

Safely beyond the reach of this dope with the camera sits the black and white Panhead that Bear had mentioned. It has a crowd gathered around it. Dude gets in on the action and moves close enough for a thorough examination. The obvious owner is answering one man’s questions. It looks a lot like George’s ’63 and Dude has some questions of his own. He starts with, “what year is it?”

The man with the answers has gray hair with a military crew cut and a matching goatee. He proudly wears a black Panhead t-shirt littered with small holes showing its age. “She is a ‘65”

The man’s answer drew Dude much closer to him. Close enough for the two men to shake hands.

“It’s always nice to meet someone who likes the old stuff. What did you say your name was?”

“I didn’t say. But my name is Dude.”

“I’ll be damned, you’re the guy looking for the missing ’63. I’m Martin, the guy who you spoke to on the phone yesterday. Did you ever go talk to the guy selling the parts here?”

“I did. Thanks for the tip. He is still trying to dig up some info about where he got those parts from. By the way, which parts did you buy from him?”

Dude is now looking into every nook and cranny of the black and white ’65.

Martin takes a minute to answer, and then he points to the back tire. "That back rim came from him."

"Is that all you bought?"

"I also got my horn from the old man." Martin walks to the other side of the bike so the two men can look at the horn together. The horn is mounted on the right side of the bike, just below the gas tank and between the famous Panhead rocker covers. The three-inch chrome circle causes Dude's mind to race. There is the legendary Harley bar and shield in the center, with horizontal louvers at the bottom, and curved ones at the top going with the flow of the round shape.

"I haven't been able to confirm whether these parts are from my friend's bike or not, yet, but this is the same horn that was on George's Pan. I have a strong feeling that whatever Willie sold you was from George's bike. I know you are innocent in all of this, but I want to ask you one serious question. I'm not going to ask you to take off your rear wheel, but I would like to make you an offer to sell me the horn. How much do you want for it?"

Martin strokes his chin hair. The wheels in his head are spinning. He can sense the desperation in Dude's voice, so he throws out a crazy number. "I'd sell it for three-hundred."

"Here's the deal." Dude straightens his back and Trixie puts her hand on his arm. "It's only worth about eighty dollars. I will give you a hundred bucks and buy you another one."

Everyone knows you can't put a price on sentimental value and Martin is no dummy.

"First of all, if I do agree to make a deal with you, I don't want to ride home without a horn. Will you be hanging around tomorrow or are you blowing out of town early?"

Dude hadn't given much thought to what time he'd be leaving, but he is in no rush to get home. "I don't have any problem with meeting you after the rally tomorrow if it means I will have a piece of George's motorcycle to give his son."

Martin gets a lump in his throat. "Why'd you have to go and mention the guy's kid, now I feel bad. Make me a cash offer I can live with, and you have a deal."

Dude reaches into his pocket, pulls out a wad of cash and starts peeling off bills. "Here is two-hundred cash. You can take the money now and I will pick it up from you tomorrow."

Martin hesitates to grab the money. He knows he can probably squeeze Dude for a little more. "Make it two twenty and we have a deal."

Dude hands him the cash. "Thank you Martin. I have your number, and you should have mine. It's the one I called you from. What time can I expect to hear from you?"

"I should be home and settled by three. Sound good?"

"Perfect. Good luck today." Dude drops two tickets into the bucket by Martin's front tire: one for his favorite vintage bike and the other for best of show.

The two men shake hands and then Dude turns around and gives Trixie a kiss on the mouth. He pulls her in for a long hug. She rubs his back as people passing by bump into the oblivious couple. He whispers in her ear. “If all I go home with, is you and this horn, I will be a happy man.”

Sure, he wishes he can catch the thief and bring home the whole bike, but it just may not be possible. Dude becomes content with just retrieving one piece at a time, if that’s what it takes. He is ready to celebrate this small victory.

“Trixie, we need to put the rest of our tickets into the buckets and go get something cold to drink.”

She drops a ticket in Martin’s bucket, then scrambles between the crowd of people to get back to her favorites. She had already dropped one ticket into the bucket of the flower bike and another into the bucket of the Road Glide that reminds her of Angel. Her next ticket goes to the military sidecar. Dude drops one of his in the same bucket.

Uncle Tucker makes a last call for people to vote for their favorite motorcycles. The judges have completed their assessment of the bikes, but the weight of the vote goes to the people.

A mad scramble of people fumbles with their tickets. In some classes, the competition is stiff, so having to choose only one can be difficult: then there are the rat bikes.

With no tickets left, Dude and Trixie make a beer run with the hopes of getting back in time to hear the winners get announced. You can hear Uncle Tucker's big mouth from anywhere on the farm when he talks into the microphone, but it's not the same as seeing who owns these mostly beautiful machines.

***

While Trixie and Bobby (Dude, to everyone but Trixie) wait in line for beer, he turns to her, "I could hear some excitement in your voice when you were talking about your dad showing you how to ride. This is the first time you've mentioned him. Is he still in your life?"

After a moment of hesitation, Trixie breaks her silence. "He is. He lives a few streets over from my apartment. He is a giant pain in the butt, so I usually only see him when he needs my help with something. He has a bad back, so, to answer your next question, yes, he did ride motorcycles, but it has been years since he sold his last one. He was just a casual rider. I'm not sure if he ever went to rallies. He sheltered me from the motorcycle culture. He drilled it into my head from an early age that guys only want one thing from a pretty girl like me."

They make it to the front of the line just in time for Dude to order the beers and think of a proper response. The man behind the table pours beer from the tap mounted to the side of a refrigerated box truck. Under the beer tent, the cover of shade is long overdue for the pair of parched patrons who have been baking in the sun for the last several hours. Dude slowly pulls out his money and pays in slow motion so he can savor the shade for just one extra minute before heading back out into the sun.

With beers in hand, on their way back to the judging area, the couple walks past a bearded man chowing down on a giant turkey leg like he is Fred Flintstone. Trixie gags when she looks at the caveman devouring what looks like the world's largest turkey leg.

Dude races to think of a response that won't offend Trixie.

"Your dad sounds like a good guy. It's nice of you to look after him. He gave you some wise advice."

"Thank you. I've done my best to stay away from guys like you." She cracks a smile. "Damn this band Carolina Country for luring me here." She lets out a lighthearted chuckle. "Actually, you are the first biker that I have ever hooked up with. When I was younger, my dad would have killed me if he knew I dated someone with a motorcycle. He always talked about how dangerous they can be. But I'm a grown woman and I do what I want now. He's too old and injured to kick my ass anyway."

Dude returns the smile. "I feel honored. Trust me, you've made a good choice."

They head back to Dude's motorcycle to watch Uncle Tucker give out the trophies from the other side of the caution tape. An older couple is sitting on chairs next to Angel when they walk up. Trixie looks at the couple who have been married for thirty years and daydreams about growing old with someone. They are wearing matching plaid shirts and look like two peas in a pod.

Dude is shuffling around in his saddlebag when the older man notices him. “That’s a nice bike y’all got there. We’ve been keeping an eye on it for y’all.”

“Thank you.” Dude approaches the man to shake his hand.

“I’m Ed and this is my wife, Sherry.”

“Nice to meet you guys. My name is Dude, and this is my girlfrie… uh, um, Trixie.”

“It’s fine, you can say it.” Trixie tells Ed and Sherry, “he’s, my boyfriend.”

Sherry says, “you two make a cute couple.”

Trixie thanks her and then turns to Dude. “See, we’re cute together. I think you’re a keeper.”

In the weeks leading up to the Mud Hole Rally, Dude focused all his energy on setting up the poker run and chasing down any last-minute leads on the missing motorcycle. The last thing he anticipated when coming here was meeting someone like Trixie. After flying solo for the past couple of years, the girlfriend experience is a welcome change. Sure, there are benefits to having no strings attached, but when that string is as cool and sexy as Trixie, Dude’s willing to roll the dice.

A tapping on the microphone gets the crowd’s attention.

Uncle Tucker, DJ Bear, and Tex Anderson, stand in front of the trophy table. The three blondes representing the NC Biker Lawyers stand beside the table waiting to take pictures with the winners.

"The first trophies we will hand out will be for the sport bikes." Uncle Tucker holds up an eight-inch-high trophy with a white marble base and an engraved plate saying 3rd place sport bike on the front. "Third place goes to Joey Simmons with the red Honda CBR."

A heavyset guy with a neck full of gold chains wobbles forward to collect his trophy. He gets a cheap feel when he wraps his arms around two of the girls' waists during the photo.

All the trophies look the same, but the size increases by four inches with each step toward first place. Second place goes to the 2012 Suzuki Hayabusa.

"First place goes to the Harley that wasn't. The Sportster engine on a sport bike seemed cool at the time, but they just couldn't get it to catch on. Everybody, give the owner of the silver Buell Blast a big round of applause." Uncle Tucker waves his arms in the air.

The winners look more excited about the picture with the blonde threesome than they do about the trophies.

The special edition Black Hills Indian Chieftain takes third place in the bagger class. Feeling cheated, the owner of the Indian looks like someone just pissed in his oatmeal. The silver Road

Glide takes Second place even though it's basically a stock bike because of all the extra chrome and mag wheels. The addition of a custom fairing and saddlebag lids with exposed sub-wolfers and a tour pack loaded with stereo amplifiers, helps the white Harley Street Glide steal the top spot.

The bare metal Shovelhead takes home the sixteen-inch trophy in the rat bike class. The other two rust buckets fought it out for second place. It is basically a tie for biggest pile of scrap metal.

The WLA military Harley takes the top spot in the three wheeled category. The Sugar Bear front end blew away the competition in the chopper class and Trixie's favorite, the flower power V-Rod, wins the biggest trophy in the custom paint category.

Martin Woods took home second place. The Knucklehead squeaked away with the win in the vintage class.

Uncle Tucker announces the final winner of the ride-in bike show. "We want to thank everyone for their participation in today's show. The best of show trophy goes to the World War Two Harley WLA and its fifty-caliber machine gun." He hands the winner three-hundred dollars in cash and tells the guy to find him later after the wet t-shirt contest for his lap dance. Then, as people walk away, he makes another announcement.

"Don't forget, as soon as we clear this area, we will start the biker games. The first event will be the slow ride. You can sign up right here at the table with the lawyer chicks." Of course, the three gorgeous blondes are offended by his remark. They all shake their heads in disgust.

Trixie reminds Dude how much she dislikes Uncle Tucker.

Dude responds by suggesting a break from the action. “Let’s go back to camp and relax. The slow ride is kind of boring unless you like to watch people drop their bikes in the grass. Plus, I need to get off my feet.” They climb onto Angel. “We can see if Santa and the rest of the crew made it back from the bar yet.”

# Chapter 13

THE CAMPING AREA IS fairly quiet because most people are filling into the main grounds to watch the biker games. Dude and Trixie are enjoying some down time at camp after a busy morning. Dude finally eats the burger he brought back from the Boone Roadhouse. Trixie eats a granola bar she dug out of her purse. They both drink bottles of water to hydrate themselves. Trixie is putting sunscreen on her fair skin when she thinks to text Peggy. She reminds Peggy to bring her bag of clothes from the hotel when the friends come to the farm later.

There is still no sign of Santa and Kat, or Chuck and Birdie. Sitting around the fireless fire pit, the happy couple's casual conversation is interrupted by the unzipping of Tommy's tent. They had forgotten Tommy was still in there. He climbs out of the tent in his tightie-whities, dripping with sweat. "Jeez, it's like a sauna in there. I'm going to drive home and get a shower."

Luckily for Tommy, *he* lives close by and doesn't have to use the shower trailer on the farm. Low water pressure and dirty underwear are what you can expect to find in the one shower trailer that is supposed to accommodate thousands of bikers. A good reason for people to get drunk is to become oblivious to the smell of the person next to them in the crowds.

Sure, Dude wants a shower, but if he's going to come out feeling dirtier than he was when he went in, he figures, what's the point. He uses baby wipes and deodorant to freshen himself up throughout the weekend. That hotel room was Trixie's saving grace. She wouldn't have lasted a minute in the shower trailer. The shower alone was worth the price of the hotel room.

If Trixie didn't get the hotel room, she may have already been gone by now. And if that happened, Dude would've been beating his meat in the tent tonight thinking about her. So, in a way, the hotel was *his* saving grace too.

"Let's go sit in the shade." Dude points at the RV in the next row over. The owner introduced himself to Dude on Thursday night and said he was welcome to stop by anytime, and right now, Dude is taking the guy up on his offer. It doesn't matter if nobody is home, he just wants to sit under their awning to avoid melting into his chair.

Dude picks up two chairs and asks Trixie to grab the cooler bag. She is enjoying the quiet time with her new man and every minute alone gives her more time for questioning. They drop their chairs in the neighbor's shade and Dude pops the top of one of the few beers left in the bag. He can see a beer run in the near future.

Trixie puts Dude's feet to the figurative fire. "You mentioned having your own RV, and that you would be willing to move it across the state. Tell me how that would work."

"Um, well, what I was saying was, that if we couldn't make a long-distance relationship work, I would be willing to relocate if that's what it will take for us to be together."

She processes his answer then follows up with, "you would really do that for me?"

"Here's the deal; I live in my toy hauler RV in a year-round campground. They have places like this all around the state. I can paint houses anywhere. I'm getting bored with the place I'm in now anyway. It's a nice campground, but my neighbors can be annoying. I think living in the mountains would be cool. I have always loved western North Carolina."

Trixie is a little shocked, but also very happy. "Well, guys make a lot of promises to get into a girls' panties. You make it sound good, but let's see what you're saying tomorrow morning after we sleep together."

"Hey, you asked what I meant, and I told you the truth. I'm ready for a change and based on the chemistry we've had so far, I'm willing to follow it wherever it takes us."

The sarcasm drains out of Trixie's body. She wants to say something clever and shoot down his sincerity, but she can't. It's like he has her hypnotized. She is blinking and her lips are moving, but no words are coming out of her mouth.

Finally, she strings enough words together to make a complete sentence. "I agree with feeling the same chemistry." She takes a deep breath. "Change is something I think about all the time. I hate my job, and I can't stand my apartment. I'm always talking about quitting this stupid job, but I never do it. The last six months have been terrible. Before we broke up, my ex and I had plans to move to Virginia together. I was so excited to get out of Asheville. I don't have anything against the place, it's just that I have lived there my whole life."

Dude rubs her back as they sit shoulder to shoulder in the shaded camping chairs. "Maybe you would rather come check out my side of the state?" He can't imagine someone living in one place for their whole lives. He likes a change of scenery.

She says, "you're giving me a lot to think about."

"Who would look after your dad if you moved out of the area?"

"My sister, Laura, lives close by. She is married with a five-year-old son, my nephew Zach."

"I understand. Change can be scary. We've all been there. When I left New Jersey after my dad died, I had no idea what would be waiting for me in Florida. I just knew I wanted warm weather and a fresh start; somewhere I could ride all year round in a t-shirt. I made the move, and it was awesome. I lived there for almost fifteen years. I got tired of all the overhead associated with living in a house, so I bought the RV and dropped it in a campground."

In a curious tone, Trixie asks, "And you moved there by yourself?"

"Basically. I did have a friend down there who gave me a lay of the land. I worked in a fish market and rented a small house when I first got there. I changed jobs all the time. I moved around the state to a different part every couple of years. I started out on the east coast, just above Daytona in Palm Coast. Then I gave the west coast a try. I bought my first RV in Fort Myers and found a place to park it close to the beach."

"Wow. You've been a busy boy with all that moving around."

"That's nothing compared to all the actual traveling I've done." Dude is struggling to stay humble and not over hype his Gypsy lifestyle.

"I miss being in a relationship and having someone to enjoy life with. I mean, my cat is cute and all, but I could really use a steady man in my life. These past couple days have been amazing, and I don't want this ride to end tomorrow. If you are being serious right now, you would make me the happiest girl in the world."

"Of course, any move across the state won't happen overnight, but I'm willing to do my part to take this to the next level if you are." Dude almost can't believe the words that are coming out of his mouth. "Plus, I would love a chance to Prove Emma wrong."

Trixie shows her excitement by leaning over to suck his face.

"Before you get me all worked up, let's take a ride to the gas station to get beer and whatever you want to drink." Dude pops out of the chair. Luckily, he is wearing pants, or he could've poked her eye out with his boner.

***

Dude tops off his gas tank and then the couple walks into the gas station store. He grabs a case of beer, and Trixie gets a twelve pack of watermelon flavored hard seltzer. When they get to the cash register, Trixie pulls him close and whispers in his ear. "Don't forget to buy condoms."

All they need now is a sign saying, *if this tent is rocking, don't come knocking.*

Dude undoes the bungee cords that are holding down the cooler bag. He leaves it sitting on the luggage rack and loads it up with half of his case and all twelve of Trixie's fizzy cans of alcohol. He dumps a bag of ice on top and zips it up and straps the bungees over the top to secure it for the quick ride back to camp. He stuffs the trash into the can next to the gas pump, then they hit the road.

***

They arrive back at camp to find Santa and Kat relaxing by the firepit. Santa perks up when he notices the stuffed cooler bag on the back of Dude's bike. "I thought someone stole our cooler."

Trixie climbs off first and picks the wedgie out of her tight little butt. Dude takes notice and wishes she would've asked him for help.

Santa asks about how the poker run turned out. Dude gives him the final numbers and then moves on to fill him in on the Panhead horn he bought from Martin Woods.

"I have to pick it up from him tomorrow. I still have to check back with Willie to see if he has any new info about these thieves. Are you guys going over to watch the biker games?"

"Yeah, we're going to watch the shit show. We just need to relax for a few minutes first." Santa wipes sweat from his brow and plops down into a chair with a cold beer.

Dude overhears Trixie telling Kat about the rapid development of their relationship. Trixie notices him eavesdropping, so she has a little fun with him. She leans closer to Kat, and then in a loud voice, she says. "We agreed to get married."

"Whoa. Get the fuck out of here!" Dude falls for it, hook, line, and sinker.

The girls laugh. Kat tells him, "You wouldn't have the balls to tell her no if she asked. You're already whipped."

Santa gets in on the action. "Boy, you better not let her out of your sight. A hot number like her won't be on the market for long."

It's three against one. Dude attempts to defend himself. "You guys are acting like I'm not trying over here. What do you want me to do, put a hose clamp on her finger right now?"

Trixie bats her eyelashes and extends her hand in his direction. "Take me off the market big boy."

"You're all crazy." Dude pulls out a joint to relive the sudden pressure he feels from Trixie's fake proposal.

If Dude wants the girlfriend experience, it looks like he hit the jackpot. Atlantic City has nothing on Trixie.

After a couple of cold beers and smoking the full joint, Dude is ready to switch gears. With the cooler bag still on the bike, it's time to ride over to the main grounds.

As the day goes on, and people consume more alcohol, the biker games get better. Watching someone tip their motorcycle over on asphalt is terrifying, but seeing them fall over on grass, now that's just funny.

Dude climbs onto Angel. "Mount up fuckers!"

# Chapter 14

A CLOUD OF SMOKE hovers over the main grounds. The smell is a mixture of barbeque, campfire, cigars, cigarettes, marijuana, burnt rubber and arm pits. The next couple of hours will be like the Motorcycle Olympics. The burnout pit has been set up and people waste no time breaking it in.

Pop! What sounds like a gunshot is actually the rear tire of a beautiful black Street Glide. The young buck went through all his gears, but the crowd wouldn't let him quit until he popped the tire. He backs out of the pit with a flat tire and what looks like cobwebs of rubber draped from the bottom of his fender and saddlebags. Now this guy has to drop two fifty on a tire or load the sweet ride onto a trailer.

Dude could never understand why someone would beat up on an expensive motorcycle this way. He would never treat Angel with such abuse.

By the time Dude, Trixie, Santa, and Kat rode into the event area, they had missed all of the Slow Ride competition and most of the Keg Roll.

The final round of the Keg Roll comes down to a little skinny guy on a Honda Rebel and a large man wearing denim overalls with no shirt on a Low Rider. The two men are lined up about twenty feet away from each other. Empty aluminum barrels rest against their front tires, just waiting for Uncle Tucker to give the green light.

With their feet dragging on the grass, the two men jerk their handlebars from left to right, trying to keep the barrel moving forward toward the finish line thirty feet away. The Rebel is going sideways while the Low Rider just avoided eating grass. The big man was going too slow and almost jackknifed his frontend. He stops to regain his composure and lights up a cigarette. He blows a cloud of smoke into the air, then gets the barrel rolling again. The Rebel straightened himself out and is now pushing his barrel on the edge of the course along the caution tape. The wide field leaves plenty of room for zig zagging.

With only a few feet to go, in a photo finish, the Honda crosses the finish line without his empty keg and the Low Rider takes first place. Uncle Tucker gives the big man his prize; a fifty-dollar gift card to the Boone Roadhouse.

Trixie cringes every time she hears Uncle Tucker's raspy voice. "Is there a way we can shut him up?"

Dude lets her know that as the Emcee, it's his job to get the crowd riled up. "You would've loved to see what happened to him last year. He was so drunk that he got himself slapped by the winner of the wet t-shirt contest."

Trixie smiles and nods her head up and down. "I would pay to see that video." She brushes her hair back and tells Dude, "I think I need to get very drunk in order to listen to his mouth all day. I had planned to be drunk by the time Carolina Country comes on, but I may need to move up the timeline. Will you promise to watch my back if I get too tipsy?"

"I've got you girl. You don't have anything to worry about. Enjoy yourself." Dude puts his hand on the bare skin of her lower back and gives her a kiss on the mouth. The combination of her strawberry lip gloss and the watermelon alcohol on her tongue is the closest Dude has ever been to tasting a fruit salad.

Trixie puts her fingertips in her ears as Uncle Tucker announces the next event. "Last chance to sign up for the Weenie Bite. We're going to get started in ten minutes."

She watches the event staff as they hammer two long broomsticks into the ground. They tie a rope from one stick to the other about eight feet off the ground. Small strings with raw hotdogs are hung from the larger rope. Trixie asks Dude to explain this to her again. Just as Dude starts to talk, Uncle Tucker sends out a bike with a guy and girl to test the height of the dangling dogs.

The man rides slowly under the rope and his passenger pulls on the man's shoulders to lift herself to her feet. She opens her mouth wide and comes up from beneath the raw wiener. She manages to bite off two inches before falling down onto the seat.

"Oh, hell no! No way will I give Uncle Dirtbag the satisfaction of watching me put that disgusting thing in my mouth." Trixie turns to Dude. "You seriously thought I would do that?"

He responds with caution, "It wasn't my idea."

Trixie tells him, "I'm not even sure if I can watch this nonsense. Can we just take a quick walk around the vendors?

Dude reaches into the cooler bag and grabs them each a cold can. "Sure. Whatever you want to do. I have to stop by to see Willie anyway."

***

Inside the official rally merchandise tent, Dude and Trixie scan the table of shirts, hats, pins, and patches. Every year, the rally merch gets a new design. This year's Mud Hole Rally emblem has a tire covered with mud in the center and mountains topped with a breathtaking sunset in the background. The words *Mud Hole, NC. Motorcycle Rally* in Old English letters are above the image, and the numbers *2019* sit just below it.

Trixie keeps holding shirts up against her chest to see how they look in the mirror. She has the size figured out, now the question becomes, long-sleeves or the V-neck? Pink or white? She is overwhelmed with choices, so she summons Dude's opinion. He walks over to her with a black XL t-shirt and a circle shaped patch in his hand.

"Which one do you like best?" She holds the white long sleeve in her left hand and the pink V-neck in her right.

“I don’t think you should have to choose only one. You buy one, and I will buy you the other. Deal?” Dude reaches out his hand.

“If you keep this up, I’m going to get spoiled.” She hands him the pink V-neck rally shirt. “Thank you.”

With their new garb all bagged up, the next vendor to provide the couple with shade has a table full of sex toys. Dude asks Trixie, “do you see anything you want?”

She responds by grabbing his crotch. “This is all I need.”

He says, “and the torture continues. I might poke a hole in these pants before this day is over.” Dude puts his hand in his pocket to make an adjustment from the inside.

Dude hasn’t seen her eat much today, so he asks, “are you hungry?”

She thinks for a minute and then says, “I could eat.”

They skip the next few vendors and head towards the food trucks.

“Hey, Dude.” DJ Bear calls out from the radio station tent. The couple cuts through the flow of people going in the opposite direction. “Big Bear. How’s it going?” The men shake hands and Dude reintroduces Trixie.

“You guys want to spin the wheel?” Bear rocks the prize wheel back and forth like a carnie trying to lure his next mark.

Dude steps aside. He says, “Ladies first.”

"Ooh, this is exciting." Trixie puts her hand on the wooden wheel. The metal pegs around the edge rub against a clothes pin until it stops. Ten sections are color coded, one for each prize. She looks it over and then pulls down like she is on *The Price is Right*. The two-foot round wheel is sitting on top of a rectangular folding table covered with a black tablecloth. Her spin almost causes the wheel to go rolling off the table. When it finally slows down, it ticks past the free key chain, then past the radio station t-shirt, and it stops on the skinniest color on the wheel. There are only three pegs on the outside of the section containing free concert tickets, and Trixie just landed in the center of the three.

She jumps off the ground, her hands shoot up above her head. "Holy crap!"

Bear congratulates Trixie. "You just won two tickets to North Carolina's biggest summer music festival."

"Get the heck out of here! Thank you so much."

She turns to Dude. "How freaking cool is this?" She raises her right hand, and he gives her a high-five.

Trixie takes the tickets from Bear and teases Dude with them. He asks, "when is the festival?"

She quickly scans the tickets. "The weekend of July 19$^{th}$, in Greensboro."

Dude gives her puppy dog eyes. "Please take me with you."

"I am going to make you earn this ticket. Don't worry, only fun stuff." She makes a sexy growling noise.

Dude wins a black radio station koozie with his spin. Much less exciting than Trixie's lucky spin, but hey, he will put it to good use.

Bear gets his picture taken with Trixie holding the two tickets and Dude standing behind her like a bodyguard. Bears says the picture is going to be on the station's website and social media pages.

They part ways with Bear and stroll up to a truck selling slices of pizza. Dude asks, "will this work?"

From the look of Trixie's lean body, it appears she spends every meal counting carbs, but her answer surprises him. "Yes, I love pizza."

A *Tony Soprano* look-a-like stands inside the open window of the pizza truck. His gold chains are covered in flour and there is a good chance his sweat is part of the recipe. Dude motions hello with his hand and then orders. "Two slices, no toppings please."

After a few minutes, the two hot slices come through the open window, followed by a trail of steam. The couple plays hot potato with their plates as they gravitate toward the closest picnic table. While waiting for the slices to cool down, Uncle Tucker's voice radiates through the speakers. He announces the new leader in the weenie bite contest just swallowed the whole hotdog. Trixie almost throws up in her mouth. "He is going to ruin my appetite."

She manages to eat most of the slice, then she offers Dude the crust. He would love it if they could each chew from opposite ends and meet in the middle like they do on TV with spaghetti. She sticks it in his mouth, then pulls her hand back like she is feeding an alligator.

Twenty steps from the pizza truck, the Delta 8 guy is working hard to get Dude's attention as the couple strolls by his tent. "Come on over here, I will give you a good deal."

Dude looks at Trixie, and she knows what he's going to say before he opens his mouth. She tells him to go ahead and get whatever he wants, but she won't take anything until later. He passes on the potent stuff this time but gets a handful of low dose gummies. He pops one now and pockets the rest for later.

As they are working their way around to see Willie, the weapons trailer catches Trixie's eye. "Those knives look familiar. Is that where you bought mine from."

"Guilty as charged. If you don't like it, we can trade it in for something different."

She grabs his hand. "No, that's not why I asked. I love my pink camo knife. I wouldn't trade it for anything."

Uncle Tucker announces that the winner of the weenie bite is the woman who swallowed the whole hotdog. He hands the woman a fifty-dollar gift certificate to the vendor selling the sex toys. She takes the envelope and flashes her big boobs to the crowd to drum up applause. He announces to the crowd, "don't go far. The Porta-Potty races are up next."

Dude tells Trixie, "You will get a kick out of these races. They are always hilarious."

"I don't understand. How are they going to race a portable toilet?"

He knows she is a motorcycle rally virgin, so he gives it to her real slow. "The plastic toilet shed is tied to a motorcycle with a rope. One person sits inside the porta-potty and gets pulled by the person riding the bike. Two bikes line up and race. Whoever gets their toilet past the finish line first moves on to the next round. Some usually tip over inside the stinky hot plastic box. At the end, everyone will be eliminated except for one. The winner will get some kind of prize. Don't worry, I'm not even going to ask. We can have our fun watching from this side of the caution tape."

Trixie continues to be amazed at the stuff these people think is fun. She feels like she needs a shower just listening to Dude describe what is going to happen with these portable toilets. Trixie says, "what's next, is their going to be a garbage eating contest?" She is mentally preparing herself to see the unthinkable now. "I really need another drink."

Dude tries to chill her out. "It's not all as bad as you're making it out to be. Let's stop to see Willie and then we will head back to the bike."

***

Willie is selling a gas tank to a man when Dude and Trixie walk up to his blankets full of motorcycle parts. He tells Trixie to bat her eyes at the guy to loosen him up. She reluctantly nods like she is agreeing, but in her head, *it's a no go*. They patiently wait for Willie to finish before Dude puts the squeeze on him.

"Hey Willie."

The old man looks up and shakes his head. Willie is getting sick of seeing Dude's face. "You again?"

"Yeah, it's me, but I also brought some eye candy this time. This is Trixie."

His eyes widen and shoot straight down her shirt. It's amazing how much power a cleavage can have.

"Willie, give me some good news."

He is talking to Dude, but looking at Trixie. "Okay, here's what I can tell you for sure. The two guys are definitely brothers. They live here in Mud Hole and, according to a reliable source, they both work at a welding shop in town."

"That's a good start. Do you know the name of the place where they work?"

Willie has a nervous look about him. "I really don't want to be involved in this. There are only a few welding shops in this town. I'm sure you can figure it out."

"What you're telling me is good, but it's not worth the thousand-dollar reward. What else can you tell me." Dude is trying to have patience with the old man.

"I asked my friend about the white van you were telling me about and he said he doesn't think either of them drives a van. He said they could have had help. You find that van and the person driving it should be able to identify the two brothers. That's all I know. As much as I'd like your money, what I'd like better is if I never have to see you again. Good luck finding these guys. Please don't mention my name to anyone. I have to make a living in this town."

"I understand. Thanks Willie."

Dude reaches out to shake the old man's hand, but Willie isn't interested. Willie pulls up the bottom of his shirt to reveal the butt end of a .38 Special. "Please leave me alone now."

Trixie questions Dude about what he will do next. "We're going to start by getting away from *John Wayne*." He tells her he'd like to ride to all the welding shops in town, but it's getting late on a Saturday and most businesses close early. He decides to call Tommy on the phone to see where he is and find out what he knows about the local welding shops in town.

They walk back to where Angel is parked before he makes the call to Tommy. Santa and Kat are standing by the bikes when they return.

"Hey Santa, is Tommy back yet?"

"I didn't know he ever left."

"Yeah, he went home to take a shower. Do you know of any welding shops in Mud Hole?"

Santa says he knows of one on Holly Springs Road, but he's never been inside. "Tommy may know of others." Dude steps away from the group to make the call.

Tommy answers from his living room couch.

"Are you coming back to the rally?" Dude is glad he answered, but it sounds like Tommy is half asleep.

"Yeah, I'm just taking a break from the heat. What time is Peggy coming back from the hotel?"

"I'm not sure. I can find out from Trixie and get back to you on that. Right now, I just need to ask you a question. Are you familiar with any welding shops here in Mud Hole?"

Tommy turns down the volume on his television. "Uh, um, I know there is one down there on Millbrook Lane. Not sure what it's called. I don't know of any others around here."

"Do you know if there are a pair of brothers who work there? They look like twins."

"Dude, I only been in there a few times, but I don't remember seeing any twins. Let me make a few phone calls. I will see what I can find out and I will fill you in when I get back to the farm."

"Do me a favor. Please ride by that shop on Millbrook and the one your uncle told me about on Holly Springs Road and see if they're open. If so, call me."

"Will do."

"Thanks Tommy."

***

Dude slinks his way through the crowd and back to his friends. He finds Trixie sitting on the front seat of Angel with her hands on the grips, looking like she is ready to ride. Santa is explaining what all the buttons are for. Her feet sit flat on the floorboards, but she can only reach the ground with her tippy toes.

Hey Santa, "Tommy is home recharging for tonight. He is going to ride by the welding shops he knows about on his way back. If you need anything, catch him before he leaves the house. We might need more beer."

Kat climbs onto the passenger seat behind Trixie. She wraps her arms around Trixie's skinny little waist. The two pose for pictures and Dude can't get his camera phone out fast enough. The girls look like they could be modeling for *Easyriders*.

Before he stuffs the phone back into his pocket, Dude does a quick internet search for local welding shops. There are only three listed in Mud Hole. The one on Millbrook Lane, the other on Holly Springs Road, and the third is on Apex Parkway. Each one is listed as being closed on weekends. Dude shoots Tommy a text, telling him not to bother stopping at the welding shops, and then asks him to pick up another case of beer.

Dude pulls a can of beer out of the cooler bag that's in the shaded grass by Santa's feet. His mind is now racing.

Trixie hears Dude mumbling under his breath as he paces around the motorcycle. She says, "I can see smoke coming out of your ears. What's going on?"

"I just looked up the local welding shops and all three are closed on weekends. I could be stuck in this Mud Hole town till Monday if I want answers."

Trixie says, "don't forget, you are getting *me* and the horn to take home."

"I know and that is plenty, it's just that I feel obligated to get some form of justice for George."

Santa offers to sniff around next week. "Me and Tommy will run these guys down for ya."

Dude looks disappointed. There is no sign of the smile Trixie has come to adore. Sure, he will have the horn, and taking home a trophy like Trixie should be enough to make him happier than a clam. The problem is that he's having trouble accepting the fact that these thieves are going to get away with no consequences. He pops open another cold can and slides it into the foam koozie he won at the radio station tent.

A flying porta-potty lands on its side. A man in a white shirt emerges covered in blue liquid. Luckily for him, the portable toilets hadn't been used by the public yet. He will have to walk around smelling like a urinal cake and looking like a dye pack exploded on him after a bank robbery. The motorcycle that was pulling it is now planted face first in the grass. Three guys go running over to lift the bike off the rider. He gets up limping and notices his windshield is cracked. The large man screams, "ah, fuck! Jesus Christ!" The Smurf looking friend comes over to see if he is okay. Clumps of grass are stuck to the highway peg, brake caliber, and the front fender. The man picks out the dirt and grass, then he climbs back onto the still running motorcycle.

Seeing the man covered in blue toilet water actually made Trixie laugh. She finally found the humor in this whole shit show.

The portable toilet drag race comes down to the final round. Uncle Dirtbag gives them the signal to start. A man on a Harley Fat Boy is hooked up to a potty containing a female partner. The second bike is a Sportster ridden by a little guy with another little guy being dragged behind him, wobbling side to side in the plastic shitter. The Fat Boy spins its back tire getting off the starting line. The Sporty is out in front, but his partner almost tips over so they stop to regroup. The Fat Boy gains some ground and the two are neck and neck approaching the finish line.

The Sportster gets going again and blows past the Fat Boy. The man riding the Sporty celebrates prematurely as his bike crosses the finish line, but the plastic toilet is still three feet away from the win when he slams on the breaks. The toilet slides forward and slams into the back of the bike, then tips forward onto the rider. With no door on the plastic outhouse, the opening swallows the rider, and his partner is now on the rider's back. The blue water splashed out of the hole people sit on and coated the whole inside of the plastic box. The blue juice is dripping everywhere, covering both men.

The Fat Boy slowly passes the Sportster toilet combo and takes the winning spot. Event staff rushes over to pull the outhouse off the Sporty. The man inside the toilet is peeled off his partner's back. He emerges with the blue juice all over his face, in his hair, and on his teeth. He stomps away from the shitter, wiping his face with the also wet shirt as he extends his other hand out, asking for water.

The rider manages to keep the bike upright during the whole ordeal so there is no physical damage to the bike, but he doesn't look happy, that's for sure. Hopefully the toilet chemicals won't eat his paint.

The lucky Fat Boy receives a fifty-dollar credit for the Delta 8 tent and another fifty in cash.

Dude got a kick out of watching Trixie get excited during the intense toilet races. She watched with the kind of amazement a child has when they go to the zoo for the first time. She sees him checking her out. "What's up?"

He says, "nothing, you just look so cute. I enjoy watching you smile and laugh."

Pointing at the remnants of the Sportster toilet pile up, she says, "That was hilarious but I kind of feel bad for those guys."

Trixie's enjoyment of the events was short-lived because Uncle You-Know-Who pushed another one of Trixie's buttons.

The rally Emcee is being obnoxious as usual, and Trixie is about to blow her top. He is slurring into the microphone and pointing at women in the crowd. "We're still looking for five more girls for the wet t-shirt contest. I don't care if you have big titties, little titties, titties with big nipples, small nipples, no nipples. Just bring your ass up here if you have tits and a vagina."

Trixie turns to Dude. "Will you please let me punch him? I may go buy one of those tasers and zap his ignorant ass. He is such a pig. I think I need a break from his voice. Can we get away from here?"

Dude tells her they can briefly chill at camp, but he wants to be back in time to watch the wet t-shirt contest. She says, "when we get back to camp, you can pour water on *my* shirt."

"Hey, Santa, we're heading to camp. Be back soon."

# Chapter 15

MOST CAMPSITES REMAIN VACANT. There are only pockets of people spread out in the camping area. One of the people lingering around is the guy with the rusted blue Panhead camping next to Dude. The older man with his long gray beard is sitting on a camping chair when Dude and Trixie pull up and park the Road Glide.

Trixie heads straight for a camping chair and Dude waves hello to the neighbor. Santa has already talked to the guy and told Dude that the man rode in from Tennessee and he wasn't here last year. His antique license plate confirms the guy is from out-of-state.

Dude grabs two cans from the cooler bag and sits down next to Trixie. On her first sip, Trixie spills some of her watermelon hard seltzer down her cleavage. She attempts to wipe it out with her bare hand. He offers her a bottle of water and says, "aren't we supposed to be getting that shirt wet anyway?"

She pours some water on her hand then wipes between her round firm 38 double-Ds again. She asks, "what is the big fascination with guys wanting to see a girl in a wet t-shirt?"

Dude asks, "do you really need me to explain it?"

"Actually, I do."

"If you insist. For the sake of this wet t-shirt contest, here's how it works. The girls are given plain white t-shirts and are asked to wear them without a bra. Water gets poured on the shirt, causing it to form tightly over the chest, exposing the nipples. And if this year is anything like last year, most of the girls take the shirts off and it becomes a full-blown topless showdown. The winner gets cash and prizes."

Trixie is dumfounded. "You can't be serious."

"You asked."

"So, all this commotion is just to see some boobs?"

Dude tells her, "Now you're getting it."

"Sounds like sexist bullshit." Trixie shakes her head.

"It's all in good fun. There's no touching involved."

She looks around and tells Dude that if the neighbor wasn't sitting there, she would pull up her shirt for his eyes only. He tries to coax her into the tent for a private show.

"I just don't understand what the big deal is. They are just boobs." She cups her chest with both hands and bounces the twins up and down. "If we go in that tent right now, I know it won't stop with me just pulling up my shirt. If you can just hold your horses, you can have this whole package tonight." She takes his hand and puts it up her shirt. "Wouldn't you rather touch them, than see them anyway?"

He circles her nipple with his index finger and licks his lips. “Don’t you think it would feel better if I was using my tongue right now?”

“Mmmm, you’re a bad boy. It would, you got me there. Just be patient and you can use your tongue on me later.”

Uncle Tucker’s voice can be heard in the distance. Trixie says, “He is ruining the mood.”

Dude walks over to Angel and digs out a joint. “Let’s take a couple puffs and then head back over.”

Trixie reluctantly agrees and he can tell that she is not enthused. As he sits down with the lit joint, he asks, “are you going to be okay with watching these girls get topless?”

She tells him flat out, “I get jealous easily, so, if I see you staring too hard, I may need to drag you away from there.” Then, in a moment of temporary insanity, (or maybe it’s the weed smoke filling her head) she stands up in front of him, takes a quick look around, and pulls up her shirt and bra, exposing her round breasts and pink nipples in all their glory. “I don’t think you’re going to see a nicer pair than these anyway.”

Dude is shocked in the best possible way. The flash happened fast and didn’t last more than twenty seconds, but he was able to take a mental photo of the twins before the shirt came back down. He files it into his spank bank and thanks her for the show. “They are amazing. You could win if you were to enter the contest.”

“You can’t put a price on dignity.”

“I respect your decision. I like that you are reserved just for me.” Then Dude adds, “And you don’t have to worry about my eyes wandering. You are more than enough for me to look at.”

The chill session comes to an end with Trixie agreeing not to judge the wet t-shirt girls for their loose morals. She puts on her cowgirl hat for the ride back to the stage.

***

Dude is riding slowly and dragging his feet through the crowd to get back to where Santa and Kat are parked. Santa welcomes the couple back to the party by handing Dude the jar of moonshine the minute he swings his leg over the seat. Trixie puts her hand out to grab the jar next. “I need something to get me through this.”

Kat asks her if she is okay. Trixie says she’s fine and tells Kat that she is ready for this part of the day to be over. “I’m ready for the bands to come on.”

All the focus is on the stage now. A group of ten girls huddle together on the side of the stage, waiting for Uncle Tucker to bring them out one-by-one. The females range from tall and skinny to short and chubby. The group is mostly made up of the girl next door types, average looking girls, some hotter than others.

“Oh my gosh, this pig is the one who gets to pour the water?” Trixie can’t believe her eyes when Uncle Pervert raises a big pitcher of water above his head and calls out girl number one.

Girl number one is short and wide. Her tits must weight ten pounds each. When the water pours over her shirt, a pair of CD sized nipples show through the thin white cloth. She rubs her tits and plays with them over the shirt. The crowd cheers then she pulls the wet shirt off and swings it over her head. Her giant balloon tits are flopping around with every swing of the shirt. She leans forward and they almost touch the stage floor. She wobbles across the stage to make room for girl number two.

Next up is the opposite of girl number one. Girl two is tall and skinny. Her A-cups are mostly nipple. The water barely touches the shirt, and she is already taking it off. With a lackluster applause from the crowd, the girl turns around, bends over, and drops her pants. Her white ass causes the crowd to kick it up a notch. Horns are honking, engines are revving, and the waiting contestants just had the bar raised. She pulls up her pants and slides down the stage. Standing next to the first girl, the pair is shaped like the number 10.

"Oh great. Now this is a full body contest." Trixie is standing with her back to the stage in protest. She pulls Dude close and reminds him not to stare. He thinks to himself, *I'm glad she wasn't with me at Topless Larry's.*

Santa's eyes are glued to the stage. Kat couldn't care less. She tells Trixie, "These girls can get him worked up and then I will finish him off." Trixie looks at Kat like she is a lost puppy. She bites her tongue to avoid offending her new friend. Kat keeps quiet about her days of swinging from the pole.

Any guy in their right mind would consider the next girl fuckable. She has long blonde hair and a cute face. If this was an ass-only contest, she would be an instant favorite to win. Her medium sized breasts look great through the wet t-shirt, and she knows it. Unlike the previous contestants, she opts to keep the wet t-shirt on and leave something to the imagination. She gets a loud cheer from the horny crowd. She shakes her ass as she moves down the stage.

A mostly naked man comes walking through the crowd. He's wearing only work boots and a G-string. His pecker is wrapped in an elephant's trunk made of cloth. Ears sit out to the sides as the trunk bounces with each step. Dude points him out to Trixie. "See, there is something for the girls to look at too."

"Oh please. You get me more worked up with your clothes on than he ever could."

Dude tells her she needs to loosen up. "Here, have one of these gummies."

Trixie hesitates, then realizes she is feeling a little up tight. "You're right. I'm sorry for being such a grouch. I do want to relax and have fun. Give it to me."

He hands her a yellow gummy containing 25mg of Delta 8 THC. Then he eats one too. He offers one to Santa and Kat, but they both decline. He tells Trixie to chew it a couple times but leave it sit in her mouth for a minute before swallowing. “It will kick in faster.”

The sound of someone burning the rear tire off their bike drowns out Uncle Tucker’s voice. The burnout receives a loud cheer, then the cloud of rubber smoke blows across the crowd.

The jar of moonshine makes its way around the foursome again. Trixie takes a big gulp, then exhales a breath of fire. Santa puts the jar into the cooler bag and lights up a cigar.

“Give it up for contestant number four.” Uncle Tucker lifts his pitcher of water, and a sexy redhead steps under it. As he pours the water, she teases the crowd by lifting her shirt just enough to expose a dragon tattoo on her stomach. She gets a rise from the crowd and then teases a little more before walking across the stage to stand next to the first three girls.

Girl number five has stripper written all over her. The tall brunet dances her way to the front of the stage wearing high heel shoes and the plain white tee. There is no sign of whether or not she has anything covering her private parts until she peels off the wet shirt. Her tits are obviously store bought. Each of the round cantaloupes has a nipple pointing in a different direction. Her skimpy thong leaves very little to the imagination. She turns her back to the crowd and shakes her ass like she is working the pole. Then she throws the wet shirt into the crowd. Guys in front of the stage toss crumpled up bills at her. She sweeps up the cash and stands next to the other girls in her high heels and black thong. Uncle Tucker encourages the crowd to keep the applause going.

Dude pounds down a beer and reaches for another, then he hands Trixie one of her cans. She seems to be mellowing out as her smile makes its way back to her face. A giggle slips out every few minutes as she converses with Kat.

Santa taps his can against Dudes as the two men enjoy the show. “She is my favorite so far.” Says Santa about girl number five. “Oh, and by the way. I don’t remember paying you for winning the bet. You done good, she’s a gem.” He hands Dude two twenties and a ten.

“Thanks.” Looking up at number five, Dude says, “yeah, she would’ve been George’s favorite too.” He pours beer onto the grass.

“Let’s hear it for sexy number six.” Uncle Tucker motions her to the front of the stage. She struts out wearing a blue and white trucker’s hat, with long brown hair hanging down to her ass. She twirls in a circle, causing the water to splash onto the Emcee as he drizzles the pitcher over her chest. She squeezes her breasts together over the wet shirt and teases the crowd by sticking her tongue out and licking her lips. A quick flash of her boobs leaves the crowd wanting more.

“The louder you cheer, the better the chance you have of seeing your favorite girl win.” Uncle Tucker motions for number seven to make her way forward.

Like a true cougar, number seven crawls on all fours to the center of the stage. The woman in her mid-fifties rises to her feet with the body of a twenty-something. Her hard work at the gym could pay off in cash and prizes today. Her muscular tan body, short blonde hair, and sexy attitude are causing some of the other contestants to get jealous. When the wet t-shirt comes flying off, her fake tits get a roaring cheer from the crowd. They look much more natural than girl number fives. At least these ones have a bounce to them. She sticks her finger in her mouth, then rubs it on her nipple. "Damn, she is sexy!" Uncle Tucker gets close enough to get clawed by this cougar.

Santa pokes Dude in the arm. "That's what I'm talkin' about."

Dude cuts his eye toward Trixie to see that she isn't paying attention anymore. She has mentally checked herself out of what's happening on the stage. Kat Miller is proving to be a welcome distraction.

Contestant number eight could give Trixie a run for her money. Another sexy redhead with one hell of a body slowly wiggles her way to center stage. She twirls around to show off the bottom of her ass cheeks, which are peeking out from her cut-off jean shorts. The wet shirt appears to be painted on her large tits. She peels off the wet shirt to reveal two of the nicest natural breasts on the farm. Her light brown, rock hard nipples could poke someone's eye out. Uncle Tucker may need safety glasses.

Another cloud of burned rubber causes the girls on the stage to cover their faces. Even Uncle Tucker buries his face inside his shirt.

The cloud passes and number nine rushes to center stage. She swings her blonde ponytail in circles, then tilts her head back while pushing up on her chest. As the water pours over her, she rubs herself like she is getting a shower. Boners are popping up across the crowd as Uncle Tucker pours a second pitcher of water over her now bare chest. She turns around and quickly pulls down her pants to flash her bare ass to the horny crowd.

Uncle Tucker announces to the sea of people, "we have some real talent here this year. Let's keep this party going for contestant number ten."

A walking pin-up makes her way to the front of the stage. She has a black bandana wrapped around her short, blonde hair. Her t-shirt has a knot tied at the bottom, exposing her bellybutton. She gets cheers before a drop of water hits her shirt. Her jean shorts are unbuttoned in the front, giving the crowd a peek of her red lace underwear. As the water flows down the front of her body, she pulls out the front of her panties to allow the water to trickle into her crotch. The crowd goes wild. The guys in the front row are tossing money onto the stage. Uncle Tucker is breaking his neck to sneak a peek. He tells her, "Stay right here." Then he asks the rest of the girls to spread out. "Make a line across the stage." He goes on to tell the crowd how the elimination process is going to work.

"I am going to stand behind each girl one-by-one. When I put my hand over her head, y'all cheer. The three girls who get the loudest applause will each win a prize."

He stands behind girl number one and raises his hand. She shakes her big titties to a half-decent applause. She bounces up and down and almost gives herself a black eye while trying to get a few extra cheers.

"Give it up for girl number two." She immediately turns around, drops her pants, and starts twerking her bare ass at the crowd. Horns honk and Uncle Tucker gives her a thumbs up.

The natural beauty known as girl number three teases the crowd by lifting her shirt halfway, then dropping it down. The applause fades fast, and she quickly realizes her strategy to tease but not show has bitten her in the ass.

The applause for girl number four is more for her dragon tattoo than it is for her wet t-shirt. Like the girl before her, she also didn't get the memo about what the crowd likes. Her pretty face is not enough to make up for the lack of a bare chest. A few horns honk but her chances aren't looking good.

Uncle Tucker stands on his tippy toes to get his hand over the head of girl number five. "Y'all are the judges. Let me hear you scream!" Her expensive boob job gets a roar from the crowd as she spins around on her high heels. She rubs her big silicone breasts while she dances in place and reaches for the pole that isn't there. Her natural instinct is to flip upside down, but there's nothing for her to climb on. The revving engines and loud screams from the crowd make her the frontrunner so far.

Still not willing to show the crowd what she is working with under the shirt, girl number six hears some boos from the crowd. She has that sexy down on the farm look, but the crowd wants to see bare breasts.

The cougar representing the older women at the rally gets positive feedback. Engines are revving and horns are honking. One guy in the crowd yells, "marry me." Number seven bounces her fake tits in an attempt to raise the crowd's decibels.

The huge natural breasts dotted with light brown nipples cause girl number eight to receive the loudest applause so far. Her cut off jean shorts leave just enough to the imagination. She lifts her hands over her head and jumps up and down, hypnotizing the onlookers.

Still dripping from round one, girl number nine asks Uncle Tucker for another pitcher of water. She recreates her shower scene to get a rise from the crowd and it works.

Before Uncle Tucker can slide his feet to the left, girl number ten has already dropped her pants around her ankles. Standing there in only a red laced thong, the crowd erupts. She wiggles her ass at the crowd then turns around massaging her husky breasts.

Uncle Tucker turns to the event staff who have been paying close attention to the noise levels. They have a quick pow-wow. Then he returns to the front of the stage. "Please give a big round of applause to all our sexy contestants. Unfortunately, there can be only one first place winner, but we do have cash prizes for second and third place as well."

The line of ladies across the stage are all checking each other out; sizing each other up. Some know they have a chance; others know they don't. Some are still shaking their asses and rubbing their chests as others quietly wait for the verdict.

"In third place, and taking home one-hundred dollars in cash, is girl number five!" She walks to center stage, shakes her tits one more time, then takes the cash and is instructed to wait by the side of the stage for a picture.

Uncle Tucker continues. "Taking home two-hundred and fifty dollars in cash, and the title of second place, is girl number eight!" There are a few boos from the crowd. People are yelling at Uncle Tucker for not giving her first place. She agrees with the crowd as she reluctantly grabs the money.

There is a group of guys in front of the stage holding hands full of cash, just waiting to make it rain on the first-place winner.

Uncle Tucker gets the crowd pumped up for the announcement of first place. He walks up and down the line of remaining ladies. He stops between girls' number nine and ten. The crowd cheers and then he lifts the arm of the woman wearing a red thong and a black bandana. "Give it up for the winner of the Mud Hole Rally wet t-shirt contest, number ten!"

She gives him a big hug, then tosses her bandana into the crowd. Her short blonde hair blows in the wind as she shakes her boobs one more time. She bends over to show her ass, then she turns around and pulls down the front of her red lace underwear to flash the crowd as they go wild.

"This envelope contains everything you've won." Then Uncle Tuckers says, "Let me tell you what's inside. The first thing you will receive is a hundred-dollar credit to the vendor with the sex toys. Next, you can head over to the weapons vendor and pick up your new taser and a box of bullets to protect yourself with. And finally, here is five hundred in cash. Now I am willing to increase the cash prize by another hundred bucks if you will give the bike show winner a lap dance. It's your choice."

Sexy number ten passes on the extra hundred but scoops up all the cash laying on the stage from the guys in the front row.

Uncle Tucker brings the three winners to the center of the stage for a group picture. He announces that his old lady will give the lap dance to the best of show winner. Then he says, "once we get the stage dried off, we will bring up the first band of the day, the Good Old Boys. You don't want to miss this awesome country rock band. Get yourselves something to eat and drink. The band will be on in about an hour."

Santa looks at his pocket watch. "I guess we can roam around till six. What do y'all want to do?"

Trixie is first to speak up. “My friends should be back from the hotel soon. I will call to see where they’re at.”

Dude says he would like to park his bike back at camp before he gets too drunk. “We can walk over with our chairs when the band comes on.” Then he adds, “Tommy should be back by now.”

Some of the crowd begins to disperse. It sounds like thunder as hundreds of motorcycles start their engines at the same time. A golf cart rides by with three topless women inside. The smell of marijuana blows across the field, causing Dude’s nose to perk up. “Let’s get back to camp and light up another fatty.”

# Chapter 16

THE RELAXATION BACK AT camp is brief for Trixie. No sooner did she think about kicking off her boots, she gets a text from Peggy saying her and Emma are parked by their tents. She is preparing to walk over when Dude says, "Go catch up with your friends. I will meet you over there in a little while to break down the tents."

Dude has given plenty of thought to how he is going to handle Trixie's cockblocking friend Emma. It's inevitable they will be hanging out together, so he plans to keep the conversation with her to a minimum. His backup plan is to get her drunk enough to become fun, assuming the stick-in-the-mud will drink the bait. He can't help but to think, *why didn't she bring two Peggy's?*

Once Trixie scampers off to be with her friends, Dude bends Kat's ear for a minute. "What kind of stuff have you two been talking about?"

"You know, girl stuff." Kat Miller is trying to stay true to girl code.

Dude tries reverse psychology. "I don't think she is really into me. I'm pretty sure now that her friends are back, I won't see much of her tonight. I guess I'll be flying solo again. What do you think Kat?"

"You've got her all wrong. Just between us, she is creaming in her undies over you. She was chewing my ear off all day about how great she thinks you are. Don't be an idiot, play nice with her friends and you're golden."

"I appreciate you telling me this. Thanks Kat."

Dude takes a big gulp of Santa's homemade moonshine and washes it down with a cold beer to prepare himself for playing it cool with *the friends*. Knowing he won't feel like dealing with the tents after dark, he makes his way toward Trixie's camp to get this over with.

***

Dude approaches the white Jeep, then stops twenty feet short to take a couple of deep breaths. He psych's himself up, then makes his move.

The three girls are sitting in camping chairs talking when he enters their camp. "Hello ladies. How's your day going?"

Peggy stands up to give him a hug and says, "good to see you again."

Emma remains seated and cracks a half-smile. She says they've had a nice relaxing day so far.

"Good to hear. You should be well rested for the big show tonight. Can I get you girls something to eat or drink?" He asks with a smile.

Peggy says, "no thanks, we've been eating all day, and we loaded the cooler on our way over."

Dude played nice, now he wants to deal with the tents and give the girls some alone time.

"Sounds good. You girls just relax while I take down your tents."

The Jeep is playing country music in the background as the girls chat away. Dude catches bits and pieces of the conversation while dropping tent number one. He's sweating, so he takes a break and stands quietly in the shade of their neighbor's trailer. Peggy is going on about some *Lifetime* movie they watched in the hotel room. It was something about a love story with a girl who returns home for Christmas and hooks up with the new guy in town. The boring story motivates Dude to work on tent number two.

He bends down to unzip the door and Trixie whistles, then she says, "nice ass cowboy." He looks back with a smile but is careful not to say anything that may ruffle the feathers of the flighty friends.

Dude stuffs tent two and its poles into the carrying bag and zips it up. He sits it next to tent one and moves to the final tent still standing. He wonders how anyone can go through life not knowing how to set up a tent. *It's a basic survival skill. Fuckin' yuppies.*

Tent number three is flatter than a pancake in thirty seconds. He pulls the two plastic poles out of their slots and folds them into fifteen one-foot sections. The rubber band running through the middle of them all keeps the pieces connected. The three-section piece above the doorway was first to come out. With the nylon tent laying flat on the ground, Dude folds it in half; then in half again.

Down on his knees, he rolls the folded tent into a cylinder shape, then stuffs it into its bag. The poles go into a narrow bag, similar to the much smaller bag used to hold the small metal stakes which are used to keep the tent from blowing away. The two smaller bags go into the bigger bag with the tent. Then he picks up all three and walks over to the backseat of the Jeep and puts them on the floor.

Dude says to the group, “make sure you lock the doors before you head up to the stage.”

They all simultaneously thank him for taking care of the tents. Trixie offers him a cold drink. “We have three different flavors of hard seltzer. What kind do you want?” She holds up three cans: watermelon, tangerine, and lemon.

“I appreciate the offer, but just a bottle of water will be fine.”

Trixie hands him a wet bottle of water, then asks him to come sit down next to her.

“I am going to give you girls some alone time. I’m walking up to the pizza truck; do you want anything?”

“Food will only ruin my buzz. No thanks.” Says Trixie in a giddy voice. “We will be hanging out here for a while. Stop by on your way back.” She blows him a kiss as he walks away.

Only five steps removed from their camp, he overhears Peggy’s loud voice say to Trixie, “Oh-my-God, you’re blushing. You really like him, don’t you?” Dude is tempted to wait for her response, but if Kat was telling him the truth, he already knows the answer and he doesn't want to risk getting caught spying. He slips away undetected. He envisions the conversation the girls are having, then he stops and tells himself, *just be cool and don't get too crazy tonight and she's yours.*

***

Standing in line for pizza, Dude feels a tap on the shoulder. He turns into a puff of cigar smoke. He sees denim overalls and a beat-up straw hat through the cloud. He hears a raspy voice. "Remember me? We met yesterday up front at the registration table."

As the smoke clears, Dude sees the short woman with curly white hair standing behind the man. "Yes, I remember you two. Buck and, um, I'm sorry, I forget your wife's name."

"Yup, I'm Buck, Buck Jones and this sweetie pie is Gretchen."

"Good to see you guys. How's the rally been treating you two lovebirds so far?"

"We've been enjoying every minute of it all. Where else can you have this much fun without any rules?" Buck winks his left eye, then whispers to Dude, "did you see that wet t-shirt contest?"

Dude reaches out to shake Buck's hand. "I agree. There is nothing like an old school biker party. Fuck the theme parks, I'd rather be right here any day."

"Dude, I have been looking for you."

"What did I do now. Don't tell me you have a daughter named Emma." Dude laughs at himself.

"I don't know anyone named Emma, but that guy Henry you were asking about is right over there." Buck Jones points out a man wearing an orange shirt with a black skull on it. "That's Henry, Henry Schultz."

"You're the man Buck." Dude says thanks and hands him a twenty-dollar bill. "Buy yourself a couple beers on me." Then Dude adds, "give me your phone number because if anything comes of this, I will have some more money with your name on it."

Dude eats his slice of pizza while walking closer to the man Buck says is Henry Schultz.

Henry is wearing a greasy derby hat with ripped jeans and an old pair of work boots. He looks like he just crawled out from under a rock. Or maybe he sleeps in the van Dude has been told about. Either way, Dude has Henry locked into his sights. He hangs back and keeps a close eye on Henry's every move. He stares so hard that he could burn a hole in Henry's shirt, the way you can light a piece of paper on fire by holding a magnifying glass under the sun.

The Good Old Boys are rocking the stage, and the crowd is swaying and bobbing to the music. Henry is standing off to the right about halfway between the stage and the food vendors. He is flanked by a woman in her late fifties wearing a leather vest covered with patches. For the past thirty minutes Dude has been watching them, Henry has been stationary and focused on the band.

The Good Old Boys play their last song and people begin moving around. Uncle Tucker announces there will be a thirty-minute break before the next band comes on. Henry and his old lady make a move towards the porta-potties and Dude follows suit, keeping a safe distance behind them.

All alone, Dude slithers along the vendor tents with his eyes glued to the dirty man with the handlebar mustache. He feels like an actual spy. He pulls out his phone and looks at a picture of George sitting on the Panhead. He keeps asking himself, *what would George do?* And based on the way George was talking and acting while the two of them were in pursuit of the missing bike together; there is a good chance bad things will happen to the thief.

Figuring he has enough cash in his pocket for bail money, Dude follows Henry and his old lady into the camping area. He is alone and unsure of how he wants to approach the situation from here. *Should I go get some extra muscle and risk losing track of Henry?* His mind is racing.

He was so focused on Dirty Henry that his tunnel vision caused him to gain a follower of his own.

"Hey. You don't know how to say hi?"

Dude turns around to see Trixie power walking up behind him.

"You just walked right past me."

"Sorry I didn't see you. I am in the middle of following that guy with the orange shirt." He points at Henry. "It was his house that we went to earlier.

You know, the place with all the rusty stuff in the yard."

Trixie takes a sip from a can wrapped in a foam koozie. "Can I come with you?"

"I don't want you to get involved. Just give me a couple minutes. I can't lose him. I will stop back when I'm done." He gives her a quick peck on the lips while keeping his eyes fixed on Henry.

A concerned Trixie stares at Dude's back as he walks away. She waits until he is a few car lengths down and then slowly moves her feet in his direction.

Henry's bright orange shirt stands out like a sore thumb, making him easy to see, so Dude keeps his distance. Henry stops to talk with a guy who is sitting on the tailgate of a truck, drinking from a bottle of whiskey. Dude ducks in behind a large RV and watches Henry through the window. Trixie comes up from behind Dude and startles him.

"Shit. I didn't realize you were behind me. Don't let them see you."

Dude pleads with her to go back to camp and not get involved. He warns her. "I don't want you to see this."

"See what? What are you planning to do?" Fright comes over her face.

"I have spent the past year looking for this asshole. There is a lot of pent-up rage. Sorry."

Henry and the woman leave the man sitting on his tailgate and continue walking towards the back of the camping area. Dude goes behind the RV and weaves through people's camps in stealth mode, keeping his eyes locked on Henry. Telling Dude, she won't let him go alone, Trixie latches on to the back of his shirt with her free hand.

Henry and the older woman in the leather vest slowly approach a camp site with one tent set up next to a black van. The woman sits down in a chair and the man identified as Henry Schultz walks up to the van and opens the driver's side door. Dude is now close enough to see that the van has been spray painted with black primer. Henry stands outside the van with the door wide open. He grabs a pack of cigarettes off the dashboard and lights one up. Dude sees the bright white door jams. "Lazy fuckers always forget to paint the jams." Alarms start going off in Dude's head. He tells Trixie, "This is the van. I can feel it." I'm going over there. She tries to talk him out of it, but his mind has already been made up.

***

"Hey Henry."

The man turns around. "Hey man. What's up."

Trixie stays ten feet behind Dude as he walks into the man's camping space.

"I stopped by your house earlier, but you weren't home."

"Do I know you?"

"You do now. My name's Dude. Do you recognize this bike?" He unfolds the missing motorcycle flyer he pulled from his back pocket and holds it up.

Dude watched Henry's face drop as he scanned the flyer.

"No, I've never seen it before." Henry glances over at his old lady.

"How long ago did you paint your van black?"

"I don't know. What the hell does that have anything to do with anything?"

Dude is trying to maintain his strategy of talking the truth out of this guy first. The lady in the vest gets out of her chair and walks toward the front of the van. Dude turns to Trixie. "Keep an eye on her. Let me know if she reaches for a weapon." Trixie looks shocked, but drifts to her right to see what the woman is doing.

"I am going to shoot straight with you Henry, and I need you to be honest with me in return. When I was at your place today, I could tell this shiny bike is not your style. I don't think you stole it, but I've had several people identify this van as being the one that was creeping around this campground at last year's rally. Now, I'm going to give you one chance to tell me the truth. Tell me your side of the story."

Henry can't look Dude in the eye. He keeps looking towards the woman like she's going to do something. Dude asks her to sit back down in the chair. Henry tells her it's okay. He says, "just sit down honey, you're making everyone nervous."

Then Henry tries to lie and say he didn't have this van last year. Dude laughs in his face.

"Do you think I'm stupid? I have been turning over rocks in this town for the past year and every other time I flip one over; your name is underneath. I have a list of people who have given me your name and told me about this van. I have witnesses Henry. I can call the police right now if that's what you want me to do."

"No, please. No cops."

"Talk Henry."

"I didn't steal your bike."

"Make up your fuckin' mind Henry. If you lie to me, I'm going to crush your fuckin' peanut head."

Dude's face is turning red, and his fingers curl into fists.

"Spit it the fuck out! What do you know about this bike?" Dude shoves the flyer into Henry's face. "If you didn't take it, who did?"

"I don't know, I swear."

"Think long and hard before you answer, because if you lie to me, I will have no mercy on your sorry ass. Give me a fuckin' name!"

"I can't remember. I swear."

Dude grabs a handful of Henry's shirt and pushes it up under his chin. He slams Henry into the side of the van. "I know about the twin brothers."

From the smell of things, Henry either farted or shit his pants.

A squirming Henry says, "who told you about the twins?"

"See, you know something Henry. What are their names?"

"Look man, those guys will kill me. Literally!"

"If you don't tell me their names, I will kill you first. Or better yet, you can take the rap for the stolen bike."

"Okay, please, let me down and I will talk."

Dude lowers Henry down onto his flat feet and releases the handful of orange shirt. The woman in the vest sits on the edge of her chair, rocking back and forth. Trixie stands at the rear of the van looking like she is prepared to take off running at the drop of a hat.

"If I tell you what you want to know, will you promise not to hurt me or turn me into the police?" Asks a pleading Henry.

Dude said he wouldn't lie to Trixie, but Henry, who gives a shit. He says, "Sure."

Henry starts by saying he doesn't know the brothers well. He just knows them from around town. Then Dude says, "but you know them, right?"

"I really need you to promise me you won't tell them I told you this."

"I promise Henry, but you haven't told me anything I don't know yet. So get to it."

The talking in circles is getting on Dude's nerves. He attempts to get Henry to relax. "Grab a beer Henry, you need to chill out. Look at you, you're shaking."

Henry walks over to the cooler and grabs a beer, then he offers Dude one. The two men crack the beers and Henry asks, "do you mind if I sit down?"

Trixie watches with amazement as Dude gives Henry permission to sit.

"They paid me to help. I swear it wasn't my idea."

"Now we're getting somewhere. Explain to me exactly how it happened." Dude circles Henry's chair as he talks.

"They approached me at the bike show and asked if I wanted to make five-hundred dollars. I didn't know what they wanted me to do for the money; they wouldn't tell me. All they said was they wanted to use my van, and they wanted me to drive it somewhere local or they were going to kick my ass."

Dude leans in. "You agreed to the deal without knowing what it was about?"

"I mean, I needed the money. Plus, I was drunk as a skunk by the time they found me later in the night. I didn't even realize what was going on. It all happened so fast."

"Exactly what happened Henry?"

"The two brothers, they grabbed me from up by the stage and drug me back to my camp. They were threatening to hurt me if I said no. They made me get in the van and drive around the campground. They got in the back of the van and then Jasper said he would tell me when to stop. I just did what he told me to do."

"Jasper. That's one name. How about the other?" Now Dude is the one shaking. His blood is boiling, and it's taking every bit of willpower he can muster not to pummel this birdbrain into the ground.

"I just know him as Catfish. They are the Rockwell brothers."

"It's about time you gave me names. What happened next?"

He mumbles, "they told me to stop, then they opened the side doors and jumped out. It was dark, so I didn't realize what they were doing at first. By the time I heard the big thump and felt the van shake, it was too late. The bike was already in the van."

"Motherfucker! You dumb son of a bitch."

Henry raises his arms to cover his face. He fears Dude is going to pound on him. Trixie is in the background half-covering her eyes. She has the same feeling as Henry.

Dude tells him, "I hope you understand that just based on what you've said so far, you can go to jail. You were an accomplice in a crime, and you were driving drunk."

"I know I fucked up. Please forgive me. I feel horrible."

"Here is the million-dollar question Henry. Where did you take the bike?"

Henry pleads with Dude to not make him snitch on the two brothers that he appears to be terrified of.

Dude says, "we have passed the point of no return. Tell me."

"If you go to the police, can you please leave my name out of this mess?"

"Yes Henry, mums the word."

"Behind their shop, there is a garage in the woods. That's where we went to unload the motorcycle. There, I told you everything I know. Are you happy now?"

"Not quite. Are you talking about the welding shop they work at?"

"Who told you about the welding shop?"

"I'm the one asking the questions asshole. Now which fuckin' shop is it?"

"Come on man, you don't have to be so mean." Henry mumbles. "You're not too far off. It is a welding shop, but they don't work there: they own it."

"Where is it located?"

"I don't know the address, but I know it's on Apex Parkway. There is no sign on the building, I don't know what they call the shop. The garage can't be seen from the road."

Dude recognizes the street name from his internet search. He believes Henry is telling the truth, so he lays off on the questioning. "You've been helpful. Thank you. I'm going to check these guys out. If you're lying to me, I will show up at your house."

Henry leans back in his chair and breathes a sigh of relief. His old lady walks over to give him a hug. As Dude is walking away, he hears the woman tell Henry, "You did the right thing."

Trixie takes Dude by the hand and says, "holy crap, what a rush! I don't know where to begin. You did it. You figured it out. I mean, that was freaking sexy as hell. I want to rip your clothes off right here, right now. Take me to your tent."

He tells her, "Tomorrow will be a busy day. I have to go snooping around again in the morning, but tonight, we are going to party!"

Back at Dude's camp, nobody is around. The sun is going down behind the mountains and Trixie is going down with it. She tells Dude to get in the tent. He unzips the door, and she pushes him in. She climbs in after him and zips the door shut. She tells him to lie down, then she says, "This should hold you over until later. No touching, just relax."

Trixie starts by kissing his stomach, then works her way down south. He puts his hand on the top of her head, violating her no touching request. She doesn't stop. She keeps bobbing up and down on his johnson like she's trying to win a prize, and it works. She unclogs Dude to win first place in the pipe cleaning competition. The eruption can be felt in the next county over. She wipes her mouth as she collapses onto his chest, gasping for air.

# Chapter 17

FLOOD LIGHTS ILLUMINATE THE main grounds for Saturday nights biggest bands. Rays of light break through the cloud of smoke hovering above the heads of the rallygoers. The vendor tents lining the sides of the event area are packed like sardines. People are hustling and bustling in every direction. The smell of gasoline, exhaust, and burnt rubber dominate the atmosphere from the line of motorcycles coming in and out of the burnout pit. Golf carts and motorcycles are parked facing the stage as if it were the 1970s and this was a drive-in movie theater.

The band, Squirrel Nuts, is kicking ass on the stage. Their mixture of southern rock and new school country make them a fan favorite. The lead singer is wearing denim jeans with a big round belt buckle, cowboy boots, no shirt, and a black ten-gallon cowboy hat. The man playing guitar has long black hair and a matching beard. He's wearing a ZZ Top t-shirt, jeans, and black boots. The drummer is dripping with sweat. Every time he bangs his head, you can see the sweat drops glisten as they fly through the stage lights. He throws a drumstick into the crowd at the end of a song, hitting an oblivious woman in the head, then it gets picked up by the man behind her.

Dude, with Santa, Kat, and Tommy, has lined up their camping chairs together with Trixie and her friends, creating a home-base for tonight's show. Set up in the center of the field, fifty feet from the stage, the group has easy access to food, beer, and the portable toilets.

Trixie is hanging from Dude's arm to keep herself from wobbling. Her white cowgirl hat is tilted sideways, and her low-cut red and white plaid shirt tied in a knot at the bottom is pushing her big tits out of the top. Her cut off jean shorts are exposing the bottom of her ass cheeks, causing the guy standing behind her to get slapped by his old lady for staring. Dude heard what happened behind them and he says to Trixie, "you just got that guy behind us slapped."

"No, I didn't. He deserved it. Another perverted man!"

He says, "stand in front of me."

The three girls came prepared to wear matching outfits for the Carolina Country show. Peggy is also wearing a cowgirl hat except hers is black and her plaid shirt is black and white. Her short shorts also provide plenty for the guys to look at, and Tommy wastes no time reminding her he's still interested. Tommy came back to the farm dressed to kill, wearing a cowboy hat and boots with a button-down flannel shirt.

Emma's outfit is just as cute. Her boobs are pushing out of her blue and white plaid top. Nobody's noticed her ass because she has been sitting on it since the moment the group set up their chairs. From behind, it just looks like a brown cowboy hat is occupying the chair.

Dude is still in his same jeans and boots, but he changed into a gray Mountainfest Motorcycle Rally t-shirt from 2012. He loves the annual rally in wild and wonderful West Virginia. His black H-D ball cap is on backwards facing the food vendors while he watches the band on stage.

A man standing next to the group taps Dude on the shoulder and offers him a puff of a joint. Dude gladly accepts, and the two men introduce themselves. Dude offers the joint to Trixie, but she says, "no thanks." The high-octane Dude juice she swallowed in the tent is still affecting her equilibrium.

"You guys need to walk over there. It's fucked up what somebody did to that man." Says Santa as he and Kat come back from the porta-shitters laughing. They just saw a man passed out in the grass who has a dick drawn on his chest with black marker.

Santa is only wearing denim overalls and a beat-up straw hat. Kat Miller is dressed like your typical biker's old lady. She is wearing a tight black tank top from Daytona Bike Week '98. Draped over her riding boots is her tight jeans. She has a fanny pack clipped to her belt loops, giving her the ability to ditch the purse most chicks have slung over their shoulders. She's wearing a black bandana on her head with a braided ponytail hanging down the middle of her back.

Apparently, Birdie had been feeling sick since she and Chuck ate at a bar in Boone while they were out cruising the back roads. They showed up at camp just after the sun set and she puked, so she crawled into the tent and is currently sleeping while Chuck sits guard.

A guy who looks like Indiana Jones cuts through the crowd on a Vulcan Voyager. He's riding 5mph while dragging his feet, honking his horn, revving his engine, and smoking a cigar. His saddlebag knocks over an empty chair.

Dude sees a woman holding a baby walk right in front of him.

Kat asks, "Did you just see that?"

"Was that really a baby?" Trixie thinks she is hallucinating.

Santa slurs, "when they said no rules; they meant it."

The band sounds great. Everyone is dancing and having a good time. The chairs have become mere placeholders. Nobody in the group is sitting down. The four girls are now dancing together while Dude fills Santa and Tommy in on what happened with Henry.

"Henry was the driver. These twins used him and his van to get the Panhead off the farm." Dude goes on. "I know where they took the bike. It's a garage behind a welding shop on Apex Parkway. Henry says there's no sign on the building, but the internet has it listed as, Rock Welding." He takes a breath. "Get this, Henry says they are the Rockwell brothers, Jasper and Catfish. I'm going to ride by tomorrow while they're closed to snoop around."

"That's great news. I've never heard of them, but let me know if you need any help." Says Santa.

Tommy also hasn't heard of the brothers. He congratulates Dude on doing a good job locating these guys and offers his support as well. Dude isn't sure what he'll find in this garage, but he welcomes all the help he can get.

"Thanks. I'm heading over there first thing in the morning. I'll let you guys know."

Trixie, as she has been all day, is eavesdropping on Dude's conversation. She can't contain her curiosity about this mysterious man she feels so connected to. She wishes she could read his mind. She can't, so she does the next best thing.

"I heard some of what you said to them. What are you planning to do tomorrow?" Trixie is getting concerned about him disappearing in the morning.

"I have to go to this welding shop to look around."

"What if you find something? What if these brothers catch you? I don't want anything to happen to you. Can you please take someone with you, like the police?"

Dude hasn't been able to picture himself walking into a police station, but if that is what justice for

George looks like, he may consider it.

"I appreciate your concern, but don't worry, I'll be careful. If I find something worth going to the police about, then I will consider it."

Trixie seems to be sobering up at the thought of Dude trying to take on this whole thing by himself. "I won't let you go alone. Take me with you."

He tells her. "Please, you have already seen too much. Besides, I could be tied up with this all day tomorrow. Plus, I have to wait around until three to meet Martin for the horn. It's going to be a long day; I doubt your friends will want to wait around."

She takes a minute to process his argument. "What if I let them take the Jeep? Would you ride me home?"

Dude is taken aback. "Seriously?"

She says, "I'm dead serious. I want to spend every possible minute with you while I still can. Who knows if you're ever going to call me again once you get home? With my luck, you will change your number and forget about me. You're not getting rid of me that easy."

Shit just got serious. It's time to put up or shut up for Dude. She just laid down the gauntlet.

"I may have to stay until Monday."

"I can't let you deal with this alone." Trixie means business.

"No offense, but if you say you're with me to the end, you can't hassle me about needing to be home by a specific time. I'm staying as long as it takes to put this whole ordeal to bed, so I never have to come back here again once I leave." Her bluff, if it was one, has just been called.

"I understand. I will call out of work, and I promise I won't slow you down."

As she waits for his answer, Trixie gets paranoid. She thinks Dude's having second thoughts about them being together, and she fears he is looking for an excuse to leave first thing in the morning. His silence is causing her concern.

*This was definitely not part of the plan.* Dude quickly tries to rationalize the pros and cons of keeping Trixie with him. Taking her home is going to add an extra three hours to his trip. Plus, he is starting to realize that this fine piece of ass could easily become a stalker if it doesn't work out between them. His long hesitation to give Trixie a definitive answer causes her to get upset. Emma's words, *he is just using you,* are running through her mind.

"I give you oral and now you're done with me?" Her mind is racing like a dragster.

"No, no, seriously, I want you with me. If you're sure about this, I would love for you to stay with me. I will ride you home, whatever you want."

Trixie breathes a sigh of relief and gives him a hug and whispers in his ear. "Please, don't scare me like that again. I felt my heart sink."

By now, they have gained an audience. Emma is chomping at the bit to put in her two cents.

"Did I hear you correctly? You're planning to let us take your Jeep and you're going to stay here with him? Seriously?" Emma is furious. She has painted a clear picture of Trixie's words.

Now Trixie is the one with her feet to the fire. What comes out of her mouth next could lead to more problems in the friends department. Her emotions are running high and any decision she makes could cause regret in the sober morning.

"I'm sorry Emma, I know you don't understand. It's what I want to do. Are you okay with taking the Jeep home without me?" Now Trixie is concerned Emma could say no. She thinks, *then what would I do?*

Peggy stands back as her friend's voices get heated. Emma is lecturing Trixie about her questionable choices. She is being stuck up and judgy. "If I am going to drive your Jeep home without you, I don't want to wait till the morning to do it. I've only had a couple drinks; I want to leave tonight after the band."

Peggy looks like a deer in headlights. She is disappointed, but not enough to interject herself into the argument.

Trixie looks at Dude before responding. She asks him, "are you sure about this?"

He reaffirms his commitment to safely getting Trixie home in one piece.

Apparently, her hormones are calling the shots. "Fine. You two can leave tonight. I'm sorry this weekend didn't go as planned. Can we at least have some fun together before you go? Carolina Country is coming on soon. Please?" Trixie just went all in on Dude's adventure.

The three girls hug each other, and a few tears are being shed by each of them. They talk amongst themselves as Dude stands in amazement at the sudden turn of events. Reality just slapped him across the face. He can't imagine any reason for needing to leave her on the side of the road, so it looks like Trixie is now a permanent resident of Dude's passenger seat.

***

Carolina Country has taken the stage and for the moment, everyone seems to be having a good time. The four girls are dancing like nobody's watching; but of course, there are a bunch of people staring. The guy who was slapped by his girlfriend earlier just got round two. Groups of guys on each side stare like they have never seen hot chicks dance before. Although, the type of grinding on each other the girls are doing is something guys usually need to pay for; so, the staring is understandable.

Between songs, Trixie takes a break from shaking her ass to tell Dude about her recent realization. She pulls him close, gives him a kiss, and then gets close to his ear. "Guess what?"

He thinks, *oh boy, what now?* But he simply says, "what?"

She can barely contain herself from the excitement. "I already paid for the hotel room for tonight. If they're leaving, we can sleep there. Well, um, not just sleep." She winks at him.

"I thought you were excited about having tent sex?"

She says, "the ground hurt my knees earlier. Plus, we will have much more room in a bed if you know what I mean."

There are some motorcycle rallies where staying in a hotel is the thing to do, but not this one. Although exceptions can always be made. With the Mud Hole rally, Sunday is mostly a packing up day, and with Saturday night working its way toward being over, Dude gives her request some serious consideration. He daydreams about getting a shower at the hotel, then he imagines Trixie in the shower with him and the decision was made.

"Sounds good to me. I will have to stop drinking soon if you expect me to ride tonight. Unless you want to call a taxi or something?"

Trixie jumps for joy and tells him, "We can get a ride back with them since they still have to get their stuff, or we can worry about the details after the band is done. It's up to you. I promise, you won't regret it. Thank you." Then she grabs his crotch.

Leaving so suddenly would feel unnatural to Dude. "I'd like to party in the camping area before going anywhere." Trixie acknowledges his request, then runs back to her friends.

Santa and Kat have been quietly observing this clusterfuck of conversation while jamming to the band. Now that Trixie is dancing with the girls again, Santa pulls Dude aside.

"Are you sure you know what you're doing with this girl? And with chasing these thieves?" Santa doesn't usually care enough to stick his nose in someone else's business, but he can't sit back and watch his friend potentially crash and burn without saying something.

"I appreciate your concern, I really do, but I got this. I trust her, and I mean, come on, look at her. I can't walk away not knowing what could have been. And as for the Panhead, this welding shop is the end of the line. If nothing comes of it, I'm leaving here tomorrow with her and the horn, end of story."

Dude digs a beer out of the cooler bag and stands quietly as Santa gives his blessing. He tells Dude, "You are one determined son-of-a-bitch. Like a dog with a bone. I hope you nail these pieces of shit. And boy, I saw the fire in your eyes from the day you met that little redhead. I hope you two can make it last. Good luck brother." The two men embrace each other with a hug and pats on the back followed by a hearty, *cheers*, and the clinking of cans. Santa reaches for the jar of moonshine and Dude pulls out a joint.

Now that everyone is on the same page, the party rages on. Trixie and her friends are now line dancing with the group of women in front of them. Two of the three cougars are visibly intoxicated; they are holding each other up while moving with the music. This is the moment Trixie originally came for. She is enjoying the music with her friends, dancing and having fun. Dude just hangs back, feeling lucky while he watches her in action.

The band announces they only have a few songs left. The girls are shaking their booties like they're on spring break. Carolina Country starts playing Trixie's favorite song, and she grabs Dude by the hand to dance with her. She drags him into the group of dancing women. Trixie has to fend off the drunken cougars from trying to claw at Dude. She pulls him close and turns him away from the other girls. They are facing each other as Trixie slides up and down the front of his body. She pulls his head down to shout in his ear. "Thank you for an amazing weekend."

He squeezes her ass cheeks and says, "It's been my pleasure."

As the song fades out, Trixie drifts back to her friends for the last song of the night. The group of ladies lets out a collective cheer when the first guitar cord is struck. The girls scream and whistle at the band. Their jumping and shaking are causing the surrounding guys to be glued to the group waiting for a tittie to pop out.

The lead singer drops the mic to signify the end of their set. The house music kicks on as the crowd begins to disperse. Roaring engines drown out the music. Clapping, cheering, and horn honking continue long after the band exits the stage. A good time was had by everyone in the group. Trixie and her friends are all smiling and laughing. Santa and

Kat are holding hands with their chairs folded up, just waiting for the slow pokes.

Peggy has been giving Tommy the cold shoulder all night, and when he asks for her phone number, she shoots him down. Emma had gotten into her head at the hotel. Score another cockblocking point for Emma. Tommy is acting like he doesn't care, but everyone knows he's disappointed, rightfully so.

On the walk back to the camping area, Trixie and Emma hash out the details of how Trixie will retrieve the Jeep when she gets home. The girls and Dude stop at Trixie's camp so she can get what she needs from the Jeep before her friends take off with it. She gets a small duffle bag, her phone charger, her house keys, a hotel room key and some hard seltzers from their cooler. The three girls share an emotional goodbye.

"It was a pleasure meeting you ladies." Dude flashes one last smile at the friends.

They wave at him from inside the Jeep. Emma puts it into gear and after one more hug through the driver's window, Trixie watches her white Jeep drive off into the darkness of the camping area.

Campfires light a path from Trixie's camp to Dude's. People are sitting around their fires, drinking, smoking, laughing, and listening to music. Wandering into strange people's campsites when he's by himself is one of Dude's favorite pastimes. He's made a lot of good friends over the years by stumbling into random camps the way he is stumbling into his own right now.

"Shhh, Birdie is still feeling really sick. We have to keep the noise down." Kat warns Dude and Trixie as they approach the unlit fire pit.

"Santa, are you going to get the fire started?" Dude wants to keep the party going.

"Chuck asked us to please keep the noise down and if I get the fire going, you know we won't be able to stay quiet. My ass is dragging anyway, not sure how much longer I can keep my eyes open." Santa is slurring and wobbling.

Tommy is sitting quietly in a chair when he hears Dude say something to Trixie about going to the hotel. "Dude, you're not planning to ride there, are you?"

"Not sure yet Tommy, but if everyone is going to sleep anyway… I wanted to keep the party going but now I'm thinking about heading over early."

They all sit down and start talking. Everyone except Tommy quietly has a couple of drinks.

Tommy's hopes of hooking up with Peggy took all the wind out of his sails. He stopped drinking hours ago. He tells Dude, "I may just go home. I can drop y'all off at the hotel on my way."

Dude looks at Trixie and she is rapidly nodding her head up and down. He tells her, "I can leave the tent and motorcycle here and we can take a taxi back in the morning. Sound good?" She is all for it. She latches herself to his arm.

Tommy says he's leaving his tent until the morning as well. Dude grabs what's left of the case of beer, then gets what he needs from his saddlebags before locking the motorcycle up tight. Kat tells Trixie she wants details in the morning. Dude and Santa hug it out one last time before the couple loads themselves into Tommy's truck.

The hotel is only ten minutes down the road, but the darkness makes the ride seem longer. Tommy lets them out in front of the Red Rooster Inn lobby. "See you guys in the morning, text me before you call a cab."

"Thanks Tommy. Thanks for everything this weekend. I really appreciate you brother."

Trixie says thank you as she dances in place with excitement.

"I want to take a couple puffs before we go inside."

"Here? Let's go over there. Make it quick, I want you upstairs." Trixie points to the back of the hotel parking lot.

# Chapter 18

THEY EXIT THE ELEVATOR and turn left. Walking down the hallway toward room 218, it feels just like any other low budget place used to simply rest your head and fuck. A musty smell is to be expected when you pay less than a hundred bucks a night. The building looks clean, for the most part.

Entering the recently vacated hotel room, the couple must have just missed the friends by a few minutes. All the lights are on, the TV is tuned to the *Lifetime* channel, and the room feels like an icebox from the thermostat being set to sixty degrees. Two queen beds are separated by a small table topped with a lamp, phone, and an alarm clock radio. To the left, through the open bathroom door, used towels are piled in the corner. Mini shampoo bottles are tipped over in the sink, and used tissues covered with makeup are sitting next to a bar of soap.

A trail of potato chip bags and candy wrappers lead to a table with empty soda bottles and a sandwich wrapper. Maps of the local area sit untouched. Both sets of sheets are disheveled. Dude suggests making the bed. Trixie says, "don't bother, we're going to mess them up again anyway."

Trixie turns off the TV and turns up the volume on the clock radio, then pops open one of her fruity cans of alcohol. Not wanting to let her drink alone, Dude opens a beer and sits on the end of the bed closest to the only window in the room.

"Your friends should have left a tip for the maid. What a mess."

"What do you expect, they ran out of here like their hair was on fire." Trixie half-heartedly defends her messy friends. "I will straighten up before we leave."

He says, "I can't wait to get a shower." Then Dude asks, "can I tell you a secret?"

Trixie is all ears. "Of course. You can tell me anything."

"When you were here this morning, and I was talking to you on the phone, you said you were getting into the shower. And, um, if I wasn't standing outside of a bar, I would have stuffed my hand straight down my pants. I have thought about taking a shower with you at least three times today."

She blushes. "That's good. I like knowing you were thinking about me. I think we can make your little fantasy come true. Let's work up a sweat first."

Trixie takes her bag into the bathroom and shuts the door. Dude takes off his boots, which almost causes a premature orgasm. He tosses them in the corner of the room, hoping they don't stink too bad. He sits his hat on the table then lays back on the bed with his heals resting on the dingy carpet.

He hears the bathroom door open while he stares at the ceiling. He turns his head for a sideways view of Trixie in a white lace bra and a matching thong. Before he can even lift himself off the bed, she is sitting on top of him. She grinds on his crotch as she leans forward to stick her tongue down his throat. Dude puts his hands on her bare ass cheeks while trying not to choke on her fruit flavored saliva.

She asks where the condoms are. Then she tells him to take off his pants while she grabs the box. She says, "I'm sorry, but we have to use these, for now. I haven't been on the pill because it's been over six months since I've had sex. We surely don't want a baby Biker Dude slowing us down, do we?" She empties the box of rubbers onto the bed.

He's at her mercy, and he knows it. "No argument here." He lays there thinking, *holy shit, six months.*

As she climbs on top of his naked body, she says, "Good, because I can't wait to feel you inside me."

If she grinds any harder, he may finish before they even get started. She tilts her head back to finish her drink, and from his angle, her boobs look enormous.

He slides his hand under her crotch and begins rubbing on top of her underwear. She squirms and slides up onto his stomach, then she reaches behind her, grabbing a handful of nuts. Using her legs to push her body off the bed, Trixie creates enough space for Dude to slide his fingers into her panties. The tip of his index finger makes small circles just below the landing strip of hair leading to the promised land.

"Slow." She tells him. "Nice and easy, we have all night."

He rolls Trixie onto her back and starts kissing her stomach. He looks up at her and says, "this is payback for the special treat you gave me in the tent." He licks her bellybutton, then makes his way down the landing strip. The moment his tongue touches her button, she grabs two hands full of his hair and turns this into a pie-eating contest. Her back is arched like a gymnast. She is squirming in every direction, and his face goes where she goes. If he was wearing a toupee, she would have ripped it off by now. She is crawling up the bed and dragging him with her. Trixie's head is cramped up against the headboard, but she won't let him stop. He alternates between using his tongue and his fingers. She is gasping for air as his slobber covers both of her thighs and everything in between. "Don't stop! I'm almost there!" She is pulling him in so tight that he may pass out from lack of oxygen if she doesn't erupt soon.

Just as he feels his jaw starting to lock up, a wave of fluid rushes out of Trixie like someone turned on a fire hydrant. She is screaming for the good lord, but Dude can't hear her because his head is being crushed by a pair of soaking wet thighs. Her legs have become a boa constrictor and Dude is now the rabbit. He's trying to tap out but, in her ecstasy, she doesn't notice. He falls limp to avoid having his neck snapped. She finally rolls her body to the side and loosens her grip.

Sometime while he was fighting for his life, she removed her bra. Dude claws his way up to her chest and puts his hand on one of her pillows, and then his head on the other. His tongue touches her nipple, and she gets goosebumps all over her body. She looks him in the eyes as he pants on her chest. She tries to talk, then stops. She takes a deep breath, then tries again. “Oh, oh, oh, my God, you are driving me crazy. You have no idea how bad I needed that.” She strokes his beard as they both lay naked in a puddle of sweat and love juice. Her legs are shaking uncontrollably, and she continues to twitch every thirty seconds.

Their breathing returns to normal, and Trixie grabs the bottle of water from the nightstand without sitting up. She pours water into her mouth, then his. They may as well be laying in a small swimming pool. She looks down her nose at him and says, “lucky for us, we have an extra bed.”

Dude says he is ready for a shower, and she tells him not to waste the water. She says, “I’m not done with you yet.” Then she rolls herself on top of him and reaches for a condom.

She lowers herself down onto him slowly. His ass cheeks are puckered together as her warm insides almost cause him to explode when she passes the tip. Trixie is using her firm thighs to raise and lower herself in a slow and methodical fashion. Her eyes are closed, and her hands push down on his chest.

Dude stares up at her beautiful face and watches her chew on her bottom lip while she groans and gradually goes deeper. He massages her breasts, then pulls her forward so his mouth can reach her perfect breasts. He sucks on her hard nipples and her moaning gets louder.

Dude rolls her over and gets Trixie on all fours. From behind her, he reaches forward and grabs both of her braided ponytails. He goes deep and pulls back on her hair; she tells him not to stop. He releases one of the braids so he can use his hand to slap her ass cheek every time he pushes in. She says, “Oh yeah, don’t stop.” Then she pushes back against him causing a rhythm so sweet you can hear a squishing symphony. His grunting gets louder, and so does hers. They are dripping with sweat and focusing solely on finishing together. He lays his chest on her back and talks dirty into her ear. The slapping of flesh has now become a slow grind as they moan together in harmony. She reaches behind her back and pulls his ass tight against her as they simultaneously let out a battle cry that was sure to wake the neighbors.

They fall flat on the bed. Dude lies on her back, but off to the side to avoid crushing her skinny frame. They are stuck together with sweat and have no interest in peeling each other apart. Trixie lies on her stomach with her arms above her head. Dude rubs her back as he stares at her ass. If he could catch his breath, he would be down there licking her crack.

Trixie turns onto her back and lays there staring at the ceiling alongside him. She turns her head to look at Dude and tells him, “You just rocked my world. I always knew you were a keeper.”

“You’re not the only one on cloud nine. Damn girl, I can get used to this.”

She laughs. “If we lived together, I don’t think we would ever leave the house.”

“I think you may be right. I’m willing to find out.”

Trixie twirls his hair around her finger and says, “I think you just earned yourself a festival ticket Mister.” Then she leans in and begins kissing him. When she stops, she says, “I’m ready for that shower now.”

Her stamina impresses Dude. He sits up on the edge of the bed and takes a sip of his beer.

Trixie stands up, giving Dude his first look at her completely naked body from head to toe. She makes her way toward the bathroom, then looks back and says, “give me a minute to pee and then meet me in the shower.”

Dude hears the toilet flush, then the shower turns on. He gives her a few minutes alone before he grabs the rubbers and knocks on the door.

“Come in and shut the door behind you.”

Dude enters the small bathroom; he can only see Trixie’s silhouette through the steamy glass. She has the water set to boil. He slides the glass door to the side to reveal she took out her braids and her ginger hair is lathered with shampoo. He steps under the raining water, and she rubs her soapy hands across his chest. He steps behind her and begins rubbing soap on himself. She rubs a washcloth on his back, then uses it to lather her body with suds. They both rinse off the soap and begin groping each other.

"Now that we're clean, do you want to get dirty again?" She grabs him by the trunk.

He turns her around and drops to his knees. He runs his tongue between her ass cheeks, and she flattens herself against the glass. She claws at the steamy window, then grabs the top of the frame to keep her balance. He comes up for air just as she was ready to tap out. She bends forward and looks back. "Finish me, now! Hard!"

The glass is shaking, and the door begins to slide open. Dude reaches over and grabs it without missing a beat. She pounds on the glass with her palms and tells him, "Harder!" He thinks they're both going to crash through the glass if he pounds any harder. He goes deep and swirls his hips. Her knees buckle: he feels her insides pulsing, then her body goes limp. Trixie slides down the glass and sits on the shower floor with her head between her knees as the water washes over her back. Dude asks if she's okay. She looks up, kisses the tip of his pecker, then tells him, "Just leave me here and go get yourself dried off. I will be out soon."

He is laying down reliving the shower scene when she hobbles out of the bathroom, flips off the lights, and slides herself in between the sheets next to him in the unsoiled bed. She lays her head on his chest and says, “I don’t want to inflate your ego, but you are the best I’ve ever had. And, if I can have it my way, you will be the last man I ever need.” Her eyelids slide shut as she mumbles something about multiple orgasms.

# Chapter 19

RAYS OF SUNLIGHT SNEAK between the closed curtains of room 218. Still wrapped in blankets, Dude feels Trixie's warm naked body pressed against him before his eyes open. He lifts his head and squints to see the time on the clock. He hadn't planned to sleep till ten thirty, but then again, the extra sleep was well deserved. Last night's fuck fest was draining, literally. He feels like there's no fluid left in his body. Dude would ask Trixie if she felt the same way, but he has a good idea what her answer would be. Besides, she looks so cute while sleeping.

He doesn't bother to wake her and slips out of the bed, then into the bathroom. He dribbles his last drops of fluid into the toilet, then turns on the shower. The sticky feeling on his junk requires another round of soap and water.

When he steps back out into the mostly dark room, Trixie Stone is still cuddled up like a cute kitten in the blankets. He grabs the room key off the nightstand and heads downstairs for coffee. Dude waves hi to the young girl behind the front desk. To the left, the continental breakfast is being cleaned up. A male hotel worker tells him the coffee is still hot. He says, "help yourself."

Dude fills two cups, grabs a handful of creamers and sugar, then gets back into the elevator.

The loud clicking of the door handle startles Trixie as he enters the room. She sits up covering her chest with the sheet, and glances at the clock.

"I can't believe I slept so late. How long have you been awake?"

He extends a cup of coffee in her direction. "Not too long. How do you like it, cream and sugar?"

"Nice shirt, I love Orlando." She grabs his belt and pulls him close. "Kiss me." Then she says, "cream and sugar sounds good." She continues. "You smell good. Did you shower again?"

As he rips the tops off three sugar packets, he looks at her and says, "I woke up feeling sticky. I had to jump in again."

"Sorry, I woke up around four with your tool in my hand, so I decided to give him a couple kisses. You were moaning, don't you remember?"

"Of course, I just thought I was dreaming. No need to apologize; you can kiss, suck, or whatever you want to call it anytime the mood strikes." He smiles and sits the coffee on the nightstand beside her. Trixie may be cool, but telling her he slept through her bobbing for apples is not worth the argument. Or maybe he was awake and can't remember, nobody will ever know.

"Honey, that was no dream, trust me. If my crotch wasn't so sore, I would drag you into this bed right now." She purrs while putting her hands under the sheet. "It's going to be a long day sitting on that bike seat. I may need to ice my kitty first."

Dude offers to get her ice from the hotel machine. She says, "no thanks, I'm sure it will become numb at some point." Trixie slowly walks to the bathroom naked.

"Take your time getting ready. I have some internet research to do before we head out." Dude puts the local news on the TV and pulls out his phone. He's trying to find a map of where this welding shop is located.

He hears the shower turn on and he has a flashback. Dude immediately feels his pants rising. He resists the temptation to knock on the door. His experience with passengers needing an ice pack tells him to cut her some slack.

Trixie walks out of the bathroom with one towel wrapped around her hair, and another covering her body. Dude is still hard from the thought of last night. He thinks, *now this is just torture*, as his stare burns a hole in the towel covering her sore kitty.

She unzips her bag and starts laying clothes out on the bed. Trixie holds up the white lace bra she wore last night. She mumbles under her breath. "But the matching thong is." She gets the chills, then stuffs the bra into the bag. Trixie pulls out a much less fancy white bra and its matching thong. Under the towel, she wiggles up the panties, then she lets the towel hit the floor. Dude's jaw falls with it.

"You're beautiful and you look even better when I'm sober."

Trixie leans down and puts her tits in his face and runs her hands along her hips. "*This* is all yours now. Aren't you glad you didn't ditch me?"

"I gladly accept. And for the record, I never had any intention of ditching you. I think you're amazing and I'm not just talking about your body. You are so genuine and unique. I think you're smart and funny. It doesn't hurt that you have *these,* but I hope you know I'm serious." He pushes up on her dangling boobs, then says, "I don't care if this sounds cheesy, but I'm going to say it anyway. 'The instant your boot hit the ground, and you stepped out of the Jeep, I got hard.' After we talked for a couple minutes and we took a few puffs together, I knew I wanted to see you again."

Trixie straddles him on the chair. "I don't think that's cheesy at all. Honestly, for me, it was the moment you embraced my friends and offered to help with the tents. I mean, I thought you were cute from the second I saw you but, as you know, I've always been skeptical about bikers, but mostly just men in general. You guys get a bad rap, but you are so kind, and generous. You're adventurous, and fun and you make me happy. I don't care whether you ride a motorcycle or not, but the bike does excite me, so don't even think about selling it."

"My back seat is all yours. I have a good feeling about us. Now put some clothes on before we get stuck in this hotel room all day. Are you hungry?"

"I can eat." Trixie responds while flipping her wet hair back. She grabs a brush and walks into the bathroom topless. Standing in front of the mirror, Trixie asks what they're going to eat.

Dude is standing in front of the window overlooking the parking lot. The sun is shining and through a maze of parked cars and trees, he sees a yellow sign with black letters.

He says, "We can walk across the street to the Waffle House."

Trixie picks up a blow dryer. "Sounds good. I will be ready soon. Help me pick a shirt."

Dude walks toward the bed covered with Trixie's clothes and pulls out her rally shirts.

On his phone, Dude is saving the address to the welding shop and looking at a street view map to scope out his approach. The welding shop building sits on the street with a house on one side, and some kind of business on the other. The map shows thick trees behind the buildings. The residential house sits off the street and is surrounded by grass running back to the woods. There's a driveway separating the welding shop from the business on its other side.

Trixie lies on the bed and wiggles on a pair of jeans. Her feet are kicking as she bounces her ass on the bed. Dude watches the show while he tells her about the map.

She holds up the two rally shirts and asks, "which one?"

He tells her to wear the pink V-neck. "It's going to be warm; you can always put the long sleeves over top if you get chilly." He goes on. "I can show you the map at breakfast. We need to make a plan."

Dude puts his clothes and hygiene stuff in a small plastic bag, then asks Trixie to put it in with her stuff. "I will carry the bag for you."

Trixie pulls her wavy ginger hair into a ponytail then wraps it with a hair tie. She sits on the chair and slides on her cowgirl boots. She pops out of the chair. "I'm ready!" Then she instantly regrets the sudden movement and grabs for her crotch. "Still a little sore."

Dude puts the trash in a can while Trixie straightens the blankets on both beds. They double check the room for any personal belongings and turn off the TV.

***

After playing *Frogger* with traffic, the happy couple makes their way into the Waffle House. A short woman in her fifties wearing a hairnet and apron greets them from behind the counter. "Sit wherever y'all like."

Dude stretches his arm forward. "Go ahead, you pick."

To the right are booths along the windows facing the parking lot. Ahead is a row of stools along the counter, running the length of the dining room. The grill is behind the counter with the chef's back to the guests. The jukebox and bathrooms are to the left, so Trixie leads them to the right, toward a booth in the back corner against the window.

Dude sits with his back to the wall with a view of the whole restaurant, while Trixie sits facing only him, a wall, and a window. Their waitress is Mary, the same woman who greeted them by the door. "Can I get y'all some coffee or water?"

"Two of each, thank you." Says Dude.

"Take a minute to look at the menu. I'll be right back with your drinks."

The double-sided laminated menu is littered with colorful pictures of food: breakfast on one side and lunch and dinner on the other.

He asks Trixie, "what breakfast food do you like?"

"If I'm not eating healthy, I love pancakes, with strawberries."

"With whipped cream?"

Trixie tilts her head. "I wouldn't have it any other way."

"Good to know. So, is that what you're going to order?"

"I think I will. After last night's workout, I can use the carbs."

When the waitress returns, Dude orders for Trixie and gets himself biscuits with sausage gravy poured over top. The Waffle House was quiet for a Sunday morning. Maybe they missed the rush, or everyone in town is still at church. Dude wastes no time showing Trixie the map on his phone.

"See right here?" He points at the driveway on the right side of the building. Then he points to the neighbor's fence line running along the welding shop.

"There are two options, maybe three. I think you should stay with the bike. I'll park in the lot of the building next door. The garage is in the back, but I can't see it on this map. I have to get behind the building by the trees. The woods are thick, not sure if I will be able to come in from behind. I will try going down the driveway first. If it doesn't get me all the way back, I can try from the house on the other side. I need to locate the garage and see if I can get a look inside. When I'm back there, if you see anyone pull up or come out, call me right away. Got it?"

Being sober and clear-eyed, he can see Trixie's wheels turning. He says, "You are so sexy when you're thinking. I love how you take the time to think before you speak. It shows intelligence."

She blushes and looks away. "Look at you trying to flatter me. You can drop the act now; you already had your way with me." She smiles, then says, "I'm just joking. I think it's cute when you talk serious, and I'm loving all the compliments. Keep 'em coming."

Mary unloads a plate and a large bowl from her round tray. A Plate of whipped cream sits in front of Trixie. She will need to dig for the pancakes. Steam rises from Dude's pool of gravy while the poor biscuits are drowning underneath.

"Thanks Mary. Do you know of a local cab company who can take us down the road?" Dude is trying to avoid hassling Tommy after all he's already done to help this weekend.

“Sure, we have a place on speed dial. As soon as someone passes out in one of these here booths, I call the cab before I call the cops. How long before you want him here?”

Dude looks at Trixie, then looks at her plate. “About thirty minutes. Thank you.”

“My eyes are bigger than my belly. I can’t eat all of this.”

“We can take the rest to go. Don’t make yourself puke.”

“Ewe, don’t say puke while I’m eating. Gross.” Trixie hasn’t even picked up her fork yet.

Dude cuts up all his biscuits before eating anything. Trixie pushes a pile of whipped cream to one side of the plate to expose her pancake and strawberries. The two get quiet while they eat.

Trixie breaks her silence. “You know, this is the first time we’ve been totally sober together in public. I’m going to consider this our first official date, and when the check comes, don’t you dare touch it. I’m paying.” She pushes her plate forward. “I’m stuffed.”

Dude finishes chewing his food. “Now were official, sounds good to me.”

“Oh, don’t get confused, we’ve been official since the first time you put your hand up my shirt. I was referring to our first date. Don’t forget June 7$^{th}$, I will be expecting an anniversary gift.” Trixie laughs then stands up and excuses herself to the ladies room. She stops to tell Mary not to give *him* the check. The waitress says, "I'll do ya one better, here girl." She hands the check to Trixie.

Dude finishes his bowl of mush and calls Santa to let him know they'd be back at the farm soon. On the other end of the phone call, Santa tells him, "Get moving boy, it's almost noon, drag your ass out of that comfy bed. We're all packed up and waiting around for you two."

Trixie returns from the restroom, goes into her purse, and takes out her credit card. She waves the waitress over and slides into the booth. Mary asks to box up the unfinished pile of whipped cream and the shards of pancake. There are no strawberries left. Trixie declines. "I won't eat it later."

"Your ride is here." Mary points out the window at an all-white Crown Vic with no lettering.

"Looks more like a cop car." Dude is skeptical.

"Don't worry, he will get y'all where y'all want to go."

As Trixie prepares to sign the credit card slip, Dude puts cash on the table. "At least let me leave the tip." She reluctantly agrees, then they make their way to the door.

Barely able to see over the steering wheel, Danny DeVito's twin brother rolls down the passenger window and waves them over. "Where are y'all headed?"

Dude opens the back door for Trixie, then gets in on the driver's side. "Just down the road, Lone Ranger's Farm."

"Yes sir. I will have y'all there in ten minutes."

Trixie reaches across the duffel bag sitting between them and grabs Dude's hand. "Our first cab ride together." He smiles and thinks, *how long is this first-time bullshit going to last?*

***

Arriving at the farm, a black dually pulling a thirty-foot RV is attempting to get out of the camping area but having a hard time making the turn. With this clown blocking the entrance, Dude tells the cabbie to pull over by the registration tent. He throws DeVito a twenty and the two climb out the back doors smelling like Camel cigarettes.

They trek through the half-empty camping area. Trixie shakes her head with disgust when she sees a recently vacated camping spot scattered with trash. Dude says, "There's always a few lazy scumbags amongst the bunch."

The sound of vendors loading up their remaining product radiates across the field. Trailer Queens load up their motorcycles. Smoldering firepits provide the inviting smell of camping.

With Trixie's off-white Victoria's Secret duffel over his shoulder, he asks, "So, camping is not your thing?"

"I never said I didn't enjoy camping; it's just sleeping on the ground that I'm not a fan of."

"Okay, that makes sense. Because you do realize my life is basically one big camp-out, right?"

She says, "I think I get the picture. I have been to campgrounds before and have seen the way people create cute set-ups around their campers."

"I don't have a flower garden, but the RV is nice, and I do have a really comfortable bed, in case you were wondering."

"Good to know because the thought has crossed my mind." Trixie looks up to see Kat Miller approaching from forty feet away. She zooms toward Trixie and grabs her for a hug. Dude says, "nice to see you too Kat."

"Yeah, yeah, morning Dude. Or should I say good afternoon?"

The girls slow down to talk while Dude goes straight to Angel and sits the duffel by the front wheel. His tent is the only one still standing at their camp. Chuck and Birdie hit the road early. Tommy came back for his tent, then left again. Santa is sitting on his Ultra Classic listening to the radio when Dude walks up. He says, "Dude man, look at ya, all bright eyed and bushy tailed. Was she worth all the hassle?"

"The short answer is yes. You have no idea; we went for a ride alright. I think I'm missing a layer of skin down there."

"Glad to hear it. Now what's your plan for the day?"

Dude pulls out his phone and shows Santa the map of the welding shop. He explains the different approaches. Santa tells Dude to be careful. He says, "everyone around here carries a gun. Don't go gettin' your ass shot."

"They are closed today so there shouldn't be anyone around."

"Well then don't get your ass arrested for trespassing." Santa appears to be serious. "These mountain folks don't play around when it comes to their property."

Dude tells him to relax. "But keep your phone close just in case." Then he starts breaking down the tent. He's had plenty of practice with tents this weekend, so dropping his should be a breeze.

The poles come out and the canvas falls flat. It's folded, rolled, and packed before Trixie steps foot into the camp. She and Kat are standing close and holding each other's hands as they bounce up and down with giddiness. Apparently, Trixie likes to kiss and tell.

Dude opens the lids to both side boxes and the tour pack. He pulls a bunch of stuff out to reorganize, making room for the extra bag. Last year, when Dude rode to Sturgis, he had enough stuff packed on the bike for three people. He has plenty of room for pretty little Trixie and her duffel bag. Then Dude wonders if she was serious when he mentioned going to see Mount Rushmore. Although, if she packs for South Dakota too, Dude may have to leave a few things behind. A compromise he would gladly make to have such a great companion for the five-thousand-mile round-trip adventure.

"Hey Trixie, when did you say your birthday was?"

"Hey Dude," in her mocking him voice. "You never asked."

"I thought you said it was in about two months, right?"

She says, "you're very observant. I don't remember telling you the date. It's the 9th by the way, in August."

"Holy shit. Your birthday is during the Sturgis Motorcycle Rally this year. You have to go, or to phrase it a different way; we should really go together. You said you would think about it if you weren't kicked to the curb by then. How about it?"

"First of all, if you ever mention my name and the words *kicked to the curb* in the same sentence again, I will kick you in the nuts. Second, yes, I think going to Sturgis for my birthday would be awesome. I would love to go."

"It's a plan. Don't worry, I will take care of all the details." Dude secretly pumps his fist with joy.

Kat says, "I like your spunkiness girlfriend. Kick him in the balls if he gets out of line. That's what I would do."

The girls exchange phone numbers and agree to keep in touch. Santa and Dude say their final goodbyes. Everything is packed up on both motorcycles. Dude turns on the ignition then fires up Angel so she can warm up for a few minutes. The sun has evaporated any morning dew that may have been. Trixie may not have ice, but she will surely have heat. If she were wearing shorts, she'd have burn marks for sure.

Dude puts the welding shop address into Angel's built-in GPS system. After one last round of hugs, they all mount up. Dude asks Trixie if she has any interest in going back to the vendors.

"No thanks. I'm ready for you to take me around the world, let's hit the road." She squeezes him around the waist.

Dude yells over to Santa. "Ride safe brother. I will call you later. Bye Kat, love ya."

The wheels start turning, and Trixie leans forward. "Let's go catch some bad guys." She sees him smile in the mirror, then kisses him on the neck.

# Chapter 20

SWEEPING TURNS UNDER THE cover of trees provides a cool breeze, causing Trixie's nipples to perk up. She presses herself tightly against Dude's back. They exit the tree tunnel to be blinded by bright sunshine. Trixie leans back in her seat and points her face and chest toward the warm rays.

Instructed by the GPS, Dude turns left onto Apex Parkway. A small hill flattens at the bottom just before a stop sign brings all traffic to a halt at the corner of Boulder Avenue. Just beyond the stop sign, the corner property on the right side shares a fence line with Rock Welders.

Dude passes the corner house and slowly rides by the welding shop. The storefront sits on the sidewalk and there is a parking lot just before a driveway with a closed gate. An auto mechanic garage sits on the other side of the gated driveway. The cinderblock building has a small parking lot in front of its three garage doors. There is extra parking on the other side, but half the spaces are filled with lemons and beaters, nothing newer than the faded green 2005 Ford Taurus.

After slowly scoping the scene, the twenty-minute ride ends when Dude pulls onto the side of the auto mechanic shop, just out of sight from the welder's side of the building. He picks the first parking space and pulls in. Trixie climbs off and scoots herself up against the building while picking a wedgie out of her crack. Dude asks her to stay by the bike but peek around the building to keep an eye out for anyone coming in or out of the welding shop.

She gives him a kiss. “Please be careful. I will call if I see anyone. Good luck.”

Dude’s method of going where he is not allowed has always been simple: act like he belongs there. He starts by walking up to the front of Rock Welding. The stucco building has a tall garage door and a people sized door next to it. The sign above the smaller door looks like it was made in the 50s and hasn’t been repainted since. Remnants of red letters are so faded they are unreadable. The metal garage door has a row of windows at eye level. Dude sees a farming tractor with a welding torch set up next to it. The welding shield hangs from the four-foot-high tank of gas. Hoses connect the tank to the torch, which is hanging from a metal cart. There’re no lights on and no movement inside.

Dude walks through the parking lot alongside the solid wall of the building. When he reaches the back, he’s met with a fence, a dumpster, and an area used for storage. He can see into the woods behind the shop through the fence. The heavily wooded tree line is deceiving at first. Dude drifts along the fence to the left until he can see the slightest hint of a structure poking through the pines.

He can barely see through the trees separating himself from the sight of the neighbor on the corner. Pulling up on the bike, Dude saw the beautiful white ranch style home with a wraparound porch overlooking the manicured lawn. The fence separating the two properties stops at the trees. On the map, the fence from the neighbor's side looked to be the fastest way to get into the woods, but with a car in their driveway, it's not the smartest play.

To the left, Dude can see the driveway running behind the building, but then it turns to the left, away from the mysterious garage. The road is not fenced, so if Dude can get down there, he can work his way to the trees by cutting across some heavily overgrown grass.

Dude heads back to Trixie and explains what he saw.

"From behind their shop, I got a small glimpse of a metal shed in the woods. I want to go check it out. People are likely home in the corner house, but the trees are really thick, so I don't think they'll see me cutting across the grass. My best bet is to hop this small gate to the driveway and walk down like I own the place. When the road curves to the left, I'm going straight across the high grass and into the woods. Then I can work my way down to the shed through the trees."

"I'm glad you came back to tell me. I thought you already went back there. Please be careful." Trixie leans against the wall and stretches her arms out in

Dude's direction. "One more hug and kiss before you go."

Dude hops the fence to the driveway. It's paved with gravel and only wide enough for one car. There is knee-high grass flanking both sides of the downward sloped driveway. When he gets to the bend in the gravel, Dude plows his way toward the thick trees. He gets deep enough beyond the tree line to not be seen from the street. Then he makes his way to the right towards the mystery garage where Henry said he dropped the Panhead.

Buried a good twenty yards beyond the tree line sits a garage wrapped with dirt colored metal siding, sitting ten feet high, twenty feet long by twelve feet wide. The rectangle tin can has a solid metal roll-down overhead garage door facing the welding shop, a regular size solid metal door on the side, followed by one small window covered with tree sap and dirt. The rear and far sides are blank, and the rusted roof is pitched in the middle. The portable garage appears to be growing roots, indicating how long it's been there. Dude thinks, *surely more than a year.*

There are pieces of metal rotting away into the wilderness all around the garage. A chopped-up car frame is buried up to the axles. Half of a fifty-five-gallon steel drum sits filled with stinky green water. Dude realizes the obvious connection between Henry and the twins: Rust.

Dude uses the sleeve of his black Orlando H-D t-shirt to wipe the bottom right corner of the small dingy window. He rubs a circle and gets his eye close enough to look in. A piece of plywood covering the inside of the window leaves only a sliver of daylight for the peep show. He wipes away a spider web, then uses his sleeve to wipe an area in the bottom left corner. Same deal, just enough room for a peek. He can see a four-wheeled ATV, a red dirt bike, and a faded Pabst Beer sign on the wall.

He goes back to the other corner, gives it a better wipe and presses his forehead against the window. He looks straight down and sees an ashtray full of cigarette butts sitting on top of a red toolbox. Just beyond the red rectangle, on the seat of a golf cart, Dude sees a Sportster gas tank. It matches the fenders and oil bucket sitting on a towel on the floor. A last scan through the slender gap doesn't reveal anything he couldn't see from the other end. He would need a ladder to try for a better view, but for now, he's seen enough. He calls Trixie.

"Hey babe, just want you to know I'm fine. Listen, I can't see much inside, but what I can see is good enough. They have Harley parts. All the tins from a bright blue Sporty. More pieces of the bike have to be around here somewhere."

She acknowledges but doesn't mention what he just referred to her as. She secretly swoons at the thought of him relaxing into the role of being her man.

"Okay, good news. Now can you get out of there, please?"

"Let me try to get some pictures, be there as soon as I can."

Dude presses his phone against the glass and snaps a handful of pictures. He grabs a few more pics from the other wiped spot, then wanders around the garage, stepping over an empty bag of Burger King. In the high weeds, a tipped-over rusty wheelbarrow reveals a motorcycle tire on a rim. Dude flips the barrow and examines the wheel. It could be Harley, but it could also be Kawasaki. Either way, it's from a motorcycle and it gives Dude a boost of confidence.

He zigs and zags through the high grass looking for anything motorcycle related. A milk crate full of engine parts sits up against a tree. Dude pulls out a set of heads from a Japanese motorcycle and sits them on the ground. He digs in again and comes up with the bottom end piece of the motor that connects to the frame. The solid piece of steel has a small amount of rust, but not enough to hide the grinder marks going across a one-inch flat surface near the top of the engine piece. Dude knows it's the spot where the vehicle identification number goes. This piece alone could be enough evidence to nail these thieves. He debates whether or not to take the bottom end with him.

Dude decides to photograph the engine pieces and put them back into the orange plastic crate. He moves through the woods away from the garage, about twenty feet behind the tree line. He works his way to where he can walk straight out to the driveway. He steps out from the trees and into the open section of high grass toward the gravel driveway. He does his best not to look paranoid. He reminds himself to act natural. He scales the four-foot fence with ease, then turns right toward Trixie.

Dude spooks her when he turns the corner of the auto mechanic building. She's in the shade sitting on a parking block. He grabs his helmet off one mirror and hers off the other. "Let's go, I will fill you in down the road."

Trixie wipes the butt of her pants, then buckles her helmet. With the engine running, her ass barely hits the seat when they start rolling. Dude glides back a few feet before turning his handlebars hard to the right. He pulls out of the parking lot and turns right, away from the welding shop. They continue straight on Apex parkway for two miles before Dude pulls into a gas station and parks by pump number eight. They both climb off the bike.

Trixie had been sitting quietly on the short ride waiting for Dude to say something. She stared at herself through the reflection on his sunglasses in the mirror. His lips remained tightly sealed while the wheels in his head churned butter.

He weighed his options while riding, and now it's time to confer with his accomplice.

"In addition to the Sportster parts inside the garage, I also found some engine pieces with the numbers scraped off."

Trixie asks cluelessly. "Is that a good thing?"

"Good for me, bad for them. Only a thief would grind off the numbers."

"What are you going to do now?"

He asks, "what do you think I should do?"

"Honestly, if you want my opinion, I think the safest thing to do would be go to the police."

Dude snickers and shakes his head. "Back in Jersey, I wouldn't get the law involved, but out here in the fuckin' sticks, I may not have a choice. Let's just hope these hillbillies aren't related to the damn sheriff. I'm going to top off the gas, then call Santa. If you need the bathroom or want anything from the store, go for it."

Trixie heads into the gas station store while Dude makes his call.

"Are you calling me for bail money or are you laying in a hospital bed?" Santa seriously waits for a response.

"Wouldn't you just love to be right? Not today old man. I just left the welding shop. Well, technically the garage in the woods behind the welding shop." Dude goes on to tell Santa all about what he saw inside and outside of the garage.

After some back and forth, Santa was able to convince Dude to take Trixie's advice. His exact words were, "don't be a dumbass."

When Trixie's boobs come bouncing in Dude's direction, he thanks Santa for the advice, then ends the call. She walks up with a black plastic bag. "Now we have snacks." Then she asks, "what did he say?"

With disappointment in his voice, Dude tells her, "He agrees with you."

Trixie doesn't understand. "What other options do you have?"

"I could get even the old-fashioned way."

"Please don't."

Showing an evil side to Trixie could be a deal breaker. He realizes no girl in her right mind would want to ride around with a guy who is talking about getting vigilante justice. So he quickly changes his tune.

The odds of George's Panhead being chopped into pieces have just gone through the roof. Dude knows these guys stole the bike, there's no more doubt about it. He thinks, *the police can arrest these guys, but they will be back on the street in no time, doing the same shit again.* Dude can picture himself ambushing these guys, but then he pictures Trixie hitching a ride with the next biker who rolls down the road.

"Okay, you win. I will go the police route, but only if you walk in beside me."

She gives him a hug. "Good choice. Of course, I will be by your side the whole time."

He looks at his phone for the address to the Mud Hole police department when he notices the time. "Oh shit, it's almost three. I need to call Martin Woods."

"Hello, Martin?"

"Yes sir. You are punctual, Dude."

"Sorry if I'm rushing you, but I have a busy day. Can we meet?"

Martin Woods agrees to meet Dude and Trixie in a bank parking lot near his house. He gives Dude the address and says he will be there in thirty minutes.

Trixie squeezes him tightly around the waist while talking into his ear as they pull out of the gas station. Her ginger hair is flowing freely from under the helmet. Blindly following the GPS, the couple leans into an upward sweeping curve. Trixie's bright smile sparkles as she squeezes Dude tighter.

They arrive in the Wells Fargo parking lot in fifteen minutes. With time to spare, Dude suggests a smoke break.

"You can't go to the police station stoned!" Trixie is astounded at the thought.

"Just a couple puffs. I need to calm my nerves."

She tells him not to walk into the station smelling like weed. He agrees to wash up before going, then pulls out the half of a joint left from last night. She is hesitant, but after he takes a puff, she says, "blow the smoke in my mouth. I don't want my fingers to stink."

"While I have this can out, give me your pipe and flower. I will stuff in with my joints."

Trixie digs in her bag then rattles off a bunch of questions about what it was like creeping around in the woods. Dude gives her a flurry of answers while reliving everything he saw. He flicks the roach and opens his saddlebag, then pulls out hand sanitizer, mouthwash and a body spray.

Martin pulls up in a gray '02 Chevy Silverado. He steps out of the truck with the shiny chrome Panhead horn in his hand. He gives Trixie a once over as he extends the horn toward Dude.

Martin says, "a deal is a deal. Here ya go. Good luck with your search for the rest of the bike."

After a brief inspection of the horn, Dude thanks him, then opens the saddlebag and wraps the sentimental horn with a sweatshirt. Martin is quick to turn back to his truck. The transaction was quick and smooth, with no surprises. Dude always appreciates a person who sticks to their word.

Trixie asks, "Are you ready to do this?"

While putting the police station address into the GPS, he says, "as ready as I will ever be."

Through the noise of the wind, the couple discusses how they will present the information to the police. Dude knows he can't say he hopped the fence to look around. The back-and-forth conversation helps to bring clarity to his story. He puts his hand on Trixie's knee. "Thanks for your support. Try not to look shocked when you hear the story I tell these cops."

***

Pulling up to the Mud Hole police station feels unnatural to Dude. The only times he's ever voluntarily entered a police station was to bail out a friend. He struggles to remember the last time he's dialed 9-1-1. Then he recalls the Sunday morning in Fort Myers when he was sitting at a red light and a car crashed into a minivan then took off. Dude got off his bike to check on the minivan driver and noticed a car seat in the back. That was almost ten years ago.

Black and white police cars are parked in a line out front of the single-story brick building. A set of three steps leads to double doors in the center of the red brick facade. A single five-foot square pane of glass is cut into the brick on each side of the doors. A small patch of grass lies at the foot of the steps on each side. Facing the building, the flagpole extends out of the right patch of grass. An American flag flies at full staff. A North Carolina state flag hangs below the stars and stripes. A parking lot on the right side of the building faces a side door and a row of smaller windows.

Dude makes a right turn into the parking lot with open spots on each side. He heads to the rear, then backs into the last parking space on the right. His exhaust blows through the chain-link fence separating the police station from the neighboring impound lot, which is full of cars, trucks, boats, RVs, motorcycles and who knows what else. Dude's blue eyes scan the impound lot as he removes his helmet. "Wow, they have some good stuff."

Trixie pops off her lid, then leans forward and shakes her head before flipping her hair back. She gives Dude a quick pep talk before taking his hand and leading him toward the street. They turn right, approaching the flagpole and three steps.

He takes a deep breath and Trixie says, “you can do this honey, just try to stay calm.”

# Chapter 21

THE PAIR ENTERS THE double doors leading into a large doctor's office style waiting room. The left side of the lobby is lined with chairs. The center of the room has a coffee table with magazines. Two vending machines sit along the back wall. One has snacks and the other has drinks. The glass wall along the right side gives a clear look at the room full of desks occupied by police officers. In the middle of the glass wall, there is a window.

Dude gazes around the room at the few patients waiting in chairs before approaching the three-foot-wide hole.

"How can I help you sir?" asks a short, fair skinned man in his thirties wearing a police uniform with a thick black mustache.

Dude stands firm, with Trixie close by his side. "Hello officer. I'm here because I have evidence of a motorcycle theft."

"Okay, sounds like you need to speak with a detective. Let me see who's available. Please have a seat, someone will be out soon."

The couple sits in the first two chairs near the front door in case Dude gets cold feet; this place could trigger a flashback.

He leans in close to Trixie and whispers. “I have to say whatever it takes to get these cops to believe me. Remember to keep a straight face, no matter what. Okay?”

“Please don’t make me laugh.” She’s giggling just from thinking about what kind of bullshit he could make up.

A light-colored oak door opens at the end of the glass wall. A tall man in his forties with curly blonde hair and a baby face walks across the room to introduce himself to Dude and Trixie. Unlike the officers floating around behind the glass wall in uniforms, he’s wearing a tan suit with a white shirt and blue tie.

“Hello, I’m Detective Zucker. I’ve been told you have information about a stolen motorcycle.”

“I do.” Dude remains seated.

“How about you two come back to my desk?”

Dude glances over at Trixie and she nods with approval. He stands up to signal his willingness to follow the detective. Trixie tugs on his hand to get his feet moving.

Through the wooden door, the sound of phones ringing and loud chatter dominate the large open room. The pair are led to a desk with a name plate reading *Detective Brian Zucker*.

Zucker points at the two chairs on the other side of his desk and motions for the couple to sit. The detective leads with, “why don’t you two start by telling me your names.”

“I’m Russell Sparks.”

"My name is Trixie Stone."

"Nice to meet y'all. Now tell me about this motorcycle."

Dude starts by telling the detective the year, make, and model of the Panhead. He tells him the colors and some other details about the '63 Pan.

"It sounds like a nice motorcycle. I'm a Harley rider myself. I have a 2007 Road King."

Dude compliments the Road King, then moves on to telling the story of how the motorcycle disappeared. He says, "my friend George filed a police report with you around this time last year."

Detective Zucker grabs his computer mouse and asks for George's last name.

After a couple minutes, he tells Dude it's still an open, unsolved case.

"I figured out who stole this motorcycle. I know where they're keeping other stolen motorcycle parts as well."

"We have a long list of unsolved motorcycle thefts. Where are you getting this information of yours?"

"These guys tried to sell me stolen parts. I even have pictures." He pulls out his cell phone and shows the motor piece with the missing numbers and the Sportster parts.

"Interesting pictures. How long ago did you take these?"

"On Friday. I met these twin brothers, the Rockwell's, Jasper and Catfish at the local motorcycle rally, and they took me back to their garage where they have tons of motorcycle parts. It's behind their welding shop on Apex Parkway. Rock Welding."

Detective Zucker is feverishly scrolling and clicking while his eyes try to keep up with the fast-moving computer screen.

"The shop itself has never had any complaints, but these two brothers, they're no strangers to the law. Give me a minute." The detective scurries away from his desk. Trixie leans over and whispers. "Holy crap. I almost believed you."

When Detective Zucker returns to his desk, he has another man with him. "Russell and Trixie, this is Detective LaRoche. He specializes in missing motor vehicles."

The short man with brown hair is clean shaven, wearing a black suit with a white shirt and black tie. LaRoche asks Dude to explain exactly where the stolen parts are located. When he says, "in the trees," LaRoche tells Detective Zucker to pull up a street view map of the welding shop. LaRoche motions for Dude to step behind the desk and look at the map on the computer.

"The garage is in the woods right here." Dude points to the thick trees on the screen.

"Can you see it from the street?" Asks LaRoche.

"If you look really hard, you can see it a little bit."

LaRoche excuses himself and goes for a CB radio to call a patrolman to ride by the welding shop and look around.

Detective Zucker continues to dig into the Rockwell brothers while they wait for the patrolman to report back. He is scrolling through the list of missing motorcycles like he is shopping for a new bike on eBay.

When the patrolman radios back to the station, LaRoche buzzes back to the desk. “Hey Zucker, blow up that map, I mean, zoom out.”

As the buildings on the map get smaller, the number of trees becomes larger. LaRoche points to the top of the screen. He says, “see here, once the tree line starts, the property no longer belongs to the buildings along the street.” He grabs the computer mouse and moves the map until the other side of the forest of trees meets a road. “What you have been looking at, is the back of the Mud Hole State Forest.” He looks at Dude. “Are you telling me that these guys have a garage on state property?”

Dude is turning his head to view the screen from a different angle. He points to exactly where the portable metal garage sits. “It is right here in these trees.”

Detective LaRoche says Dude is pointing at a state forest. He excuses himself and says, “the chief needs to hear about this. Be right back.”

Trixie’s right leg is shaking when Dude sits back in his chair. He puts his hand on her knee and whispers, “just relax, you look nervous.”

Detective Zucker asks Dude, “the pieces you saw, are they inside the garage or outside?”

“Both. There is a ton of stuff inside, but the motor pieces with the missing numbers are outside next to a tree in a milk crate. There’s other stuff scattered in the weeds too, but I didn’t get to see it all.”

Suddenly, the commotion in the station gets louder and officers begin scrambling around. Dude hears a voice in the distance say, "we’re burning daylight." Detective LaRoche comes back to the desk and says, “we’re going to check it out now. You two stay here.” He tells Detective Zucker, “the team will enter the state forest from Chapel Hill Road, on the other side of the large jungle of trees. Keep them here with you until we verify his story.”

Dude tells LaRoche about where he can find the orange crate of pieces.

“Don’t worry mister Sparks, we will leave no stone unturned.”

Dude and Trixie are offered coffee and asked to sit in the waiting area. They are told not to leave until instructed. The couple accepts the caffeine boost and returns to their seats by the front door.

“How long do you think we will need to sit here? I’m just curious.” Trixie blows on the hot cup of coffee.

“The way these guys ran out of here, we should hear something soon. Try to relax, you look nervous.”

“I’m not nervous. I am excited. If what you saw are really stolen parts, the police should be able to arrest these guys, right?”

"You watch a lot of police shows on TV, don't you?"

Trixie looks at him. "How can you tell?"

"We are not on television, although we may be on camera right now, but things work different in the real world. At this point, we're just lucky they are taking us seriously. But the fact that these nitwit twins were stupid enough to put their house of parts on state property does increase the odds of getting them arrested. If those woods weren't state land, the cops would have needed a search warrant, and who knows what would've happened then. Let's just be patient."

Trying hard to bite her tongue, Trixie can't resist using her TV watching experience. "But on the Mentalist..."

Dude cuts her short. "I'm sorry, but first off, they're usually working murder cases on the Mentalist."

Her eyes widen. "So, you've seen the show?"

"Sure, Jane is a trip, but what happens on the show is not what happens in real life. Don't forget, it's just mindless entertainment."

"Okay, if you say so. I like that we have the same taste in shows." She winks at him.

Detective Zucker pops his head out of the slab of oak in the corner. "Our people are there now. So far, your story is checking out. Hang tight, I'll come back out when I get another update."

Trixie shakes Dude's knee. "See, we're going to get these scumbags." Then she glances over at the girl who is curled up on a chair at the other end of the waiting room. “Jeez, she could really use some new clothes. She is a hot mess.” The twenty-something has blood on her shirt and holes in her pants. Her dirty blonde hair is extra dirty today, and her face appears to be bruised on the left side. “I feel bad for her.”

“Please don’t go over there to console her.” Dude holds Trixie’s hand and brings her attention back to him. “What other shows do you like?”

She thinks for a minute, then says, “I’m not a big fan of blood and guts. I really like funny cop dramas, nothing too serious. Have you ever heard of Psych?”

He smiles. “Shawn, Gus, and the blueberry, please. I love their hilarious, obscure ‘80s movie references. Maybe one of the most underrated shows on Prime.”

Trixie shakes his shoulder. “I thought I was the only person who has ever seen that show. None of my co-workers have ever heard of it. I can’t wait to cuddle up in front of the TV with you.” She squeezes his arm.

The couple exchanges witty references from their favorite shows to kill time. A break in conversation causes Trixie to check out the magazine selection. She finds one about hiking and starts flipping the pages. Dude makes a quick call to Santa with a status update.

***

Detective tan suit swings open the oak door. “You two, come with me.”

Dude feels like he’s being perp walked into a line-up room.

Trixie’s head is on a swivel trying to compare this office to the one from the Mentalist in Houston. She scans the piles of folders sitting on one officer’s desk. She tries to remember the case number, but it is too long and has too many dashes.

“Please have a seat.”

They each take the same seat from earlier: Dude to the detective’s right, and Trixie to his left. Detective Zucker’s view of Trixie is partially blocked by his oversized computer monitor.

“I have some good news and some not so good news. I have been back here running the five vehicle identification numbers LaRoche has sent me so far. They are still very early in their investigation, but so far, nothing looks old enough to be your Panhead. But the good news is, three out of the five so far are listed on the hot sheet.”

Trixie tugs on Dude’s shirt. “That’s good news, isn’t it?”

Dude opens his mouth and is cut off by Detective Zucker. “Yes ma’am, it’s excellent news. We have enough to issue warrants for the arrest of the Rockwell brothers based on your boyfriend’s testimony putting them in the garage.”

“Whoa, I never said anything about wanting to testify!”

"Mister Sparks, you came to us, remember? Don't worry, you may never need to see a courtroom. All you need to do is sign your statement. Oh, and we will need a copy of your driver's license and current phone number. You too Miss Stone. Please sign here and allow me to make a copy of both of your licenses."

Detective Zucker's phone rings. He tells Dude and Trixie to go sit in the lobby.

The not so happy couple goes back to their corner of the waiting room, but this time they remain standing, talking, and pacing.

Dude drops his voice. "What the fuck, I don't want to testify against anyone."

Trixie tries to calm him down. "You may never need to go to court. It's just for the paperwork, you know, like a formality."

"Let's hope so." Dude hangs his head in disgust.

When the oak door swings open this time, there is no tan suit.

"Can I please speak with you two?" A distinguished gentleman with a short white comb-over waves his hand in Dude and Trixie's direction. His slender figure and custom-made blue pinstripe suit stand out amongst the office of off-the-racks and uniforms. The gold pin on his breast pocket catches Dude's attention as the man holds the door open for the couple as they pass through the glass again. This time they are led to an office with a large cheery wood desk sitting in front of certificates and pictures covering the walls. The door to the office is wood but the wall facing the large room of desks is glass. The man points to the two chairs, then steps behind the cherry slab. "Please, have a seat."

Dude takes the left seat again. Trixie slides her hands between her jeans and the red leather chair as she sits.

"My name is Chief Dexter. It is a pleasure meeting you two. You have proven to be a big help." He hands them both their driver's licenses. "We have over thirty unsolved cases of motorcycles, dirt bikes, ATVs, and the like. My men have barely scratched the surface of what's in the metal garage. So far, we have identified several stolen machines and we are confident more matches will be uncovered over the next several days. Thank you for coming forward."

Dude says, "You're welcome, sir."

Trixie nods with amazement.

"This next part isn't official yet, but there is something I want to share with you. Our local crime stoppers program made a reward available last year because of a string of motor vehicle thefts ravaging this area. If this bust you've led us to becomes as fruitful as it appears, I will be pushing for you to receive the reward."

"Holy shhhh… I'm sorry, say what?" Dude is dumbfounded.

"Yes, Mister Sparks, we haven't had a bust this big around here in years."

"I want the reward to go to my friend's son, George Walker Jr., I will leave you with the name and mailing address."

"Sir, the reward is ten-thousand-dollars, are you sure?"

"Yes, I'm sure, but wait a minute. Just for a couple small time thieves?" Dude's wheels are spinning.

The Chief says, "we are not only talking about stolen motorcycles here. Didn't Detective Zucker tell you about what the boys found over there once they got inside the garage?"

"Ah, um, no, not sure what you mean."

"Mister Sparks, in addition to the motorbikes, there have been several firearms found in the garage. Plus, they have found evidence of organized crime."

"Wait! What? No, this is not why I came here. I was just trying to catch the guys who stole my friend's motorcycle. What do you mean by organized crime? Like the mafia?" Dude is standing and pacing. Trixie is tugging on his shirt.

Chief Dexter tries to get Dude to sit. "Sir, I am sorry. I thought Zucker told you first. The detectives at the garage found evidence of a motorcycle club's presence hanging from the walls. The county sheriffs have been trying to catch these guys for years. Are you familiar with the Tortured Men Motorcycle Club?"

"No sir, I'm not from this area." Dude bows his head in silence, but he's thinking, *motherfucker! Not a motorcycle club!* Then he remembers why the name sounded familiar. *These are the assholes Anchor fuckin' told me about. Shit!*

The chief tells Dude, “This case is a really big deal and if we can tie the guns to the motorcycle club, this case could wind up in the hands of the Feds. So, if they call you, you’re obligated to cooperate. I hope you understand the gravity of the situation.”

“Yes sir. But the Feds? How will I even know if you arrest these guys?”

“If the Feds want in, we can’t stop them. Detective Zucker will be in touch. Thanks again. You two are free to go. Have a good day. You can see yourselves out.” Chief Dexter shuffles through papers.

“What the hell just happened in there? My mind is doing cartwheels! What the fuck?”

“Calm down, you did the right thing. Just relax, I’m right here with you.” Trixie struggles to keep Dude quiet as they fly through the waiting area and out the front doors.

Dude throws his hands in the air before taking the three steps down to the sidewalk. He turns to Trixie, “Now I’m a fuckin’ snitch! What the fuck? I thought I was just throwing two low-lifes behind bars. Now these pigs are going to pit me against a club. I don’t know about this. I mean, it’s a fuckin’ M/C!”

***

“You could wind up in witness protection.”

“Trix, seriously, not funny, don’t even joke like that. Please, give me a minute to think.” Dude puts on his helmet and climbs onto Angel. “We need to get away from here. Get on.”

Five miles away from the police station, Dude pulls into the parking lot of Shirley's Place, a hole in the wall pub with no windows. "I really need a drink."

Once inside, Dude sips on a bottle of Bud while telling Trixie, "We have one more stop to make before we can hit the highway and get you home."

She asks what else there is to do.

"Buck Jones, the man who led me to Henry. I owe him a reward."

Trixie doesn't understand, so she asks him to explain.

"The reward I'm offering is for anyone who could lead me to catching the thieves. I could wait until the police arrest and convict these guys, but that could take forever. I don't want to come back here again, and I'm confident the twins took the Panhead. Sure, I would love to get George's bike back, but I'm not sure if it's possible. I'd hate to admit it, but these brothers sold it for parts, and I just want to be done with this whole ordeal."

"But technically, Henry is the one who led you to the brothers. Shouldn't you give the money to him?" Trixie makes a valid point.

"Technically, yes, but don't forget, he helped steal the bike to begin with. So, fuck him! He is lucky I didn't give the police his name too; that's his reward."

"Another beer please." Dude waves at the bartender, then asks Trixie, "do you want another White Claw?"

"Just one more. I don't want to pee my pants on your sexy seat. We have a long ride ahead of us."

"One-hundred miles is not far. You will be fine. Let me call Buck to find out where to take his money."

The half-empty bar only has some quiet chatter and the sound of the television. Dude makes the call from his barstool.

Buck Jones is surprised to hear from Dude when he answers the phone. "So, the guys were arrested?"

"Not yet Buck. The police have issued arrest warrants."

"That is good news."

Dude explains how Henry spilled the beans and rolled on his accomplices. "I want to deliver you some reward money. Can we meet right now?"

Buck is taken aback. He is yelling for Gretchen. "Sweetie, please come here." Dude listens to Buck speak to his wife. "This Dude guy is on the phone. He wants to give us a reward." Gretchen can be heard saying she doesn't want any blood money. Buck tries to explain how his information led to Henry, who will lead to the inevitable arrest of two local motorcycle thieves. The squabbling on the phone becomes muffled. Then Buck's voice becomes clear. "Gretchen says you should give the money to your friend's family. The one whose Panhead was stolen."

Dude is practically speechless. "Ah, um, I, I don't know what to say. Are you sure?"

"Yes sir. The queen has decided. We don't need your money. Take care of your friend's family with it. Please."

"Thank you, and Gretchen so much. You are a saint, Buck. I can't even express how much all your help and generosity means to me. God bless you two."

"Have a good day." Buck fumbles to hang up the phone.

Trixie, who has been eagerly listening, sits like a puppy waiting for a treat. "What did he say?"

"They don't want the money. He and his wife want the money to go to George's family."

Trixie springs off her stool and onto Dude's lap, sort of. She is sliding down his legs when he wraps his arms around her waist. She claws her way up to his face and lays a wet kiss on Dude's mouth. "Wow! They are amazing people." Then she says, "And how about you? You're just as generous. I can't believe you're willing to give George Jr. your ten-thousand-dollar reward. You are an amazing man."

"Now it's time to get home and deliver the poker run money to Julie and give George Jr. the horn. Are you ready?"

"I'm ready to leave this bar, but I'm not ready for you to go home without me. When we get to my place, will you please spend the night?"

"Honestly, at this point, I'd really like to get home. Nothing against you, it's just all this cop bullshit has my mind racing."

Trixie leans in and slides her hand up his thigh. "It will be late by the time we get to my apartment. Please just stay one night. Get a good night's sleep and I will cook you breakfast before you trek across the state. Please?"

"You can be very persuasive. I'll think about it while we're riding."

Dude puts cash on the bar and pushes his empty bottle and Trixie's can forward. "Thank you." He waves to the bartender as they head toward the door.

The daylight is dwindling, and the temperature is dropping. Dude puts on a sweatshirt and gives Trixie his jacket. He hands her a pair of clear glasses. "These may be a little big, but they will keep the bugs out of your eyes."

They stop at a red light, and Trixie leans forward. "I really want to see where you live. If you're willing to hang out in Asheville for a couple days while I take care of a few things, I will go back with you. You could mail the stuff to George's family if you want to get it there faster. Pretty please?"

This police business has subdued his enthusiasm. The smile Trixie has been used to seeing in his mirror is gone. His clear glasses allow her to see his eyes while riding for the first time. Trixie does her best to see into his soul before the dark of night settles in. She stares at him, waiting for a response. The light turns green, and his focus is on the road. She sees no reaction when her hand slides down his belly and onto his crotch. Trixie imagines the worst. Now her mind is racing faster than his. *Is he just going to drop me on my doorstep and pull away? Will I ever see him again once he leaves? Does he have a girlfriend at home? Should I start massaging his balls?* Her hands dive deeper.

A sign for NC 105 south appears on the right side of the street. The open road is only one traffic light away. When Angel's wheels come to a stop, Dude turns his head. "Come closer. This weekend has been one hell of a roller coaster ride. Thank you for going on the adventure with me. You're an amazing woman and if you want me to stay with you for a few days, how can I say no? I have been looking forward to meeting Boots anyway."

Trixie pulls herself out of the seat with her strawberry lips puckered. A peck on the cheek leads to a tongue down Dude's throat. "Thank you for trusting me, you won't regret it."

"I will stay for as long as you're willing to keep me around."

Trixie chews on her bottom lip and tightens her arms around Dude's waist. "I'm never going to let you go. I'm starting to feel like a real biker chick."

**Coming soon.**
**Book #2 in the Motorcycle Rally Adventure Series.**

WANTED
DUDE
A NOVEL
RESTRICTED
R
BEN POVLOW

Ben Povlow has been riding on two wheeled motorbikes since he was five years old. He has logged tens of thousands of miles in the saddle. He has been attending motorcycle rallies since he was seventeen. Ben's love for motorcycle culture has inspired him to put his witty sense of humor, imagination, and real-world experience on the pages you hold in your hands. Ben is a recovering party animal who loves to have fun and enjoys telling a good story.

Join Ben's newsletter to be kept up to date with his new book releases and more.

www.BenPovlow.com

www.ingramcontent.com/pod-product-compliance
Lightning Source LLC
Chambersburg PA
CBHW031630200726
48288CB00019B/549

* 9 7 8 1 7 3 5 4 2 2 3 8 1 *